Small Blue Thing

S.C. Ransom

nosy
crow

SMALL BLUE THING

Published in the UK in 2011 by Nosy Crow Ltd
Crow's Nest, 11 The Chandlery
50 Westminster Bridge Road
London, SE1 7QY, UK

Registered office: 85 Vincent Square, London, SW1P 2PF, UK
Nosy Crow and associated logos are trademarks and or registered trademarks of
Nosy Crow Ltd

Printed and bound in the UK by Clays Ltd, St. Ives Plc
Typeset by Tiger Media Ltd, Bishops Stortford, Hertfordshire

Papers used by Nosy Crow are made from wood grown in sustainable forests.

ISBN: 978 0 85763 000 1

www.nosycrow.com

Small
Blue Thing

'Small Blue Thing'

Today I am
A small blue thing
Like a marble
Or an eye

With my knees against my mouth
I am perfectly round
I am watching you

....

Today I am
A small blue thing
Made of china
Made of glass

I am cool and smooth and curious
I never blink
I am turning in your hand
Turning in your hand
Small blue thing

For Ellie
and her big brother Jake

Amulet

The swan was thrashing about at the edge of the water, its huge wings beating the gravel and scattering all the other birds. We watched in horror as it twisted and turned, making loud, ominous hissing noises.

"I can't stand this," I shouted over the din, "I have to see if I can help it. Can you call someone – the police or a vet or whoever? I'm sure it's going to be hurt." I moved towards the bird cautiously.

"Alex, don't be so stupid," cried Grace. "It'll break your arm."

"I have to try," I muttered to myself as I edged down the little beach towards it.

The swan was frantic now, and as I got closer I could see why. The ring on its leg had got caught on a piece of curved wire which was sticking up out of the compacted sand and gravel. I stopped and dropped to a crouch, and tried to appear less threatening. I wasn't sure how to make soothing noises to a distressed swan, but no one could hear me so I had a go.

"There, there," I cooed, "nice swan. I'm not going to hurt you."

It fixed me with a baleful eye, but slowed down a little. I edged closer, keeping a wary eye on the vicious beak and those powerful wings. It suddenly stopped hissing and in the unexpected silence all I could hear was the strange sound of its huge webbed feet scuffing the beach. It held its wings out wide, looking as threatening as possible. It was doing a good job. At least if I broke my arm now, I reasoned, the exams were all over. We had finished the last one just this morning and our afternoon was supposed to be spent partying. At this point though, only Grace and I were left, the others having long since gone home to get ready for tonight.

I got to within a few feet of the bird when it suddenly decided that I was close enough. With a huge cry it strained up, flapping its wings wide. It was so close that the tips of the feathers brushed across my face. There was a sudden cracking noise, and in a flurry of white it was gone. I fell back in surprise and ended up sitting in the muddy sand.

Where the swan had been were the remains of the identification ring it had worn, next to the wire which had caused all the trouble. In all its thrashing about, the bird had kicked up the ground fairly well, and the wire still hadn't budged.

"Are you OK?" called Grace anxiously, peering at her mobile. "Do you still think I should call someone who knows what they are doing?"

"Not much point now," I grumbled, wiping the muck from the backside of my new jeans. It didn't make much difference. "I'm already filthy, so I'm just going to see if I can fix that wire," I called back.

It was only a little beach, one of several that appeared at really low tide on this part of the Thames at Twickenham. This one was overlooked by the terrace of The White Swan pub. The swans, geese and ducks were a regular feature, always wandering up to the terrace on the lookout for stray chips or a bit of unwanted bun. Usually when I was here it was packed with customers enjoying a pint in the sunshine, but late in the afternoon on this Tuesday in early June it was almost deserted.

Various bits of rubbish appeared on the beach at low tide, and the birds were clearly able to negotiate most of it safely. But I was angry about this particular bit of wire, which had come so close to breaking the poor bird's leg. I reached forward and tugged at it, not really expecting to be able to move it. It was stuck fast. Perhaps I could twist it over so that it was no longer a danger. I searched about for something I could use to bend it with, as my fingers were obviously not up to it.

I found a solid-looking piece of rock and started to hit the wire with it, bending it back down into the gravel. As it started to curve, I suddenly caught a glimpse of a brilliant blue. Curious, I stopped hitting and started trying to clear the gravel from around the wire. Deep in the mud it was wrapped around a small blackened circle of metal, about the size of my palm, with a round, blue stone attached. As the sunlight hit it, the stone sparkled and danced like an opal. I carried on digging. The wire went down and seemed to be wrapped around a large rock. I wasn't going to shift that in a hurry.

The wire was old, though, and this far down in the mud it looked a bit more fragile. I got a good grip on it and started to twist, and soon enough it snapped in two. I lifted the band to get a good look at it.

The stone was beautiful, a deep azure blue with flecks of gold and pinks and reds, all glinting in the sun. I rubbed at the band, shifting some of the ancient filth, and a dull silver colour appeared. Even through the dirt I could see the craftsmanship. Why would someone tie something so stunning to a rock and throw it in the river?

I took it into the Ladies at the pub, and washed it off a bit, trying to dig through all the grime and Thames muck that had clearly accumulated over some years. I tried to tidy myself up a bit too, but that was plainly hopeless: I was just going to have to go home and get changed. That was going to make me pretty late for the night out in Richmond that we had planned as a celebration.

My mind began to wander as I rubbed the band dry. If I arrived at the film late, I might miss the chance of sitting with Rob. I knew that Ashley was after him too, and she might make a move first. I had to avoid *that* happening.

I continued to rub the band as I thought about the evening ahead. It was gloomy in the Ladies with only a dim light bulb and I couldn't see the detail of the stone. I peered into it, and for a brief second it looked as if the surface of the stone rippled, almost as if it had blinked. I dropped it in surprise, then picked it up again cautiously from the basin. It must have been the light, I decided, as I considered it from every angle and nothing happened. I finished drying it and went back up to the bar to get more drinks. The barman was standing looking bored drying the glasses. He eyed me suspiciously, almost looking as if he was hoping that I would try to order something alcoholic so he could refuse me. He never liked it when we came into his bar, but the terrace more than made up for his attitude.

Although the bar was empty, the beach was getting busier. Two fit looking guys turned up with a couple of kayaks and attempted to launch them. I watched them from the balcony for a minute as they tried to impress Grace, but they really weren't very good. There was a lot of wobbling and swearing, and at one point I was sure that at least one was going to fall in, but eventually they made it and paddled off.

When I got back on the terrace with the long cold glasses, Grace and I examined my find. With the help of a spoon left on the table, we were able to prise the wire off the band, and get a better look at what it really was. It seemed to be a silver bracelet, set with a large, round blue stone. It looked a bit like an opal, but it was subtly different from the much smaller one my mum had in her jewellery box.

As I examined the stone the flecks of colour inside shimmered in the light, and I opened my mouth to tell Grace about the blinking I had seen earlier, but shut it again. What would I say that wouldn't sound a bit weird? I must have imagined it.

"It must be worth a bit," said Grace, taking the bracelet from me and turning it over in her hands. "I wonder how it ended up in the Thames."

"Well, whoever put it there wasn't expecting it to surface again," I told her. "It was tied on to a really big rock with the wire. Someone must have thrown it in, and from the look of the wire it's been there a while."

Grace peered at the inside of the band. "Of course, it's really too mucky to tell, but I can't see a hallmark. Perhaps it's fake after all," she giggled. "Or maybe a jealous lover threw it into the river, determined to get rid of his rival's gift."

"He might have thrown it in after the rival, or the girl," I mused, imagining a dark, brooding presence. I could almost visualise the scene, watching an angry lover hurling the bracelet and rock into the river. The thought made me shiver.

I took the bracelet back, rubbing it gently and wishing that there was a way to know. There had to be a story and I longed to know what it was. Whose hands had twisted that wire into place, securing it to the rock so tightly?

"Well, it will be interesting to see how it looks when it's all cleaned up," said Grace, interrupting my thoughts. "And speaking of cleaning up, what are you going to do? You can't come to Richmond looking like that." She gestured at the blackening mud was drying on my jeans. As she mentioned it, I became aware of a bit of a pong. I took a surreptitious sniff; I didn't smell good.

"By the time I get the train home and change and come back, it will be too late to get into the cinema," I realised, looking at my watch and groaning. I wouldn't just be late: I would miss a huge chunk of the film – if they let me in at all. I didn't live that far away, but it was on a very slow branch line and there was only one train an hour.

"Hmm," Grace appraised me with a mischievous eye. "If you want my help, I could fix you up…"

I felt my shoulders slump as I realised that I had finally given Grace the opportunity to play fairy godmother with my clothes. She and I had battled for years over my stubborn view that, out of school, jeans were the only practical things to wear. Grace always looked gorgeous in fabulous vintage finds from the local charity shop, which set off her dark colouring beautifully. I never had the patience. Even my mum had stopped buying me anything other than the most practical of clothes.

"OK," I laughed, admitting defeat. "Do your worst!" I threw the bracelet in my bag, finished my drink and took Grace's arm as we headed on back to the high street.

Unfortunately for me, Twickenham had a huge selection of charity shops, so Grace was able to choose from an eclectic mix of second-hand outfits. She fussed and considered, holding clothes up against me and making sucking noises through her teeth.

"Honestly, Grace, if you don't get a move on it would have been quicker for me to go home," I moaned.

"I think I have it," she announced triumphantly. "We can get you changed at the station." She paid for the last item and gathered all the bags together. "I'll be glad to get you out of those clothes. Really, the whiff is getting worse."

I could only agree with her. Whatever I had sat in back on the beach now smelt as if it had been dead for some time. Yet again, my thoughts were drawn to the bracelet in my bag, and the vision of that dark presence throwing it in.

"You know," I said as we walked towards the railway and the police station came into view, "I really ought to report that I have found that bracelet. It could be valuable, and I have no idea who is supposed to own stuff found in the river. I don't want to be accused of stealing from the Crown."

"Well, I guess you could," replied Grace dubiously, "but they might just take it off you."

"Maybe. But at least I wouldn't feel guilty. Come on, let's find out."

The police station had seen better days. I walked up the worn steps and took a deep breath, opening the heavy door. Grace followed behind me and went to sit gingerly on the edge of a seat, clearly trying not to look around her too carefully. Everything was nailed to the floor.

The policeman at the enquiry desk looked almost old enough to be my grandfather. He had a huge pile of papers and seemed to be searching through them for something. He ignored me completely as I stood in front of him. Eventually I gave in.

"Hi. I found this in the sand down at the river, and was wondering if I should hand it in." I dropped the bracelet in the drawer underneath the thick glass divider.

He gave a heavy sigh, and finally looked up. He stared at me, then fished the bracelet out on his side. "Do you know how much paperwork I have to complete to catalogue something found in the river, young lady?" he asked in a bored voice as he dangled the bracelet from his pudgy fingers.

"Um, no, not really," I mumbled, wondering if he really wanted an answer.

"Looks like junk to me," he announced with a decisive tone. "I'd just hang on to it if I were you." He tossed it back in the drawer and slid it over to me.

"Are you sure?" It looked real enough to me, and valuable too.

"Oh yes, we get this sort of stuff all the time. Junk." He looked at me and winked. I took the hint.

"Thank you, officer, sorry for bothering you." I grabbed the bracelet and shoved it back in my bag, grinning at him.

Grace had abandoned the long line of plastic chairs, and was standing by the exit, tapping her foot impatiently. "Come on," she urged. "We won't have time to get you changed before the train comes."

In the Ladies at the station, she positioned herself at the door so no one else could come in, then handed me the bags. It was just as bad as I had imagined, but I had to admit, peering at myself in the grubby mirror, that I looked OK. All but my feet – the very muddy electric blue Converse I had been wearing didn't really go with the floating chiffon dress and cute asymmetric cardigan. Grace looked me up and down with a critical eye.

"Not bad," she appraised. "But the shoes don't work. Luckily I have a secret weapon." She whipped another bag out of her little rucksack and threw it to me. Inside was a pair of sparkly flip-flops which clashed perfectly with the buttons on the cardigan.

"I can't," I protested. "You know I can never keep flip-flops on, not even on the beach."

"Well it's about time you learned," she announced decisively. "Anyway, those are as filthy as the jeans." She gestured towards my blackened shoes. She was right of course.

"And I'm sure Rob will appreciate the change in look," she smirked.

"He'll never recognise me," I muttered, but I had to agree: I did look different. Perhaps it would be the push he needed.

"This is what we need now," said Grace, pulling the clips and bands out of my hair and letting it fall down to my waist. "Absolutely gorgeous!" she pronounced as the train thundered into the station and we scrambled to get the bags together. "I think you'll have a memorable night."

The sparkly sandals really were not the best footwear for negotiating public transport or walking any distance. As I limped up the stairs at the pub in Richmond I made Grace promise that she would give me back my Converse for the journey home.

"No gain without pain," she smirked at me as we finally made it to the bar.

"There is no point in looking 'absolutely gorgeous' if I can't stand without wincing," I grumbled. "I just hope the others got here in time to get a seat."

We were in luck: they had grabbed the best table in the place, by the big window overlooking the river. There were a lot of us out tonight. We had just finished all of our exams, and now had a few weeks left of term with only a few structured activities and lessons before the long summer break. It had been a lot of hard work, and we were all relieved that it was over for now.

The plan for the night was to gather in the pub, go to the cinema to see the new James Bond film at the really big screen, and then see if we could get into Richmond's only club. It wasn't much of a place and the drinks were ridiculously expensive but it was the only option we had. I wasn't convinced that we would be able to sneak in as most of us were underage, but we were all up for having a go. Tom had been able to get most of the boys some reasonable fake ID, so they were all pretty confident.

We were a mixed bunch, with the girls from one school and the boys from the school next door. Our group had grown over the years we had been together, meeting up on the school buses and over the fence which divided the playing fields. Once we had started in the sixth form, we were allowed off the school grounds at lunchtime, and that was when some of the relationships had got more complicated. Right now, there were no particular pairings, but I felt that with the end of the exams that might change.

I knew that Grace was pretty keen on Jack, and she and I had spent many long hours considering our plans of attack on him and Rob. Unfortunately we knew that some of the others had the same idea, and at that point everything was up for grabs.

Rob's look had been thoughtful as he had eyed me speculatively in the pub before going to the cinema. "Nice outfit." He nodded his approval. "What's brought about this change of image then?" With his head inclined he looked me up and down, a small smile on his lips.

"Ah, well, actually it was an emergency Oxfam shop visit," I admitted sheepishly. I heard Grace groan in exasperation behind me.

"Don't tell him that – let him think you have made an effort," she whispered in my ear. I groaned inwardly – I really wasn't very good at being as cool as I was trying to look.

"Really?" he smiled, leaning in a little closer. "What sort of emergency?" The rest of the group fell silent, intrigued by what had made me change my fashion principles.

"Well," I hesitated, suddenly unwilling to tell them all about the bracelet, "I sort of fell into the river when I was trying to rescue a trapped swan."

My friends all roared with laughter. That was the Alex they knew, not the one sitting in front of them with the floaty dress.

"You're not a vet yet Alex," chuckled Jack, ruffling my hair. "I'd leave the animals alone for a bit until you know what you are doing."

"I think the swan would agree with you," I admitted ruefully, smiling back at Jack.

"Nasty, vicious things, swans," he added. "I wouldn't mess with one."

"I guess Alex is braver than you then, mate." smiled Rob, edging closer towards me. I could see the smile didn't quite reach his eyes. Although they seemed to get on most of the time, I wasn't sure that Rob really liked Jack, and that disappointed me.

Jack was one of my oldest friends and we had pretty much grown up together. He was also one of the best looking boys in town, and as captain of the football team, incredibly fit. It was such a shame that I could never see him as anything other than another brother. His older brother had been in the same class as my brother since they were four, and our parents had become close friends. As a result we ended up doing all sorts of things together. As the only girl I had regularly been over-ruled and had quickly learned to climb trees, play football and generally join in. Jack and I had a long, shared history that Rob could only guess at.

Now, listening to Rob, I realised that actually he was jealous of Jack. No wonder he was tetchy. I looked at Grace as she raised her perfect eyebrow in amusement at Rob's behaviour. I just knew that I had won the battle with Ashley before it had even got going. Rob Underwood – the fittest guy in the whole school! I couldn't quite believe that, if I just kept my head, he was mine for the taking. I tried to keep my breathing even to settle the sudden and unexpected butterflies in my stomach.

Rob had made himself comfortable next to me, with an arm along the back of my chair. I stole a quick glance at him in the window opposite. He was classically handsome, but tall and blonde, not dark like Jack, and as always he was dressed well in casual but expensive clothes. His brown eyes sparkled as he caught me checking him out. He leant in close.

"You do look really lovely tonight," he murmured. "You should fall in the river more often."

A shiver ran down my spine as he let his fingers trace a line down the back of my neck. How long had I been dreaming of this moment? I wasn't going to be able to resist.

I sat back in my chair and his hand fell across my shoulder. Out of the corner of my eye I could see Ashley stiffen. She was not going to be happy, but that was her problem, not mine. I was going to enjoy my night out.

Rob made sure that he was sitting next to me in the cinema. Grace had been able to manoeuvre herself next to Jack, so we were guaranteed a decent amount of post-night-out gossip. The movie was not a good one for romance though, with far too much action and violence. However, during a more peaceful scene Rob casually brushed his hand against me as I reached for my bottle of water, then smiled at me and wrapped his long fingers through mine. I was just beginning to relax and stop worrying about whether my palm was too hot and sweaty when there was a particularly horrific torture scene. Without thinking I squeezed his fingers really hard and he surreptitiously sneaked his hand back. Luckily in the dark he couldn't see me blush, but after that he slung his arm across the back of my chair where I couldn't hurt him.

After the film we quickly decided that we needed food, not the nightclub, so we all piled into the local branch of a pizza chain. We waited a few minutes while the staff rearranged some tables in a far corner of the room, and as we walked over, I realised that yet again Rob was manoeuvring so that he and I were sitting together. On the way to the restaurant I had noticed that Grace and Jack had hung back together, and I was positive that he took her hand at one point as we walked over the road. Sure enough, they ended up sitting together too.

I caught her eye as we sat down and raised my eyebrows slightly in a question. She immediately blushed and hid behind her menu, then peeked round at me and nodded minutely.

Rob was acting in a very possessive manner towards me, making sure I had a menu and a drink, that I had a decent chair and wasn't sitting in a draught from the open window. It suddenly got to the point that I wanted to scream at him to relax. What was wrong with me? Just yesterday I would have given anything to have him fussing over me, but today it was starting to annoy me. I couldn't understand why I wasn't making the most of tonight. I had been waiting for Rob to make a move for months, and now that he had, I wasn't sure he was what I wanted. The trouble was, I realised, I didn't know *what* I wanted.

I tried to unwind. Maybe it was just a reaction to the end of the exams. I forced my tense shoulders to relax and turned to Rob with a smile.

The waitress got more and more harassed as our large

group got rowdier waiting for the pizzas to finally arrive. Then we were suddenly silent, tucking into our favourites and exchanging slices with others. We sat there for ages polishing off every piece on every plate, dissecting the plot of the film and considering the relative merits of this particular James Bond actor.

The restaurant stayed open late to cater for the post-cinema crowd, but some of us had a time limit as we had to be back in school the next morning. Grace and I were on an Art Club trip into London first thing, and she was going to sleep over at my house that night so we could catch the last train home together. It looked like we would have plenty to discuss on the long walk up from the station.

Part-way through a lively discussion with Eloïse on whether the last Bond was better looking than this one, or just too old, I glanced at my watch and saw that we'd have to leave the restaurant soon or we would miss the last train home.

"Hey, Grace," I called along the table, "we really ought to be going soon."

It looked as if I had shaken her out of a dream, she was so entranced by everything Jack had been telling her. I wondered for a minute if she was going to change our plans.

"Oh. Right. Yes..." she stuttered. "Um, I'll just finish my coffee..."

At that moment, Rob took my hand and pulled me round to face him.

"Now, listen, Little Miss Workaholic," he said, "as the exams are over, you can allow yourself a little time off to relax. My parents are renting a cottage in Cornwall in the summer holidays, and they've said that I can use it in a couple of weeks if I want to take some friends down." He tucked a lock of my long blonde hair back

14

over my shoulder as he spoke, not quite meeting my eyes.

"That would be lovely," I enthused. I had never been to Cornwall and really wanted to try the surfing. "How many of us will it hold?"

A sly look flashed across his face so fast I wasn't sure if it had really been there.

"Well, it can hold eight," he admitted, "but I was thinking of something a bit more ... intimate." He emphasised his point by running his finger gently across my thigh and squeezing my knee.

What messages had I given him? We weren't even officially going out and he had already sorted out a love nest.

"Um, I'm not yet sure when I'm supposed to be going to Spain with my parents," I blustered quickly, completely unsure of how to dig myself out of this one.

I glanced around. No one else had been listening, thankfully, but it meant that there was no one to help me either. I didn't know what to do.

"But it's a lovely idea," I continued, not wanting to hurt his feelings. "Can we talk about it later in the week? I mean... It is a little sudden, and I'm not sure..." I confessed sheepishly, all pretence of sophistication gone.

He took my hands and stared deep into my eyes.

"Of course," he murmured, reassuringly. "It's just – seeing you tonight has made me realise that we could have a *lot* of fun together." I tried not to gulp too loudly and to remember to breathe. His fingers caressed the inside of my wrist.

"Why don't we discuss it over dinner on Saturday?" he urged. "I can borrow my mum's car and we can go to a little place in the country, just the two of us." It wasn't a question: he had it all planned out, and I could tell that he wasn't expecting a rejection. It was all moving scarily fast.

But it was what I had been hoping for all these months, I reminded myself. Rob had finally asked me out, and to dinner, not just on another group outing. "I'll have to see what I've got arranged," I said, as casually as I could muster, "but I think I'm free on Saturday."

He laughed, seeing through my attempts to remain cool. "Excellent, we can sort out the details tomorrow." He leaned forward so that his face was really close, our noses almost touching. "I'm really looking forward to getting you on your own."

I could smell a hint of mint on his breath. How had he done that? I tried not to think that he was so sure of himself that he had managed to find and eat a mint before starting this particular conversation.

At that point he leaned in just a little further and brushed his lips over mine. I melted. Whatever his motives, he was gorgeous. I deserved a break after all that revision.

I looked up at him from under my lashes. "Me too," I breathed, pleased that I had refused the garlic bread earlier.

I was suddenly aware of a silence around us. I looked round at the table into the curious faces of our friends.

"So you two are finally getting it together, are you?" chortled Jack, who had his arm slung casually around Grace's shoulders.

"Look who's talking," flashed back Rob, gesturing to Grace, who immediately blushed a deep crimson. Then there was a loud scraping noise from the other end of the table as Ashley leapt up from her chair and ran for the Ladies.

I straightened up. "Oops," I whispered. "This is going to be awkward." I stole a glance at Rob. For just a second he looked smug, then he frowned.

"Mia," he called down the table, "is Ashley alright? Should someone go and see…?" He managed to get just the right level of concern into his voice, but Mia was already on her way. He turned back to me. "What's her problem?" he asked.

"Oh come on. You must know that she has been drooling over you for months."

"Really? I had no idea." I bit my lip and fought back my irritation: he wasn't that dumb. But I really didn't want it to ruin the evening. Term was nearly over, I finally had a date with Rob, and he had kissed me. I should be over the moon. He carried on. "And now that she has seen me with you, well, no wonder she is upset."

I needed time to think. I glanced at my watch again.

"Oh crap!" I exclaimed. "Grace, we need to leave now and make a run for it, otherwise we'll have to pay for a taxi." We grabbed our bags, threw down some cash to cover our share of the bill, and waved at everyone as we dashed for the door. At least I wouldn't have to look at Ashley's face when she finally reappeared. I wondered whether Rob would try to comfort her, and couldn't work out why that thought didn't bother me. Then all other thoughts went out the window as I ripped off the silly shoes and ran with Grace down the high street.

Vision ✑

Grace and I didn't get a huge amount of sleep that night. We only just made it to the last train, and spent the entire journey and the long walk deep in a dissection of the night's events.

Grace was glowing. She had been longing for Jack to notice her for years, and now she was finally in with a chance. We discussed in detail her best approach to maintain his interest over the next few weeks. If she could keep the other girls off his radar until the start of the holidays, she would have a much better chance of hanging on to him longer term, we reckoned. There was so much to debate, and I encouraged the conversation along so that I didn't have to spend too much time talking about Rob.

However, she wasn't going to be completely deflected. "So, it looks like Rob's finally taken the plunge and committed to taking you out," she said, as we continued trudging up the road between the station and home, with me finally back in my Converse after a quick wrestle with her on the train.

"Yes, that seems to be his plan ... but there is rather more to it than that: he wants me to go to Cornwall with him in a few weeks. His parents have rented a cottage."

"That's brave of you, volunteering to spend so much time with his family at this stage!"

"Ah, well, that's the problem. You see," I admitted, "his family won't be there. It would just be the two of us."

There was a sharp intake of breath, and I stole a quick glance at her face as we passed a street light.

"He's a fast worker, isn't he?" There was a pause. "Are you thinking of going?" she added, suddenly lightening her tone.

"How can you even think that?" I exclaimed. "It's way too soon."

"I know," she agreed, "but sometimes even the best plans can just evaporate in the face of extreme temptation." There was a far-off look in her eye as her voice faded away.

I spotted a weakness. "That sounds like something you might have been thinking about yourself," I challenged. "Does this mean that you and Jack will be..."

"Huh, chance would be a fine thing. I was only thinking about the pact."

Grace and I had made a pact a long time ago that we would look out for each other if either one was thinking of stepping over the line with a boyfriend. We had seen too many of our friends leap into disastrous, short-lived relationships during the last year, and neither of us wanted to be hurt as they had been.

In fact, earlier in the week I had been wondering if Rob might be the one, but I seemed somehow to be seeing him a lot more clearly now, and the whole thing just felt ... wrong. I couldn't work out why: he was gorgeous, popular, and available, and now he was interested in me. Why wasn't I happier?

We couldn't resist dropping into the little playground by the bridge and having a quick go on the swings in the moonlight. When we had first moved here, I was nine and had felt far too sophisticated to enjoy the equipment. Now, though, Grace and I regularly used the swings as a place to stop and gossip where no one could overhear us.

We talked about Ashley. I had known Ashley forever. We had been in the same school since reception, but not always in the same class. In a way we were too similar, too competitive, and we were never the best of friends. But we had shared some good times, like the trip to France in the junior school where she and I had led the raid on the boys' dormitories, and the more recent choir tour. Unfortunately though, the situation with Rob had soured all that. As soon as I realised that we both fancied him it was clear that the fragile truce in our relationship was going to crumble.

Life with Grace was much simpler. We were quite different in our looks, outlook and cultures, but were somehow best mates. And luckily we never fancied the same boys. Instead we had shared catastrophic dramas and crushes over the last six years, then the traumas of being dumped at fourteen by boyfriends we never really spent any time with, and, throughout it all, the general irritating nosiness of our mothers. But by now we always knew when the other was in trouble, and had an uncanny ability to ring each other at exactly the right time. I trusted her completely, and I knew that she and I would be friends forever.

We were still laughing quietly about the boys as we finally crept into the house, trying not to disturb my parents too much. It was a shame that we had to be up early the next morning: we could have gone on gossiping all night.

I was thinking back over the day, and despairing over the state of my new jeans when I remembered the bracelet. I jumped out of bed and rummaged in my bag to find it. In the low light, the silver gleamed and the stone looked like a deep cobalt pool. I hadn't realised that I had cleaned it so well earlier. It looked nothing like the blackened twist of metal I had fished out of the mud.

I slipped it on to my wrist to see how it would look. It

fitted really comfortably, as if it had been made exactly for me. As I looked at the stone, a soothing calm settled over me. It felt right, somehow, to be wearing it, and so wrong that it had spent so long lying under the gravel and dirt. I moved it closer to my bedside light to get a better look, and when the fire in the stone danced, it was breathtaking – almost as if it were celebrating its rescue. It was without question the most stunning piece of jewellery I had ever seen. I finally dragged my eyes away, promising myself that I would give it a really thorough clean the next day.

I was about to turn out the light when Grace started to cough.

"It's nothing, just a tickle," she protested.

"You'll need a drink of water," I decided. I didn't want her keeping me awake. "I'll nip down to the kitchen and get you a glass." I had shared a room with her plenty of times before and knew the danger – she could cough all night in her sleep.

It was very dark downstairs, as everyone else had long since gone to bed. I got a glass from the cupboard and filled it from the kitchen tap, and walked back into the hall glancing down at the heavy band on my wrist. I touched the still-cold silver absently and my head was suddenly filled with the image of a gorgeous boy. It was as if he had appeared in front of me. It was so surprising that I jumped back, stifling a scream and dropping the glass. His face was noble yet fierce, with piercing blue eyes, chiselled cheekbones and a strong jaw. His skin was just perfect: smooth-shaven and lightly tanned, with a small mole just by the side of his mouth. He was, without doubt, the most dazzling person I had ever seen. He also looked puzzled and sad, his brow creased, and his perfect lips pressed together in a thin line.

The image stayed in my mind for just a second longer,

enough for me to register the dark blond hair, the tension in his shoulders, and that he was swathed in a dark coat or something, then, just as I started to reach for the light, as quickly as he had appeared in my head he was gone, and I was back alone in my dark hall, standing in a puddle of water.

"Crap," I muttered under my breath as I realised that I was imagining things and that I had made a mess on the floor. I heard my mum open the door to their room, coming to investigate the noise. She was always very crabby if I woke her up.

I ran up the stairs to head her off.

"Sorry, Mum," I whispered. "I was getting Grace a glass of water when I tripped over the shoes and dropped it."

Mum was always complaining about the shoes left in the hall, so she was bound to believe that.

"Do be more careful, Alex. And make sure you collect all the broken glass."

"OK. Sorry I woke you up."

"Well, at least I know you are home safely," she smiled. "Did you have a good evening?"

"It was OK," I conceded. I didn't want to start her off on one of her lengthy interrogations just now. Thankfully she got the hint.

"Tell me all about it tomorrow. See you in the ..."

"... morning," I finished for her, leaning in for a kiss.

She disappeared back to her room, and I ran back downstairs to turn my attention to the floor. I finally switched on the light and surveyed the damage. There wasn't much mess, the glass had broken cleanly in two and I hadn't overfilled it, so there was just a small puddle on the floorboards.

I searched through my memory as I wiped the floor. I couldn't imagine where I had seen that face before. It must have been somewhere – probably on the TV, I decided: he was far too handsome to be just my imagination. And such a blinding image too, as if he had been projected directly into my head. That was the really strange thing: somehow he didn't just feel like the recollection of someone I had seen before; it was almost as if he was really there. I couldn't make any sense of it at all, and in the end I gave up. It was late and I was tired – perhaps I would have a better idea in the morning.

I fetched another glass from the kitchen and went back upstairs, where I was expecting an interrogation from Grace. But it was late, and she had fallen asleep. It seemed like a detailed discussion about my weird experience would have to wait until tomorrow.

In the morning I realised that I was still wearing the bracelet. It was so comfortable I hadn't noticed. I went downstairs to get a coffee for Grace and smoothed a minuscule mark off the stone while I waited for the kettle to boil. For the briefest of moments I thought that I could see a moving shadow flitting across its surface again, but as I did a double take there was nothing there. "I'm going mad," I muttered to myself, thinking of the night before. "Bracelets can't blink and pictures of strange guys can't be projected into your head." I had been hoping that it would all somehow become clear in the morning, but I was no further forward in trying to work out who or what had caused it.

As ever there was a last-minute scramble to be ready and Grace and I each grabbed a biscuit in place of breakfast and dashed to the bus stop.

The advantages of going to an all girls' school that was right next to an all boys' school were immense. It was possible to avoid the boys if you were feeling grumpy or had a bad hair day, but easy to meet up at the dividing fence during break. We also had a joint coach service, so students from either school could get a bus in from their local area. The coach had been the hub of my social life since I was eleven, from the first week, when I'd learned every possible swear word in the language from the boys, to now, when it was where the girls discussed tactics for attracting the same boys.

Things had changed a little since we had moved up to the sixth form. Now we were officially seniors and no longer required to wear uniforms, we were able to watch the younger kids on the coach with an indulgent eye, occasionally wincing when we realised that we used to behave in exactly the same way.

My elder brother, Josh, at eighteen, was in his final year of school and had managed to spend most of the last six years ignoring me completely on the coach. But that too had changed in the last few months as he and some of his friends had got more interested in my friends, and very occasionally they acknowledged our existence.

The coach arrived, and there was time for some uninterrupted chat with Grace. I was about to tell her all about the whole thing when one of our friends dropped into the seat in front and started quizzing Grace about Jack: the grapevine had clearly been working overtime. It would wait, I decided. We had all day to talk on our day trip to London.

The school trip had been organised for those of us in the Art Club, an optional lunchtime activity. Most of us in the group were OK at art but didn't have the talent or the dedication needed to sit the exams, and membership of the club allowed us to have a bit of fun. The project for the term was to look at art in public buildings, and that day we were off to St Paul's Cathedral. My special interest was in the carvings of people and faces, and having done lots of research on the Internet I was planning to draw the figures adorning the tomb of the Duke of Wellington, the famous soldier. Unfortunately I hadn't done quite enough research before I submitted my plans, and found that all the angels were perched on the very top of the enormous monument. I was going to get a very hard lesson in foreshortening.

We were driven up into London in the school minibus by one of our art teachers. It was a subdued group as we had all been out celebrating the night before, and a few of the girls had been up really late. Unfortunately, Mrs Bell was a surprisingly aggressive driver, and some of us didn't look good as the minibus tore around the one-way system south of the river. At one point I was sure that Melissa was going to heave. She went very pale and someone quietly handed her an empty carrier bag and opened a window. No one dared to ask Mrs Bell to slow down.

We finally made it to the city, where the great dome of the cathedral still managed to dominate the much larger corporate buildings nearby. The huge white stone edifice, recently cleaned of hundreds of years of London grime, seemed to glow gently in the sunshine. The two large towers that flanked the western entrance were dwarfed by the pale grey dome which sat at the centre of the building. As we drove up Ludgate Hill, I could see the sunlight glinting off the gilding on the tops of each of the towers, and catching the railings on the Golden Gallery at the top of the dome.

I loved coming to St Paul's. As a kid I had come here regularly: Mum and Dad raved about the view out across London and every foreign visitor we had was made to come and admire it. From the top, looking to the east, you could see the Tower of London and Tower Bridge nestling between the tall smooth buildings of the city. The hills of Hampstead and Highgate reared up to the north, and if the weather was good enough, you could see Richmond Park in the far south-west. It was a long walk up to the Golden Gallery, the highest point you could get to: hundreds of steps, but worth it. I had always been fascinated by the construction of the dome, with the latticework of the internal wooden structure through which the stairs climbed to the top. I just had to be careful not to look down too often, as some of the drops were dizzyingly precipitous. Worst of all was the glass peephole at the top that let you look down at the tiny people hundreds of metres directly below your feet. It always made me feel queasy thinking about that drop, wondering if they could see me hundreds of feet above them, looking down at what they were doing.

But today I wasn't going to have the chance to go up to the top, there was too much to do on the project.

The cool and gloom inside St Paul's was a marked contrast from the dazzling sunshine and frenetic activity outside. As we walked through the entrance it was as if someone had pulled a shutter down over the brightness, noise and twenty-first century living going on outside. We shuffled through the turnstiles with the rest of the class as our eyes adjusted slowly to the muted light. Something about the atmosphere was strangely intimidating, and all the chattering in relief that the drive was over petered out as we all gazed up into the height of the roof. Every visitor was the same, I noticed: no one was able to come in and not be awed by the huge space. At this end, the cathedral was empty, with no pews or monuments, just a vast expanse of chequerboard floor and towering columns reaching up to the vaulted ceiling. No matter how many times I had been here before it always took my breath away.

Grace and I got out our notebooks and maps and began to

look for the monuments we needed to sketch. As we walked up the centre of the nave Grace started to giggle.

"Imagine Lady Di walking all the way along here in that dress," she snorted. I shuddered: I couldn't imagine anything worse, talking that long walk with the world watching, to marry a man who didn't really love her.

"If I ever get married I'm going to run off to a beach," I agreed, "not get dolled up in a huge frilly dress and cost my parents thousands." Dad might disagree though, I thought wryly. He was the only reason I might consider the whole white meringue routine. Rob's face flickered into my mind, but as I glanced down at the bracelet on my wrist, he was instantly replaced by a memory of the stunning face I had seen last night. I shook my head to clear it – I really should concentrate on what I was supposed to be doing.

Grace and I had reached the central part of the cathedral, under the spectacular dome.

"Wow," she breathed and we both stared up. The dome was magnificent, curving majestically high above us. There was a quiet buzz of conversation, and we saw people up in the Whispering Gallery, trying out the famous acoustics. You were supposed to be able to sit around the edge of the huge circular balcony that ran around the inside of the dome, and whisper against the wall. Then someone on the far side, the whole width of the building away, should be able to hear the whisper. I had never been able to make it work, but the tourists seemed to love it.

"I need to check out Nelson," Grace muttered, biting her lip as she consulted her map.

"Nelson's in the crypt. The entrance is over there, I think," I said. "I'll be there in a second; I just want to look at something in the middle." Grace started rummaging in her bag for a pencil as she went to find the tomb.

I walked slowly forward until I was below the exact centre of the dome, which was marked on the floor by a large mosaic star. High above me I could see the glass panel of the peephole, but before I could work out if anyone up there was looking down at me, I felt dizzy from leaning backwards. I straightened up and froze with shock.

Directly in front of me was the boy whose face I had imagined last night. He was even more gorgeous in the flesh, with spectacular bone structure and tousled dark blond hair. I could barely breathe and was struggling to regain my composure when I realised that he was looking at me with an equally stunned expression. He quickly looked over his shoulder, as if to check that I was looking at him and not at something behind him. It seemed a strange thing to do given that his looks could stop traffic. His eyes were a vibrant, stunning blue, and now I could see him properly there was a very slight kink in his nose, as if it might have been broken years before. As I stared I realised that I had seen the colour of his eyes before – they were exactly the same blue as the stone in my bracelet. Not really believing what I was seeing, I touched the bracelet and stole a quick glance towards it.

His eyes flicked down towards my wrist and I saw them widen in surprise. His hand flew to his own wrist, and I saw he was wearing an identical band. Another expression transformed his face. Was it alarm? He looked back at me and took a couple of steps closer.

"Keep cool," I muttered to myself under my breath, as I tried to look a little less startled and more composed and interesting. I went for a tentative half smile. He really was stunningly handsome, and I couldn't imagine what he wanted with me, but it was worthwhile trying to keep his attention for a minute longer.

He seemed to be struggling with something which made him frown, but then he too smiled, with a strange look of wonderment. He was even more beautiful when he smiled, with a deep crease in one cheek and a flash of perfect white teeth.

"Hello," I whispered, surprising myself for speaking out. He continued to stand there, smiling more confidently now, but saying nothing. This was going to be harder than I imagined. Maybe he didn't speak English.

"Alex!" called a voice behind me. Grace was looking at me strangely. "Are you coming…?"

"I'll be right there," I replied over my shoulder, trying not to lose too much eye contact with my silent companion. "I'm supposed to be working on an art project…" I started to explain to him, then tailed off. How lame was that? Not exactly the sort of thrilling conversation that was going to hold the interest of someone like him. He was still standing there, and I noticed that he was wearing a strange, full-length cloak that was pushed back behind his shoulders, secured by a thick cord by his neck. Weird. It would be just my luck if someone this lovely was a monk.

He looked as if he was about to say something, but before he could speak a group of German tourists suddenly appeared, with a guide who was telling them about the peephole in the dome's roof. The guide was right behind him, pointing up while walking backwards and talking to his group. I could see that the guide was about to walk into him, so I instinctively reached out to pull him out of the way. As I touched his arm I felt a slight tingling sensation and my hand went right through him. I pulled back as if I had been electrified. This wasn't possible. I looked at him again in puzzlement. His face was struggling with several emotions. One was clearly joy – he was still smiling – but he also looked really frustrated.

After a few seconds the German tourists moved on, so he wasn't about to be trampled any more. I must have made a mistake, I decided; perhaps his clothes were made of some strange slippery fabric, or perhaps I was just distracted by his astonishing beauty. There was no way my hand had actually gone through him – people were solid, so there had to be a rational explanation. I tried again, spotting a good conversation opener.

"I, um, I see you have the same bracelet as I do." I gestured towards my band and to his. He looked down at his arm, then directly into my eyes.

He couldn't have been much older than me but those beautiful eyes hinted at pain and sorrow. He raised his arm to show me his wrist. The band there seemed identical to mine. Thinking it would be better to compare them side by side, I smiled and took a couple of steps towards him. As I moved, the air around him seemed to swirl, and he was gone. I looked around wildly, but he had completely disappeared. Grace was right behind me though, arms folded, with a quizzical look on her face.

"Where did he go?" I demanded, continuing to scan the crowds of tourists flowing past us.

"Who?" asked Grace in surprise.

"That guy! The one in the cloak. Where has he gone?"

"I didn't see anyone in a cloak."

"You must have done. He was right here; I was talking to him…"

"Alex," Grace put a gentle hand on my arm, "you were standing here on your own, and you looked like you were talking to yourself. That's why I came back over."

"But he was standing just there, the best looking guy I have ever seen…" I faltered. She *must* have noticed him.

"I think maybe you need to have a sit-down," Grace said soothingly, pulling me by the arm over to the front row of the pews.

"There is nothing wrong with me," I protested, still straining up on to the tips of my toes to catch a glimpse of him in the crowd.

"Sweetie, you have been standing on your own in the middle of the church looking slightly demented," Grace murmured. "One of the others was going to notice pretty soon, and I didn't think you'd want that sort of abuse."

I sank into the pew, defeated.

"Perhaps you need some water," she continued. "Or maybe some fresh air."

"I'll be fine," I sighed. "Just give me a minute." She wasn't going to let me off so easily.

"Soooo, you were talking to a man in a cloak who I couldn't see. Does that sum it up?"

"When you put it like that it does seem unlikely," I admitted. She hadn't seen him then, that much was clear. What could I say? She already had a slightly disbelieving tone, and what I could tell her would only convince her that I was completely nuts. An invisible guy who I couldn't touch? That was going to be hard to swallow.

Suddenly I was relieved that I hadn't mentioned the strange incident last night – she was my best friend but I didn't want to have to push her too far. I needed to try and make some sense of this myself before sharing it with anyone, including Grace.

I sat back and closed my eyes, running through the scene again. The guy whose image I had seen last night had been standing right in front of me. He no longer looked as fierce; he had looked positively stunning. I couldn't help grinning when I thought of his smile and of how much better he looked when he was happy. In fact, he was so gorgeous I could feel myself starting to blush.

"Alex?" Grace touched my arm. "Are you OK? Do you need me to get Mrs Bell?"

I shook my head. The last thing I needed was more questions. "I'm fine. I think maybe I should have had something for breakfast. I went a bit wobbly there for a minute."

Grace heaved a great sigh of relief. "You had me worried," she admitted. "You were acting pretty weird."

"You have no idea," I murmured to myself, slightly surprised that she accepted the excuse. "Shall we get on with Nelson and Wellington?" I said, standing up. I was going to have to think about this later, once I was on my own. Was I going mad? An involuntary shiver ran down my spine at that thought. I looked around again furtively but there was no sign of him anywhere.

Reflections

After that the St Paul's project felt pretty irrelevant. I couldn't stop searching around me to see if I could see his face in the crowd. But there was no sign of him, only a slightly unsettling feeling of being watched. I peered at the bracelet a few times, and a couple of times I thought I saw the suggestion of movement in it, but nothing like the blinking I thought I had seen yesterday. The whole thing was bizarre.

Grace kept checking up on me as if I was some sort of invalid, and I was really relieved when it was time to get back on the minibus and go back to school. It was parked just round the corner and I jumped on and grabbed a seat at the back.

Grace still wasn't letting up.

"Any more apparitions yet?" The question was clearly meant kindly, but I didn't want to talk about it. I needed distracting, and the easiest way would be to distract her.

"Not a single one." I tried to laugh, and nearly made it convincing. "I think it must just be all the stress, especially now I've got Rob to worry about…"

"Good point," she agreed. "That is going to be a tricky decision. Tell me again exactly what he said?"

"I'd much rather you tell me exactly what your plans are with Jack," I countered, suddenly inspired. "Has he spoken to you yet today? I've never seen him take so much interest in anyone before."

We had been over all this in minute detail last night, but I had a hunch that it was one topic that Grace would be delighted to return to as often as possible. She radiated happiness.

She was soon off on a long description of all the texts he had sent so far today and what she had replied. It only took the occasional prompt from me to keep her on track. It was lovely to see how excited she was.

When the minibus finally made it back to school we had free time in which to work on our projects. Grace went off to the art department to stock up on the supplies she was going to need for her pictures. I quickly made my way up to the library and found a quiet computer in the corner.

It was a well-stocked library with a long bank of computers, but it was generally busy and you had to fight for spaces. By the middle of the afternoon though, there was no problem in finding one free. I sat in a quiet corner by the window and tried to organise my thoughts, reassuring myself that if I was going mad I wouldn't be so keen to find a rational explanation for everything I had seen.

My usual way to solve any problem was to Google the question, but this time I didn't even know what to type in – cloaked, untouchable people in St Paul's? I couldn't imagine that there would be much information on that. My fingers hovered over the keyboard for a moment, but I couldn't bring myself to type anything so stupid. I looked down at my hands and considered the bracelet. I rubbed the stone pensively, staring out across the playing fields where the netball team were thrashing some poor visiting school on a summer tour. As I watched I saw our captain, Helen, slam in another goal. The visiting team, their heads down low, really looked as if they wished it was all over.

As I glanced away from the window and down at the stone, I thought of the boy's face again. I smiled to myself and turned my attention back to the computer. At that point the sunshine suddenly broke through the clouds and lit me up, giving a clear reflection of my face in the screen in front of me.

He was right behind me, the sunlight illuminating his hauntingly beautiful face. I was so startled I shouted out loud and whipped my head around.

I was quite alone.

A finger of ice ran down between my shoulder blades. What was going on? Looking back at the screen, I could see the surprise on his face as I jumped up, knocking my chair over as I went. A few curious eyes lifted from books across the library, and as I quickly scanned around it was clear that there was nowhere he could be hiding. I felt another shiver of fear.

"What is going on?" Miss Neil came bustling over, talking very pointedly in a loud whisper.

"Um, I'm really sorry," I mumbled, searching for inspiration. Clearly I couldn't tell her I was seeing things. "A wasp!" it came to me suddenly. "There was a wasp in my hair but I managed to get it out before it stung me."

"Well, that is unfortunate, but do please try to keep the noise down. Not everyone has finished their exams," she hissed.

"Sorry," I muttered, picking up my chair and sitting back down as she retreated around the corner to her desk. I waited until I could hear that she was sitting down before I looked again at the screen.

The sun was behind a cloud, so the image wasn't so bright, but I could still see a faint shadow over my shoulder. As I watched the sun emerged, and, as the light brightened he came back into focus.

He was breathtaking.

The sunlight touched his dark blond hair, making it almost gleam. His eyes seemed a darker blue in contrast, with impenetrable depths. But they were friendly, and a gentle smile played around his soft, full lips. The dimple reappeared in his cheek.

I took a deep breath, then stole a quick glance over my shoulder. There was nothing there.

I looked back at the screen, where my reflection was still crystal-clear. He was right beside me. I stifled the urge to panic – there had to be some sort of rational explanation for this. I closed my eyes for a second, steadying myself. When I opened them he was still there, with a look of concern creasing his perfect features. As I looked at him he smiled gently, almost hopefully, and I felt my heart lurch.

I glanced around me. The library was silent, interrupted only by the occasional rustle of a page turning and a keyboard being tapped. The world was going on as usual. And in front of me something strange and supernatural was happening.

I took another breath and tried to rationalise things. I didn't believe in ghosts, so that was unlikely. Someone from another dimension? That was just plain silly. A trick? Josh just loved using the latest gizmos to wind me up, but he didn't have the technology to create this. Hallucination? It was the only option which made any kind of sense, even if it did mean that I was losing my mind. At least I was hallucinating an extremely high-quality fantasy man. The thought made me smile wryly.

As I smiled his whole face lit up, changing from concern to something which looked a lot like joy, and maybe relief. His beautiful eyes crinkled up, the gold flecks dancing in the sunshine.

How could my imagination have conjured up someone so spectacular?

This was ridiculous. I shut my eyes again, tearing myself away from that compelling gaze. I couldn't be going mad.

I thought back. This had all started just yesterday, when I first put on the bracelet. I had been wearing it when I first saw his face. And I had been wearing it again today. How had I managed to conjure up this vision of beauty from a piece of jewellery? The thought made me look down at it, the light in the stone dancing lazily in the summer sunshine.

I looked back at his face, and saw he too was considering my bracelet, his brow furrowing very slightly. He raised his hand, and I could see again the matching piece on his wrist. Despite its weight it looked fragile on his well-muscled forearm. My hand reached for the heavy silver on my own slimmer wrist. Was I going crazy, or was this exerting some strange influence over me?

Without stopping to think about it, I ripped the bracelet off my arm. As I did his face shimmered and was gone. I was alone again at my desk.

I gasped at the sudden change, looking around me to be sure. Nothing in the library had changed. The gentle sounds of pages turning and keyboards tapping continued around me. I fought back panic. What was happening to me?

I looked at the bracelet lying on the desktop. How had it done that?

I twisted and turned to examine it closely without touching it, thankful that I was in a very secluded part of the library. The bracelet sat there in the sunshine, flecks in the blue opal flashing red and yellow as I moved around it. Beautiful, but surely that was all? How could something that looked so lovely and harmless do something so weird? I realised that my heart was pounding and tried to relax, to slow things down a little. But almost immediately I had to try it again. I took a deep breath and edged my finger towards it, resting just the tip on the still-warm metal of the band.

The stone darkened, almost as if a shadow had passed through it from the inside. I lifted my finger and the movement stopped. I touched it again, more firmly this time, putting my fingers inside and curling them around the metal. The shadow rolled across the stone again and suddenly he was back behind me, his reflection clear in the computer screen. His face was a picture of confusion, and panic. That was odd – why would he be panicking too?

I moved my hand away from the bracelet, and just as quickly he was gone. I realised that my hands were shaking so I took a deep breath, held on to the table tightly and sat up straight in my chair. The whole thing was bizarre. I seemed to be conducting an experiment on paranormal behaviour involving antique jewellery. Perhaps I should be in the physics lab where Miss Deeley and her instruments could record what was happening. Suddenly, part of me wanted to laugh out loud with the absurdity of it all, but a much larger part was beating back a wave of fright. I shook my head. "Focus!" I told myself sternly. I must try not to panic: becoming hysterical wasn't going to help. There was definitely no way I could share this with anyone, not even Grace. How could I begin to explain it? It was all far too peculiar, and I needed to work it out for myself.

My first priority was to go somewhere else. I couldn't risk doing anything more in here that would bring Miss Neil and a detention flying to my side. I needed to do this at home.

Luckily it wasn't long until the final bell, and I raced down to the coaches, my mind spinning. I had picked up the bracelet with a pencil and stashed it securely in my bag, not daring to touch it again. I could almost feel it there, waiting for me. But however weird this was, somehow it didn't feel too threatening. Scary, yes, but only because it was inexplicable. I couldn't see how it could be dangerous, and the more I thought about it I realised I was actually more excited than anything else, and could hardly wait to get home and test some more theories. I almost managed to fool myself that I just wanted to test it, that the thought of seeing him again wasn't my main motivation.

Grace was on the coach, but I didn't want to talk about what had happened earlier, or what the next steps should be with Rob or Jack. I knew that if she started asking me questions about what I had seen in St Paul's I wouldn't be able to lie convincingly, and I wasn't ready to share it with her just yet. I wanted to think, as my head was bursting with ideas about what I needed to do, and I needed to consider each one.

"I'm feeling a bit off," I explained, guiltily. "My head aches. Maybe I did eat something odd earlier..."

Grace looked concerned for me, but she took the hint and didn't press me. I could hear the usual buzz of conversation, but managed to fade everyone out and consider my options. It seemed to me that there were three possible explanations, some more likely than others. It could be Josh and his tricks, but I was sure that something of this scale was beyond him, so that wasn't really worth considering; it could be some sort of projection from the bracelet; or it could be that I was going mad and hallucinating. The best-case scenario was the projection answer, but I was getting increasingly afraid that I was losing my mind.

When Josh and I finally got home, Mum and Dad were

out. I needed to make sure he wasn't going to disturb me, so was pleased to see that he was helping himself to an enormous quantity of food from the fridge. He was clearly going to be busy for a while, so I ran upstairs.

My small room was still a complete mess from last night's sleepover. Ignoring it all, I shoved all the junk from my desk to one side, clearing enough space to work. I went back and checked the door. Downstairs I could hear the sound of Josh watching the kitchen TV, so he wasn't about to disturb me. I carefully shut the door and turned to face my desk, my heart hammering.

My bag was sitting there, its secret waiting for me. I thought about what I was going to need. My desk lamp was pretty bright, but my laptop was not terribly reflective. I took my mirror off the wall and propped it up in front of me. Next I got out my mobile and called up Josh's number. Then if I needed help I just had to press the green button, I reasoned.

I could barely contain myself as I reached for my bag. I fished the bracelet out with a pencil and laid it gently on the desk. It sat there glistening in the lamplight, and I felt my heart rate increase. I knew now that it definitely wasn't just excitement about the strange phenomenon I was about to test. I was excited because I was about to see his face again. Whatever the consequences, I wanted to be able to look at him properly; I wanted to see him smile again. I hesitantly reached forward for the band.

His face appeared in the mirror immediately I grasped the silver. He was behind my right shoulder, looking just as if he was about to whisper something in my ear. My heart leapt at the thought. His eyes, which were so blue they ought to be cold and threatening, looked unbelievably inviting. The mirror gave a much clearer reflection than the screen in the library. I could see his perfect skin, the highlights in his hair, and the gentle curve of his lips as he started to smile.

Taking a firm grip on the band in one hand, but holding my mobile ready with the other, I turned to check behind me. Nothing. He was still only in the mirror. I couldn't begin to work out how this was happening: the laws of physics just didn't allow it. But there he was, smiling gently, almost as if he could read the argument going on in my head.

As if he could read my thoughts…

I dropped the bracelet as if I had been electrocuted, and his face was gone in an instant. Could he read my mind? My cheeks flamed as I considered the implications of that. What exactly had I been thinking?

I took a deep breath. "Stop it," I told myself sternly, "just finish checking it out." And, anyway, did it matter if a strange reflection could also read my mind? It wasn't as if he was real. I looked at the bracelet. I *had* to figure it out. I was sure Josh wasn't responsible, so that left projection or insanity as my choices. I considered the stone, peering at it from every angle. There was absolutely no way it could generate any power. There was no space for even a tiny battery, so it seemed unlikely that it was projecting an image. The only way to check though was to put it inside something thick, then try again. I rummaged quickly in the pile of junk in the corner of my room, and found an old metal cash box. I dumped the contents on my bed and laid it on the desk.

I sat back down and turned the box so that the lid opened away from me. Really carefully I hooked the bracelet with a pencil and lowered it inside. I closed my eyes tightly for a moment as I felt a small bead of sweat run down my back. This was worse than the exams. Slowly, slowly, I reached around the half-closed box lid and grasped the bracelet tightly.

In a flash his face was back behind me, reflected in the mirror. Not a projection then. I realised that he was actually looking quite distressed. My heart lurched again at the thought that I was upsetting him in some way. But suddenly he seemed to understand that I could see him again, and his face broke into a huge grin of relief. His beauty astonished me. Every time I looked at him he seemed more flawless than before. His high, straight cheekbones gave him an aristocratic air, and his lips... I sighed to myself looking at his lips. Curved in that inviting smile, his mouth looked strong but soft.

I took in the rest of him. He was wearing a loose white cotton shirt of some sort, open to reveal his throat and the top of his chest, and a heavy black cloak which was tied at his neck in a thick cord. The hood was thrown back, and I could see the strength in his neck and shoulders. If he was just a fantasy I had conjured up, I was doing a remarkably good job.

He watched as I completed my assessment, still smiling, then arched an eyebrow as if in a question. All I could do was smile back, blushing again.

So now I had managed to eliminate all the options but the most frightening one: I was going mad. But the more I looked at him and thought about what I had done, the less likely that seemed, too.

Maybe there was another option. I had never believed in ghosts, and as I thought about it, I realised I didn't believe in anything irrational, anything that couldn't be tested. But I *had* tested this, and it was proving that there was something – someone – there that couldn't be explained by anything I knew or understood. I felt another shiver of fear while I considered the possibilities. Maybe he was a ghost, or from a different dimension, or even from another planet: suddenly all those ridiculous alternatives became real possibilities.

Fear had crawled through my stomach, making me feel sick. How was I supposed to deal with this?

The expression on my face must have been transparent, as his expression turned from amusement to concern as he watched me. So whatever he was, he had some compassion. I took a few shallow breaths to settle the queasiness. I had so many questions and I needed to start answering them somehow. Where could I begin? I decided to start with the mind-reading.

I sat up straight, looked him in the eye and bellowed in my head – WHO ARE YOU? His expression didn't flicker. I tried again. WHAT DO YOU WANT? Again there was nothing.

Well, it wasn't exactly scientific, I thought, but in the absence of any other means of testing it would have to do. He couldn't read my mind.

I realised as my arm began to cramp that I was still holding on to the bracelet inside the box. Feeling a little silly I pulled it back out and looked at it for a moment. When I looked back at him he was looking down at his own band, which was firmly clamped on to his left wrist. I thought I could see some strange emotion in his eyes: he seemed to hate it. And as I watched him, I realised that my fear was receding, that whatever he was I didn't really care: I just wanted to be able to see him.

I shifted in my seat and my hold on my bracelet loosened for a second. His image shimmered. His head shot up and I saw a new, pleading look on his face. He shook his head as his lips moved – *No! Don't go, please!* My lip-reading wasn't good but that wasn't difficult to decipher. His reflection then solidified as I realised what I had done and I took a firmer grip on it.

It seemed that he was as keen to look at me as I was to look at him. I could hardly believe that his view was as good as mine. I decided to make the most of it and slipped the bracelet back on to my wrist, smiling shyly at him.

His whole body relaxed, his shoulders dropping as a broad grin spread across his face. *Thank you*, he mouthed, his melting eyes finding mine. I was mesmerised, and couldn't help putting my hand out to touch him. He was so clear in the mirror, just inches from my shoulder with his arm next to mine on the desk. I watched in the reflection as my hand slipped through his arm.

"What are you?" I whispered.

He looked pensive for a second, and started to reply. I couldn't make out the words so I shook my head. I couldn't understand anything he was trying to tell me. He started again slowly and I was concentrating so hard that the sound of a bell clanging made me jump.

I looked around me, feeling as if I had just been woken from a dream. My room was still there, still ordinary, but now touched with something wonderful. The demands of real life seemed irrelevant. The old school bell meant it was time for dinner, but I wasn't remotely interested. The bell rang again and I groaned. "I'll need to go downstairs for a minute. Will you wait?" I didn't even stop to think how silly it was to be talking to a reflection. Then he nodded and smiled.

I'll wait. At least that was easy to lip-read, I thought.

I smiled back, then leapt to my feet and ran downstairs, my mind racing with the implications of what had just happened.

Expectation

Dinner seemed to drag on and on. Both my parents were now back home, and as a treat my mum had ordered a takeaway curry. It was my favourite, and was why I hadn't been summoned earlier to help with the cooking. But today I couldn't enjoy the chicken tikka masala. I pushed most of it around my plate as I tried to work out how to get back upstairs.

Mum and Dad were both keen to hear how I had got on with my final exam. Grace and I had got back so late last night there hadn't been time to talk. Josh had also done an exam that afternoon, so there was a long discussion as Mum and Dad tried to prise out of him how well he felt he had answered the questions. I was trying not to fidget too obviously. I had no idea how long the strange phenomenon upstairs was going to last, and I didn't want to miss a minute more than I had to.

Eventually Josh managed to get away from the table with the excuse of more homework, but they knew that I didn't need to do any more revision, so I couldn't disappear so easily. Mum was particularly interested in how I had got on during the art project, and asked to see how it was all going, but all the time I was talking her through my work, I was desperate to get up to my room again.

I was just edging towards the stairs when there was a knock at the front door. "Do get that, Alex," called Mum, "it's a surprise." What had she done now? I opened the door to find one of our neighbours with their new Labrador puppy. Mum knew I was dying to see it and had obviously fixed this up as a treat. I couldn't believe the bad timing.

I excused myself for a moment, and ran upstairs to my room. Down the corridor I could hear music from Josh's room and occasional bursts of laughter. It sounded like he was watching videos of people falling off things and hurting themselves on the Internet again. He clearly wasn't working too hard. Hopefully he was also making enough noise not to hear me.

I slipped into my room and sat myself down at my desk, ignoring all the clutter and the mess. I looked into the mirror, stroking the band on my wrist. He was there, behind my shoulder, a contented smile on his face. The look then became concerned as he saw my frustration.

"I can't stay up here at the moment. I need to be with my family downstairs – we have a visitor," I explained.

He looked philosophical about it. *Tomorrow*, he mouthed.

"No!" I exclaimed, rather too loudly. "I'll be free in an hour," I added in a whisper.

He shook his head and looked at his bracelet as if it were a watch. *Tomorrow.*

The music in Josh's room had stopped and I could hear him coming down the corridor, calling. "Alex? Are you OK?"

The face in the mirror gave one last dazzling smile and was gone, as Josh stuck his head around the door.

"What's up, Titch? What are you shouting about?"

"Nothing," I hissed, furious and spinning around from my desk. "Just leave me alone." He retreated, looking puzzled. I repositioned myself in front of the mirror but there was no sign of him. I was alone again.

46

"Crap," I muttered. "Might as well go and meet the puppy then." Taking one last peek in the mirror, I turned off the lights and headed downstairs.

It was about an hour later when I finally managed to get back upstairs. I wasn't in the habit of having early nights, but I said I was tired after my exams. Once I was back in my room I shut the door firmly and resumed my seat at the mirror. I was still wearing the band, and I rubbed the stone firmly, just in case that made any difference. Once or twice I thought I saw a shifting shadow in the sparkling depths, but there was no blinding vision in my head, and no figure appearing behind me. He really did mean tomorrow then.

I took off the bracelet to consider it in a bit more detail. It had left a big black mark around my wrist and around the cuff of my shirt. If I wasn't going to be seeing him again tonight, I reasoned, I could take the opportunity to give the thing a thorough clean.

All the cleaning materials were under the sink. I knew we had some silver cleaner as I had seen Mum use it, but I had no idea how to use it or what it looked like. I started to rummage through the various bottles lined up on the shelf. I kept on moving bottles until I saw a small tin at the back – that was what I wanted. I fished around until I had a cloth as well, and started putting the bottles back in the cupboard. I was nearly done when Mum walked in.

"Alex, whatever are you doing down there? I thought you had gone to bed."

"I was looking for the silver polish." I quickly decided that there was no harm in giving her the truth. "I decided I didn't feel like going to bed, and wanted something soothing to do. I have some things which have tarnished and are making my clothes go black."

"I wish you had thought about it a little earlier. There are a few things of mine which could do with cleaning, and as you are in the mood…" She tailed off, realising from my look that she was unlikely to get a positive response to that. "Never mind, just be careful that you don't make too much of a mess."

"I'll be OK, Mum," I promised quickly. "I've got some old papers upstairs which I can work on. Goodnight."

She frowned slightly as she kissed me, somehow suspecting that something wasn't quite right. "Goodnight, love, see you in the morning. Don't be up all night playing with that stuff."

Back in my room I laid an old newspaper across my desk and examined the instructions on the silver cleaner. It didn't look too hard. The tin was full of wadding of some sort that was soaked with the cleaning stuff, so all I had to do was pull off a chunk and start to smooth it over the band. The wadding quickly went black and more of the silver colour began to shine through. I worked at it really carefully, ensuring that I got into all the crevices. Finally I took the duster and polished the residue of the cleaning stuff off. The silver shone warmly in the light from my desk lamp, and finally I was able to examine it more closely. The bracelet was "C"-shaped, able to fit securely on to my wrist without the need for hinges or fasteners. The stone was oval, about the size of the end of my thumb, and held in place by tiny silver ropes that twisted and turned over and around it. The ropes all merged together at each side to form the rest of the bracelet. The ropes were exquisite – the detail on each was stunning. I quickly rummaged around in the back of my desk drawer and found an old magnifying glass which Mum had confiscated from Josh years ago to stop him and his friends setting fire to things, and which I had promptly liberated because I thought it would be useful for fixing earrings.

I adjusted the light to get a better look, and peered through the lens at the setting. Each silver rope was perfectly made, the individual strands twisted around just like a real cable, but in perfect miniature. And each was subtly different from the last. As I turned the band I could see that the stone wasn't actually attached to the silver in any way: the ropes formed a sort of cage around it, keeping it secure, but allowing it to rotate a little.

On either side the ropes joined together into a band about as wide as the stone was long, and which on the outside was strangely rough. It looked as if the ropes had been beaten together, and the marks from the hammer were still visible, dimpling the surface. Why make a piece of jewellery which was so fine in one place but almost rustic in another? It didn't make sense.

Now the silver was clean the stone gleamed darkly, moving slightly in the setting. Its ability to move seemed to enhance the fire inside and the fabulous colours glinted in the light. Although it was mostly blue there were hints of the brightest green, all studded with the flecks of reds, pinks and gold.

The inside of the bracelet was also now clean, and I had a moment of excitement when I thought that I could see some engraving, but the more I squinted at it the more it just looked like shadows in the silver where the ropes had been welded together. I couldn't make anything out. Grace had been right: there was no hallmark, and no clue as to who had made or owned it.

When I had finished, I laid it gently down on the desk and considered it. How had something so beautiful and innocent-looking conjured up such a strange apparition? I thought about his face, initially so angry looking and then so content. Where was he from? I had so many questions and no way of answering them. I sighed, and started getting ready for bed. The bracelet may have been clean, but I was now comprehensively filthy, with silver polish and black tarnish all over my hands and up my arms. The shirt wasn't going to recover in a hurry either. I grabbed my pyjamas and headed for the bathroom where I could hide the shirt in the bottom of the washing basket.

The next morning I slipped the newly cleaned bracelet on after my shower and peered hopefully into the depths of the mirror. I saw nothing, but I could feel my heartbeat increasing at the thought that I would see him in a few hours.

It was a driving lesson day, and so instead of going in on the coach I went in the Mini with Josh. I usually had my driving lessons at lunchtime when it was a little less busy on the road. I wasn't able to practise on the way to and from school as Josh hadn't had his licence for long enough to supervise me. He was gutted about that, as he really fancied being able to boss me about officially, but I was quite relieved. So on my driving lesson days he got to take the car to school and park it in my school car park.

He loved driving past all the girls and then casually sauntering over to his school, swinging the car keys from his long fingers. Very few of his classmates had cars, so it really helped his image. Luckily most of them hadn't seen the actual vehicle.

It wasn't much of a car. It was old and beaten up and a disgusting custard yellow colour. Mum refused to buy anything worth much for us, and the insurance was already far more than the value of the car. She had promised that when we had both got our licences she would add us to the insurance for her car, but I wasn't holding my breath. In the meantime I did my best to cover over the custard paint with weird abstract murals in clashing colours, which had the added benefit of winding Josh up.

We were supposed to share the car, as Mum and Dad had

bought it for both of us, but until I passed my test I was stuck with Josh and his superior attitude. He had passed his test first time but my lessons were not going that well. Technically I wasn't too bad, but I had an unfortunate habit of speeding. I hadn't even put in to take the practical part of the test yet, and my teacher hadn't been too encouraging so far.

Josh was ready to leave in good time, as usual, while I was still trying to find all the things I needed for the day. He started drumming his fingers impatiently on the kitchen work surface.

"Come on, Alex, what else do you need to collect? If I had an exam this morning I would have left you by now." I knew this wasn't an idle threat. He had abandoned me one morning when I had lost my PE kit. I quickly grabbed my bag and made for the door.

"Ready," I mumbled, through a last mouthful of toast as I pulled on my jumper.

"About time. You really have no sense of urgency, you know," he complained as we got into the car. "One day you'll miss something really important."

"You sound just like Mum," I countered, knowing that the comparison would get him quickly off the subject.

The route was busy as usual, but with no major hold-ups, so we were on time.

"See," I said triumphantly as we drove through the gates. "There was no need for all that fuss after all."

I should have kept my mouth shut: Josh circled the car park twice before he found a space then squeezed the Mini into a tiny corner, despite my complaints. I had no idea how I would get it out of there at the start of my lesson.

"You need to practise getting out of difficult parking spaces," he laughed as he pulled his rucksack out of the back. "And this one has the added benefit that no one can see your dodgy artwork."

"You are so mean," I grumbled, hoping that I would be able to get Miss McCabe, my driving teacher, to move it for me.

"You do have your keys, don't you?"

I checked quickly in my bag. "Yup, all present and correct. See you here just after four." He waved in acknowledgement as he loped off, jogging gently across the grounds to the gate nearest his playing fields where the early morning kick-about was in progress.

I heaved my bags out of the car, locked it carefully and slowly made my way into school. I couldn't believe that so many weird things could happen in just twenty-four hours. I sighed gently, looking hopefully at the bracelet. He had promised that he would come back today, so maybe he would appear in any mirror I passed. I was smiling at the thought as I made it to my classroom just in time for registration.

The day's post-exam programme was pretty dull, and seemed more like ordinary lessons. I spent half the morning trying to catch my reflection in windows and on computer screens, hoping for signs that he might appear, and the other half peering at the stone for any mysterious movement. It stayed stubbornly still, and the more I looked, the longer the morning seemed to stretch.

Lunchtime finally came around and I grabbed a sandwich for later, then went to the staffroom to wait for Miss McCabe. She was one of the student teachers, who also had a qualification as a driving instructor, so we could book her at lunchtimes to practise as long as we had our own cars. She was much cheaper than the usual driving schools, and she didn't take me for any classes so it wasn't too embarrassing.

Luckily the car next to the Mini had gone, so I was able to get out of the car park easily, and she directed me down through Twickenham and over the river to Kew. We finally found a quiet corner to practise reversing around, and then made our way back to the main road. The road was a dual carriageway with a 40 mile an hour limit, and I always had to try really hard not to overdo it. Today I was OK, with just a few warnings from Miss McCabe as I cornered the roundabouts near school a little too enthusiastically.

When we got back to the car park there was even more space so I was able to park easily. She always gave me a pep talk after a lesson so I settled back to wait.

"Not bad today, Alex," she said, almost grudgingly. "Although you still need to keep an eye on your speed. They'll fail you for that, you know."

"I know. It's just that I start to enjoy it and I forget."

"Well, if you can keep it down I think it's about time you put in for your test. Everything else is fine."

I was thrilled. If I could pass quickly I would be able to use the car in the summer holidays and not be dependent on Josh or my parents to ferry me about. She gave me the form as we walked back into school, with instructions to get it completed as soon as possible. With a bit of luck I could begin counting down the remaining driving lessons.

I ran back up to the sixth form common room in a great mood, fishing around in my bag for my mobile as I went. Seven missed calls: someone was keen to speak to me. We were not supposed to use our phones in school, but I quickly rang the voicemail service. It was Rob, with a long, rambling message about going out on Saturday night. It sounded a bit as if he thought I was playing hard-to-get. How ironic, given that I really wasn't sure any more. He promised to call me later, and I snapped the phone off before his message had ended. As I walked down the long corridor past the main hall I puzzled over my reaction. There was no doubt that Rob was considered to be the alpha male in our pack of boys, but I had given him no thought at all since the night out in Richmond. The face that made me smile was the strange one I had seen next to me in the mirror. Even thinking about him made my heart flutter.

The common room was heaving, with dozens of girls lounging about before heading off to the afternoon's activities. Grace and the others were sitting in our usual corner, and they shifted to make space for me as I approached.

"So," drawled Mia, "Rob. Tell us all about it."

There was an expectant hush around the group. I quickly scanned the faces – no Ashley. That was a relief: I wasn't looking forward to her reaction.

"Not much to tell really," I smiled at Mia. "He's asked me out on Saturday, but I'm not sure yet where we are going. He seems quite keen," I added. "He's left loads of messages already today." I saw Grace nod her approval.

"Oh, wow, you are sooo lucky. Rob Underwood! He really is gorgeous," exclaimed Alia.

I knew they were expecting me to be much more enthusiastic than I felt. "I know – I couldn't believe it when he made a move at the cinema. It's all down to Grace's make-over skills, of course." I tried to deflect the conversation to her.

"Rubbish," she snorted. "It's only been a matter of time. I just helped to speed things up a little, that's all. I have to say though," she said teasingly, "you did look pretty gorgeous compared to how you look most school days." She gestured towards my tattered jeans and faded T-shirt, and I did my best to look offended before we both burst out laughing.

"So is he serious, do you think?" Mia clearly wasn't about to be moved off the subject. She probably had instructions from Ashley to find out what was going on.

"I doubt it. I've never known him be serious about anyone before."

"But he is taking you out on your own on Saturday?"

"Well, yes, but only to a country pub. I think that's the plan." I thought I'd better not mention his other plan about Cornwall.

I could see that she was about to launch into another question so was really relieved when the bell rang for the next lesson.

"I'll see you later." I smiled at Mia as I leapt up, hoping she wouldn't think I was running off. I still couldn't fathom my own reaction. Why was I not more enthusiastic about getting a date with the school heart-throb? Just two days ago I would have been delighted to sit there with them for hours analysing everything he said, reading all sorts of things into his every action. Now I didn't even want to listen to his messages.

I couldn't help thinking about that other face, and quickly glanced in a passing window just in case he might be around, but there was still nothing. Was he real in some way? Had I imagined it all? My heart twisted at the thought that I might never see him again, and I dismissed it quickly: he had promised that he would come back today. I smiled to myself. I could hardly wait to see him again in the mirror.

The afternoon dragged on, but finally we were free for the day. I managed to avoid Grace and the others and ran down to the car park where Josh was waiting for me. Back home both Mum and

Dad were in, so I ran upstairs quickly, with the excuse that I had to do some research on my art project. I couldn't help darting into the bathroom first to check that I looked reasonably presentable.

I sat at my desk with the mirror and held tightly to the band on my wrist. Nothing happened. I took it off and rubbed it gently, carefully examining its depths. There was nothing unusual about it at all. No movement, and no face behind my shoulder. I battled with my disappointment. If he suddenly appeared I didn't want him seeing me looking desperate, but that was how I felt.

I must have sat there for the best part of an hour, trying to call him back. If he had been the product of my imagination, I reasoned, I wouldn't be having this difficulty: I would have been able to see him immediately. But if he was real, if that were possible in some weird way, then he obviously didn't want to come back, or he would be with me.

I continued to torment myself until I remembered that it had been quite late when I had last seen him. Perhaps he'd come back twenty-four hours after that? Part of me knew that I was clutching at straws, but I stubbornly clung on to the hope. I needed to fill my time until then. I searched around for something diverting, glancing every few minutes at the bracelet, just in case. The bracelet: that was diverting enough. There must be something on the Internet which I could look up.

I set up my laptop on my desk, and took the bracelet off. It shone enticingly in the light from my halogen lamp. How could I go about searching for that? I tried "ancient opal silver bracelets", but that gave me nothing useful. I turned it over to look again at the strange shadows on the inside, and for a fraction of a second, as my eyes found the spot it seemed as if there were words there. Startled, I looked again and I could have sworn that they blurred and faded back into the dimpled metal. Maybe all my late night reading did mean that I needed glasses, as Mum kept warning me. I rubbed my eyes and looked again. Nothing.

This searching was going to be harder than I thought. Maybe antiques would be a better way. I looked that up, and found myself dragged into a world of strange bric-a-brac and poorly-organised websites. I must have spent hours going down the antiques track. Some of the bracelets were beautiful, but none of them was anything like mine. What most of them seemed to agree on was that a bracelet with an opal that large and clear, and with that weight of silver, was worth a lot of money.

Why had it ended up in the river? It had been buried very deep, so whoever had thrown it in tied to that rock hadn't intended it to be found in a hurry.

I sighed. I was no further forward – I just had more and more questions. Still, I realised as I stretched, I had successfully used up a lot of time. It was about this time last night I had last seen him. I slipped the bracelet back on to my wrist, where it felt so comfortable and right. I closed my eyes and composed myself for a moment before turning to face the mirror.

There was nothing there.

I felt the crushing disappointment before I was able to gather myself. It felt like a wave that winded me and left me breathless. He had promised to come, but he wasn't there. I shut my eyes and tried to control my feelings. How had I got to the point where I cared so much about it? I had never felt like this before.

As I sat there for the next hour, all I could think of was his glorious face, with those piercing blue eyes, and strong, soft lips. I tried not to think too much about the lips, about how they would feel, gently pressed on mine. But the memory of his face was a normal, indistinct one, not like the blinding vision of that first night; he wasn't here, and I had no way of working out how to change that. I felt the tears prick my eyes as I struggled with the loss of something I had never had.

Date

The next morning I had a moment of lightness as I woke, then the memory of the night before washed over me. He hadn't come back – he had promised, but then let me down. In the cold light of day I realised that I couldn't go on tormenting myself over something that was probably a figment of my imagination. What I had seen before couldn't possibly have been real. The figure at St Paul's, the face in the mirror – I had to assume it was all nonsense as there was no rational explanation. I felt like rolling over and hiding under the duvet, but I couldn't stay there forever. I took a deep breath, and sat up. It was time to get on with the real world.

My exams were finished, it was Friday, and I had a date tomorrow with one of the hottest guys at school. I really couldn't complain.

I thought about Rob's face, with his deep brown eyes and his knowing smile. He was handsome, I acknowledged with a half-hearted attempt at a smile, and he was incredibly fit. I just needed to decide how I was going to deal with him and his expectations. That was the tricky question I should be wrestling with, not how to summon a strange hallucination.

It was a dull day at school, and we were all pleased to be back on the coaches after the final bell. We had plans to be back in Richmond that night, at one of the pubs on the river. Grace had persuaded her dad to give her a lift, so they stopped to pick me up.

As usual, she assessed me critically during the trip, adjusting my clothes and adding a couple of accessories from her huge handbag. I managed to convince her that I was looking scruffy because I was saving the good stuff until my date with Rob the next night, which seemed to satisfy her.

Neither Rob nor Jack was with the group that night; there was some sort of cricket activity going on. Both Grace and I felt that cricket was the dullest game in the world, and could never be persuaded to watch. So it was a girls' night out, and we were always much more raucous than when the boys were with us.

We were the first ones at the pub. We grabbed a table on the balcony where we could watch the sun go down over the river and keep an eye on the activities in the terrace. It was a large area beside the Thames which went all the way up to Richmond Bridge. There were pubs and bars at both ends, and lots of grass and seats in the middle. On an average summer Friday night it would be busy, and tonight looked as if it would be no different. It was full of students, most of whom had clearly finished their exams for the year so there was a lot of exuberance. I was fairly sure that someone would be thrown in the water before the night was out.

Grace was in a very lively mood, her dark eyes sparkling with excitement, clearly still thrilled about Jack.

"Come on then," I cajoled, keen to get her talking before she started asking me questions. "What's the latest with you and Jack? I mean, it's been four days now."

"Well," she started, looking like she was about to burst with excitement, "he has been texting me every day."

"What, just once a day?"

"Well, no. More like once an hour, or once every ten minutes." She glowed with happiness. "I think that's probably a good sign."

"I think you're right," I agreed, feeling very happy for her. "I've known him for years and he's never been great about texts. You must be making an impression." She beamed at me again as I reached out to squeeze her hand. "You and Jack: it's a such great combination."

"I hope so. I've been waiting so long for him to notice me. I just need to make sure that I don't put him off by being too keen. In fact," she added, "I should be taking lessons from you. I've never seen anyone play it so cool."

"I don't know what you mean," I mumbled. But she was determined.

"Huh! From the minute Rob played his hand in the restaurant the other night you have been acting as if you could take him or leave him. It's probably driving him crazy. I can't imagine any girl has done that to him before."

"Oh." I didn't know what to say. "Well ... there's no point in just giving in, is there?"

"It's a smart move. I've never seen him so wound up over a girl."

I spent a few seconds wiping the condensation off my glass while I considered how best to answer her. "The thing is, I'm really not sure that I do want him." I didn't dare raise my face to look at her – she was never going to buy it.

"What!" spluttered Grace. "But you've fancied Rob for ages! What's made you change your mind?"

"I really don't know. It's just that, well, I'm not convinced that he's the sort of guy I want to be going out with."

"You can't be serious. Every other girl in our year has been drooling over him for months. You can't turn him down."

"Well, I can, if that's what I decide I want." I put my drink down rather too abruptly, spilling some of it on the table. Grace sat back, looking shocked.

"I'm sorry. Of course you can do whatever you want, I'm just surprised."

"I'm sorry, too. I didn't mean to be so sharp. I'm really confused," I whispered, reaching for her hand apologetically.

"But why? What's happened? Has he ... well, has he done something wrong?"

"No, not yet." I could see a way to explain my strange behaviour which wasn't too far from the truth. "But I know what he wants, and I'm not sure he's going to take no for an answer."

Grace nodded. "If you're not ready, you're not ready, and he shouldn't make you."

"But I'm really not sure he'll take it well. And I feel confused because ... well, if we went out for a bit of time ... I mean, you never know, I might feel ... different." It felt strange and somehow mean not giving Grace the whole story, but the whole story was just too odd. The fact that I seemed to prefer a figment of my imagination in a mirror to one of the most desirable boys in our year wasn't easy to explain. And anyway, I still really didn't know what I felt about Rob.

I was almost grateful when the rest of the girls turned up: I knew Grace wouldn't want to have this debate with an audience. Conversation quickly turned to other things, and although my friends did tease me a bit about my date with Rob, they were easily deflected. Many of them were planning to enjoy the end-of-exams party season in a big way, so there was a lot of gossip about which of the boys they were targeting. We all knew that the planning was futile, that the boys had ideas of their own which rarely matched ours, but we just loved talking about it. The evening passed quickly, and I was surprised when my phone buzzed with the message from Mum to say that she was on her way to pick us up.

I couldn't resist a glance in my mirror when I got home, but as expected there was only my own pale face staring back at me. There were dark circles under my eyes and I hoped that I would be able to sleep.

I was lucky: sleep came quickly and deeply, and the next thing I knew Mum was putting a coffee on my desk.

"Morning, sleepy-head. It's just gone ten, and I didn't think you would want to stay in bed all day."

"Ooh, thanks, Mum," I groaned, stretching. "Do we have any plans for today, or..."

"I'm glad you asked," she grinned, with a gleam in her eye. "There are a disturbing number of weeds out there in the garden, and I was thinking that maybe the two of us could get them thrashed."

I dropped back on to my pillow, realising I was beaten. When Mum was in one of these moods it was easier to go with the flow.

Actually, the gardening was pretty therapeutic. I had to concentrate enough to make sure that I was pulling up the right plants, and that kept my mind from wandering too far. I had kept the bracelet on, and occasionally my gaze settled on it, but just like yesterday, the stone stayed quite still.

After we had finished a particularly overrun bed Mum brought out some cold drinks and we sat together in the shade of the shed, considering our handiwork.

"That's a pretty bracelet," she commented. "Is that the one you found in the river?"

I nodded, holding out my arm so that she could see it more easily. "It's cleaned up really nicely," she said, approvingly. "But I would be careful of it. Opals have a reputation for being unlucky, but that's just because they smash easily. And this one is such a size it would be a tragedy to ruin it." She was turning my arm to and fro to admire the stone when she gave a little gasp and suddenly had me in a much tighter grip.

"Mum? What is it?" I hardly dared hope. Had she seen something? She was staring intently at the beautiful blue gem.

"Very odd," she said thoughtfully. "Must be a trick of the light."

"What? Is there something wrong?"

"No, nothing." She shook herself. "Such a strange stone, the opal. Hidden depths, you know." She paused. "I really wouldn't wear it all the time. Keep it for best. Now, how about helping to dig some of those new potatoes?"

I helped as quickly as I could, diving into the shed when I had an excuse, but there was nothing at all that was reflective in there. Even the windows were too grubby to be helpful. I finally escaped and ran to my bedroom, hoping that Mum had seen something in the stone that meant that he would be there. But again I was disappointed, alone in the mirror.

I jumped into the shower to wash off the grime of the garden. Afterwards I looked at the bracelet on the bathroom shelf, and for a minute considered just putting it into my jewellery box, but in the end I couldn't resist easing it on to my wrist, where there was now a faint tan line showing where it had been.

I really hadn't got a clue what to wear for the date with Rob. I didn't want to give the wrong impression by making myself look too available, but I didn't want to look too boring either. After an hour peering hopelessly into the far corners of the wardrobe, I did what I should have done first: I called Grace. She had an encyclopaedic knowledge of my clothes and quickly talked me through a few options. Some we had to discard because the clothes were sitting in a grubby pile not having made it to the washing basket, and other combinations I flatly refused. She even offered to cycle over with her new Topshop dress, but I thought that was going a bit too far. We ended up choosing an outfit I would never have thought to put together myself.

Her advice was obviously good, because even Dad whistled appreciatively as I came down the stairs.

"You look stunning, darling. I hope your date will behave himself."

"Me too, Dad; me too. You can rely on me to sort him out if he doesn't." At that point my phone buzzed. "Rob's here, Dad. I'll see you later." He gave me a squeeze and kissed the top of my head as I made for the door.

"Next time he can come in and introduce himself," he said pointedly.

"Yeah, sure." I shrugged as I sidled out of the door. I really didn't want that complication this evening.

Rob was waiting in his car, engine running, clearly wanting to avoid an opportunity to speak to a parent. I jumped in, and he was off immediately.

"Hi, nice car."

He grinned. "Not really, but my mum lets me use it whenever I want, so I'm not complaining. Now, we just need to do this..." He pulled the car into a lay-by just around the corner from my house, and killed the engine. "Time to say hello properly, I think." He pulled me towards him and kissed me. I didn't resist, but I couldn't help thinking about the premeditation involved in the manoeuvre. He smelled nice though, a combination of shampoo and aftershave.

I kissed him back, trying to show the right level of enthusiasm but not overdoing it, but he instantly took it as a signal to go further. I pushed him back as his hand slid over me. "I thought we were going for dinner," I said, keeping my voice light. "So where are we going?" Thankfully he settled back into his seat immediately.

"It's a really cool bar in Chertsey. Used to be the old town hall. They have some great bands on there midweek. You won't have heard of it," he added and I thought that I heard just a touch of condescension.

I hid a smile. The bar he was describing was one of my parents' favourites, and I had been going there for as long as I could remember. It was a great place, though, and it also did fantastic food, so at least I knew I would enjoy the meal. There didn't seem to be any point in letting him know that I was a regular.

He was in an upbeat mood as we drove there, relaying the details of the cricket victory last night. I made encouraging noises in all the right places, and he went on and on, and I started to feel a little irritated. I tried to get a grip on myself. I really had to stop questioning everything he did and start enjoying myself.

The Old Town Hall was an imposing building. A colonnade ran the length of the ground floor with imposing double doors at the centre. They led directly to a wide, sweeping staircase which split into two and doubled back to a magnificent balcony. Through the main doors into the restaurant I could hear the low buzz of conversation, laughter and, in the background, some unobtrusive jazz. The smell of garlic and flowers mingled, and I could see huge vases of lilies scattered around the room.

"What do you think?" asked Rob.

"It's beautiful – I love the decor." The room was huge, with a twenty-foot ceiling and about a dozen full-height French windows. The night was warm so all the windows were open and the long, light drapes billowed gently in any passing breeze.

I tried to look suitably surprised and I thought I was doing well until my cover was completely blown by the guy at the front desk. Rob had leant in to give his name when the waiter caught my eye and beamed.

"Great to see you!" he exclaimed. "It's been a while. How are you?"

"Oh, you know, exams." I smiled, looking down quickly at my shoes.

"It's a table for two, and the name's Underwood," Rob announced, clearly flustered.

"Right, here you are, and seeing as it's you, let's see if we can just rearrange things a little." He got out his pencil and started crossing things out in his reservations book. "Got you somewhere nice and private now." He winked at me and I felt myself go even pinker. He led us through the crowded restaurant to a great table in the corner, with beautiful leather chairs and next to one of the huge windows. We had clearly been upgraded.

I had never seen Rob at a loss for words before, and I found myself feeling sorry for him. "My parents come here a bit, and sometimes I come too. I'm surprised they remembered me, though."

He seemed to relax a little. "Yeah, well, I guess your parents have reasonable taste then. Mine wouldn't dream of coming to somewhere like this."

"Oh, you know: most of the time they're pretty dull, like most parents," I said with a big smile. "So how did you come across this place?"

He was soon off in a complicated story about one of his friends who was in a band that had played there once. I carried on with the nodding and appreciative noises. Really, this guy could talk, I thought. A wicked idea crossed my mind, and I considered it quickly as he droned on about the band I didn't know: I wondered if I could keep him talking all night without imparting a single piece of information about myself. It was a game that Grace and I played occasionally and it worked really well with some of the girls at school. All I had to do was sound interested and ask questions, and he would keep going.

He turned out to be almost too easy to direct for the game to be fun. We talked for hours, and I found out all sorts of things about his family, his last holiday, what he thought of the other guys in his class, and a whole lot more. He kept going all through the meal. Every time the waitress came to the table I smiled at her while Rob continued his monologue. She smiled back knowingly while he ignored her completely. It wasn't until we got to the coffee that he finally asked me the only question that really interested him.

"So, Alex," he murmured, taking my hand as I absently stirred the sugar bowl. "Cornwall. The place we are renting is in Polzeath, within walking distance of the beach, and the surfing's great." He paused briefly. "How about it?"

"I'm really not sure," I tried to sound determined, "not when it's only the two of us."

"But that's the fun bit, no one to check up on us, a free run of the house, late nights and later mornings…" He took my other hand and stared into my eyes, his pale blond hair glinting in the candlelight. "We could have a lot of fun."

"I'm just not sure that I'm ready for this," I said. "I mean, what's the hurry? We have barely even started going out."

"Alex, just because we haven't been going out for months, it doesn't mean that I don't care for you." He stopped for a moment to gauge my reaction. "I mean, I care for you a great deal."

I hesitated, unsure of what I could say that would let him down gently, but he leant in further towards me and twisted a strand of hair behind my ear. "Truth is, Alex, I think I, well – I think I love you, and I'd like to show you how much." His dark eyes were fixed on mine, and as I deliberated for the briefest second I saw the corner of his mouth raise in a triumphant smile.

"Rob, we both know that's not true." He looked puzzled for a second, then pulled his hands away.

"What do you mean? Of course I do. Have done for months," he began.

"Look, I know why you want to take someone to Cornwall while your parents are away, I'm not stupid. And I'm sure that we could have a good time going out, but we haven't done enough of the going out yet for me to want to spend a weekend with you."

His face looked like thunder.

"So are you saying that you won't come to Cornwall with me?" His voice was suddenly icy.

"That's right. It's too soon."

He slapped his hand down on the leather seat, and the sound made the people around us raise their heads to look at us curiously. "I thought we had an understanding," he hissed, his handsome face suddenly looking harsh and uncompromising.

"Well, I didn't. I like you a lot, Rob, I think I'd like to go out with you, but not if it's all on your terms." My voice had turned sharp, and I saw the couple at the next table stiffen as they tuned into our conversation.

His lips were pressed into a thin line. "I've seen how you've looked at me. You've been leading me on, you know. That's not very nice."

I gasped at the injustice of his comment. "That's so unfair! I'm glad I've found out what you're like now. I think you had better take me home."

"Huh. Well, at least I haven't wasted Cornwall on you." He sat back, looking furious. I needed a few minutes to think, so I got up from the table.

"I'm just going to the loo. Can you please ask for the bill? I'll be back in a minute." I tried to keep my voice even.

There was a queue in the toilets, so I didn't have much time on my own, which was probably for the best. I was upset and angry, so I quickly splashed some cold water on my cheeks, smoothed my hair and took a deep breath before heading back out into the restaurant.

Rob wasn't sitting at our table, but the bill was there with some notes folded under it. Perhaps he had gone to the loo as well. I sat back down and looked out of the window down the high street while I waited. There was something slightly furtive about one guy walking away from me down the street. He looked vaguely familiar, so I paid a little more attention. In fact, he looked very familiar, and I wasn't surprised when he unlocked the car we had come in. He couldn't resist looking up at the window as he got into the driver's seat, and I could see that he had seen me looking at him. He quickly ducked his head into the car and was gone.

I felt slightly sick. How had I been taken in by someone

quite so shallow? Another thought occurred to me, and I reached for the bill. The notes he had left covered his half exactly. I gasped: his behaviour was so bad it was almost laughable. I was so relieved that I hadn't let things go any further.

But I had a problem: I was stuck with no lift home, and by the time I had paid the other half of the bill I would have no money for a taxi. There were no buses, and I really didn't fancy calling my parents. They would be really lovely about it, I knew, and angry on my behalf, but I really didn't want to face their sympathy. I needed someone reliable who I could trust to keep his mouth shut. I pulled out my mobile and called Josh.

As I'd hoped, he was brilliant. He came without question, leaving his mates in the pub. He gave me a big hug and said just one thing. "Do you want me to sort him out?" I shook my head.

"He's not worth the trouble, really. But thank you for the offer."

"Do you want to come back to the pub with me, or would you rather go home?"

"Home, I think. You could drop me outside and then I won't have to answer a million questions from Mum and Dad."

"OK, if you're sure."

"You're the best brother in the world, you know." I leaned over and gave him a quick kiss as I got out of the car. "I owe you big time."

"Too right," he said, laughing as he drove off.

I gave him a few minutes to get away, and then I opened the front door. It was still early so I knew there were bound to be questions. I decided to get them over with, so I marched straight into the sitting room.

"Hello, sweetheart. You're home early," said Mum with a

hint of surprise. "Is everything OK?"

"Fine, thank you. Just not as much fun as I had hoped. It seems he really is just a pretty face."

My parents exchanged a quick glance. "Come and join us, we were just about to start watching a film," said Dad, patting a space on the sofa.

"No, thanks. I think I'll have an early night. I've got a bit of a headache." I gave them each a quick kiss and ran up the stairs. I shut my bedroom door gently behind me, then sank to the floor, exhausted by the need to keep up appearances. I felt the tears well up in my eyes at last.

I couldn't believe Rob's behaviour. The injustice of it all overwhelmed me. The tears ran down my face and my shoulders heaved as I tried not to cry too loudly. I pulled my knees up and rested my head on my arms, making myself small. As I sat there I felt my body tingle, and I shivered involuntarily.

"Don't cry."

My head snapped up. "Who's there?" I whispered, peering round at the corners of my obviously empty tiny room, ignoring for a moment the fact that the voice had plainly been in my head.

"My name is Callum."

It was a dark, silky voice, full of emotion. I jumped up and headed for my desk, flicking on the light and nervously pulling the mirror towards me as I tried to wipe the tears from my cheeks. He was there at my shoulder, his beautiful face full of concern.

"Hello, Alex. Please don't be upset. I'm not going to hurt you."

I felt my mouth drop as I stared at him in wonder.

Callum

I tried to settle my breathing as he watched, my heart bursting with conflicting emotions: fear of the unknown and an overwhelming joy that he was back. The part of me that had been agonising over Rob was instantly silenced.

He smiled gently, letting me come to terms with what I was seeing.

"Callum? That's your name?"

He nodded, still smiling.

"But you can talk. I can hear you. I mean, hear you in my head. How did you...?" I knew I was rambling but I suddenly couldn't think of anything sensible to say. He had come back, and he was talking to me.

He put his finger to his lips. "Shhh, you only need to whisper. If your family hear you, they'll come up and eventually I'll have to go."

"No!" I exclaimed. "Please don't go, not again."

His face was suddenly full of concern. "I'm not planning on going anywhere. I'd much rather stay here with you."

I smiled weakly. That was good, however strange the rest of this was. I tried to compose myself.

"So, what are, I mean, who are ..?" I stuttered. "I don't understand."

"I know." He sighed, a small frown creasing his forehead.

"It's complicated, and it'll take a while to explain. I'm not really sure where to start."

I could feel the excitement in me turn to something else; I had to ask, and I didn't know if I was ready to deal with the answer. Finally I gathered up enough nerve to speak.

"Are you a ghost?"

It was his turn to hesitate. "To be honest, I'm not sure. I know ... well, I know I should be dead, but ... I'm not ... not really, anyway. But I also know I'm not what I was before." The pain was evident in his eyes. He took a deep breath and smiled. "For now, let's just say that I'm very, very happy to have found you."

I sat there, stunned and speechless. How do you respond to someone who is "not really dead"? I took a couple of deep breaths. He was clearly waiting for me to come to terms with what he had said. His features were made even better by the slightly shy twist of his mouth, and by the gentle way he looked at me, as if he were worried by what I would say or do next.

I couldn't resist smiling: whatever he was, he had come back, and that was what I had been hoping for. My fear was slowly being replaced by a strange and unexpected feeling of contentment. I felt that I could sit there for hours, marvelling at his beauty, without asking any more questions. But I needed *some* information; I just didn't know where to start. After considering for a moment I asked him something I hoped he'd find easy to answer. "Where have you been for the last few days? You promised to come back and you didn't. I was beginning to think that I had imagined everything." I didn't add that I had been desperate to see his face again.

"Yes, I'm sorry about that. It took a little longer to do what I planned."

I raised my eyebrows in a question.

"Well, it was really frustrating being able to hear you but know that you couldn't hear me. So I went to investigate how I could change that. I didn't want to practise on you: you might never have spoken to me again."

"Well, it worked! It's a bit odd, though. In the mirror you look as if you are talking normally, but somehow I seem to be hearing you inside my head. How are you doing it?"

He gestured towards the bracelet on my wrist. "The amulet. It acts as a conduit between us. Well, you know that, you were experimenting on me the other day."

His tone was teasing but I was instantly abashed. I had been experimenting, not realising that it would actually affect him in some way.

"I'm sorry about that, but well, you have to admit it was a bit odd. I'm not used to reflections of gorgeous guys suddenly appearing at my side."

"You think I look good?" There was disbelief in his voice.

"Of course," I mumbled, suddenly embarrassed. "You are better looking than anyone I have ever seen. Don't you have a mirror where you come from?"

He continued to look stunned.

"Do you really have no idea?" He was clearly lost for words, but as I watched he pulled himself together.

"I ... well, I don't know what to say." I smiled: his response was so unlike the self-satisfied preening of Rob, and it quickly banished the last remnants of my fear. My heart was still racing, but now I knew that the cause was excitement. I couldn't believe that I was actually talking to him, whatever he was.

"But apart from your stunning good looks," I couldn't help teasing, watching a faint flush of red move across his face, "what are you doing here? What is all this about? How does this bracelet do all this?"

I waved my arm in the air to make the point, looking at the identical band on his strong wrist. He put his finger to his lips again, reminding me to be quiet.

"The amulet is a powerful device. It's lots of things, but it's also a communicator of some sort, but I really can't explain how it does what it does. I just know that I can't be without mine."

All trace of humour was gone from his voice as he regarded the intricate piece.

"I wish I knew all of its secrets, but all I care about for now is that it seems to be able to open a window to you, and for that I'll put up with some of its other … habits." He paused for a moment. "But where did you find yours?"

"Buried in the sand at low tide on the Thames in Twickenham."

"Oh, the river. I guess that makes sense. Some very odd things happen around the river." His voice went quiet. "It's not my favourite place, or at least it wasn't." He was suddenly more upbeat. "But it brought you to me, so that's finally something in its favour."

The wry smile was back, causing my heart to beat even faster. In our reflection in the mirror his thick hair looked as if it were mingling with mine. He was so real, standing just behind my shoulder. I had an almost overwhelming urge to reach out and touch him. Being held by those strong arms, resting my head against that chest … a sigh escaped me before I could stop it.

His smile widened as the blush appeared on my face this time.

"You can't read minds, can you, along with all your other spooky talents?" I asked, rather later than I should have done.

"Not at all," he laughed, "although I think I might have enjoyed knowing what you were thinking just now."

I blushed deeper. "So what did you do to learn to speak to me? Are there lots of other people wearing these?"

"No, no one else. And that made it more difficult. I had to think through all the times I have seen you and heard you and identify what made a difference. In fact," he gave a quick grin, "your experiments with the box came in quite handy."

"So what is it that you have to do?"

"This may seem a little weird, so promise me you won't scream or do anything like that."

I tried to give him a scathing look. "Do I strike you as someone who is easily scared?"

"No, I guess not," he laughed. "OK. Well, my amulet has to be in exactly the same physical space as your amulet. Look: right now our arms are doing impossible things, but it lets me into your head."

I looked down into the mirror where I could see the reflection of my arm. His shoulder was next to mine, then at the elbow the edges of our arms seemed to blur together – it was as if I was struggling to bring them into focus. There was a strange pale edge to my fingers too, and as I flexed them I could see his long hand surrounding my much smaller one.

As he spoke I became aware again of a strange, but not unpleasant, prickling sensation. "I can feel a sort of tingle in my arm. Is that you?"

His eyebrows rose. "You get that too? I assumed that was just me. I always shiver when people walk through me."

This was getting weirder, but I was determined to seem nonchalant. "Does that happen a lot?"

"Oh, yes. All the time. I spend most of my time walking around the streets of London, and when you don't have to move to avoid people, why bother?"

"I guess," I agreed, reeling slightly. "So if you stood away from me, I wouldn't be able to hear you?"

"I'm pretty sure that's what will happen. Let's see."

With that he stepped backwards. I could still see him in the mirror, but he was no longer right at my shoulder.

"OK then, try talking to me."

He appeared to speak, but I could hear nothing. I shook my head. It seemed oddly silent inside my own brain, as if suddenly something important was missing. I frowned, and Callum was instantly back at my side, but this time he sat to my left, reaching in front of me to where my arm was resting on the table. In the mirror I could see his long fingers stretching towards my elbow. As I saw our arms touch, I felt the tingling return and a feeling of contentment swept through me.

"Is everything OK? You look worried."

"I'm fine, just trying to work this out."

"But that's how it works, isn't it? You can only hear me when I'm right here."

I nodded and managed to smile at him. I was astonished by everything that was going on. I somehow felt that I had known him forever, and I could barely contain the noise of my thumping heart. I didn't understand how this was possible, but as I looked into his eyes I felt that everything had changed, and that nothing would ever be the same for me again. No one had made me feel anything like this before. We gazed at one another in silence for a few minutes then he lifted a hand as if to stroke my hair. I instinctively leaned towards him and was amazed to feel the lightest, gentlest of touches.

"I can feel you touch me," I breathed. "How are you doing that?"

"I … I don't know." He held up his hand and looked at it in puzzlement, then tentatively reached out to me again.

"It must somehow be because you have an amulet. No one else – well, no one like you – that I have ever come across has one." He hesitated, and then touched me again. "It seems to be only my fingertips you can feel. When it's my whole arm you just get the tingling." He stroked the length of my long blonde hair, making me shiver. He stopped instantly.

"I'm sorry, that's obviously a bit too freaky for you."

"No," I admitted, not daring to meet his eyes. "That's possibly the nicest touch I have ever had." I felt myself redden again as I lifted my head meekly, wondering how brave I could be. I decided to go for it. "You don't have to stop."

His face lit up and he reached for my hair again. The sensation was like nothing I had ever experienced before: a combination of the softest touches but charged with something like gentle electricity. Part of me wanted to close my eyes and just focus on the feeling, but that would mean I couldn't watch him, and I didn't want to miss a minute of that.

"Can you feel my hair?" I asked, suddenly conscious that this could be a one-way thing.

He grimaced. "A little. I can feel a slight resistance, but no real substance."

"Is it freaky for you?" Looking at his pained face I was suddenly filled with doubt.

He gave an unexpected laugh, then looked at me, his blue eyes melting. "Hardly. It's just hugely frustrating when all I want to do is gather you in my arms and kiss you. And I can't."

I looked at him in wonder. He watched me anxiously, searching for a reaction from me.

"I would love that too," I admitted, trying to hold his gaze.

His shoulders relaxed and he seemed to exhale deeply. There was a look of profound tenderness in his eyes.

"Really? Even with all of this?" He gestured towards the mirror and the amulet.

"I can't begin to understand any of this, and I don't understand what you are," I admitted, "but I can't think of anything I would like more than getting to know you better."

Somehow, it was the wrong thing to say. The hope which had filled his face suddenly faded, and he dropped his gaze to the floor.

"There's nothing worth knowing," he whispered, a bitter edge to his words. "There is nothing of me left. Really, there is no point in my being here."

"That can't be true. It just can't be," I said quickly, trying to soothe him. The last thing I wanted was for him to decide to leave.

There seemed to be a huge struggle going on inside him. He sat there silently for a few minutes. As I watched he seemed to come to a decision. I couldn't bear it if he left and didn't come back. The only thing to do was to persuade him he had to stay before he could speak.

"Please, just let me say something." I cast around desperately for inspiration, hoping to find some persuasive argument with which to sway him. Nothing came to me. The only option open to me, I decided, was to be as honest as possible. He waited, a guarded look on his face.

"Thank you," I breathed, "I want to get this right." I gave

myself another few seconds to calm down.

"I don't know where you are from, or how you got there, or what you are now. All I do know is that you and I can talk to one another and see one another, and … I can feel your touch. I just want to spend some time with you, in whatever strange way that's possible."

As I finished, I realised it had turned into more of a speech than I had intended, so I watched as he struggled with his emotions, but said nothing more.

He looked at me frowning slightly, as if weighing up the alternatives. I suddenly couldn't resist giving it one last shot.

"Please stay. What do you have to lose?"

"Well, if you put it like that, I guess not a lot." He smiled at me as he visibly relaxed. "OK, you win: I'll stay until you get bored."

I longed to throw my arms around him, but had to satisfy myself with leaning my reflection towards him. "You'll find I have an extremely high tolerance for boredom," I murmured as he started to stroke my hair again.

"I have so many questions I don't know where to start," I said finally.

"I don't want you to ask them. I don't want to put you off so soon. Will they wait until tomorrow?"

"Of course," I yawned. I suddenly realised I was exhausted. "But please, just promise me you will come back this time."

"I promise." He dipped his face towards me, bending down over my shoulder so his lips could brush my collarbone. I could see it all perfectly but could feel just the gentlest of touches.

"I wish I could feel your lips properly," I whispered.

He sighed sadly, shaking his head. "This is never going

to work." He paused, then suddenly grinned. "But it could be enjoyable trying, don't you think?"

I laughed. "So you're sure you'll be here tomorrow?"

"Nothing could keep me away. And keep that on," he said, nodding towards my bracelet. "Don't take it off, and I'll be back in the morning." He leaned further towards my reflection and I saw him gently kiss the top of my head.

"Goodnight," he whispered, and was gone.

Walk

Even though I was exhausted, I tossed and turned for most of the night, my mind racing, only dropping asleep as dawn started breaking. When I finally woke it was too late to spend too much time reflecting on what had happened, but I was careful to shower and conceal the bags under my eyes before I sat down at my desk. I whispered his name, feeling rather self-conscious. He was there in an instant, and I welcomed the tingling feeling as he moved his arm into the same space as mine.

"Good morning," he smiled. "I was wondering if you were going to stay in bed all day. I didn't think I'd get here early enough and I've still had time to have a good look round. Nice house."

"You haven't been walking through my family, have you?" I asked in mock-seriousness, wondering how I was able to make a joke about something so bizarre.

"Not guilty," he laughed.

"So, can you walk through the walls then, like a real ghost?"

"I can, but most of the time I choose not to. It makes me feel a bit more normal that way. But at least it means I don't have to do any breaking and entering to get to you." He gave a crooked smile. "In fact, I'm the perfect burglar. I just can't pick up any of the loot. But I can tell you what your neighbours are up to though, if you want."

"No I don't want!" I exclaimed quickly.

I sat back and took a long look at him. He was dressed exactly as before, his hair just as casually ruffled, his skin smooth.

"This may sound as if it's an odd question, but do you change at all? I mean, does your hair grow, do you have other clothes stashed somewhere, do you need to eat, that sort of thing?"

"That's a lot of questions. The quick answers are no, no and no, but I suspect you are going to want more detail than that. Shall we go somewhere where you don't have to whisper?"

"Good point." I quickly dropped my voice. "Do I need to be able to see your reflection to hear you?"

"No, I don't think so."

"We could go outside, but then I won't be able to see your face." And that would be a real shame, I added to myself.

"You'll still be able to hear me though, I think. Does it matter if you can't see me?"

"It's just easier to believe that you are real when I can actually see that you are there."

"Do you have a little mirror which could fit in your pocket? Then you could whip it out if you wanted to see if I was serious or not." He was teasing me now.

"How about if I'm walking?" I wondered. "Would you be able to keep pace with me so that we could keep talking?"

"That might take a bit of practice." He pursed his lips, a thoughtful look on his face. "I don't see why it shouldn't work though. It doesn't look as if you'd be able to outrun me." His face crinkled into a grin.

"I get enough abuse from my brother, thank you, without having to take it from you as well!"

"Shhh," he cautioned. I heard noises from Josh's room.

"Let me grab some breakfast and I'll find an excuse to go

84

for a walk."

My parents were already at the table, having a leisurely Sunday breakfast and reading the papers. The sunlight streamed in through the open French doors. It was going to be a lovely day.

"Morning, Alex," smiled Dad, putting down his paper in order to give me a hug. "Are you feeling better now?"

I hesitated, confused, then a small voice appeared in my head.

"You went to bed early last night with a headache, remember?" I could hear him laughing quietly.

"Oh, yes! Thank you," I smiled at Dad. "No headache at all this morning."

"So I guess the date with Rob didn't go that well?" asked Mum. "Where did he take you?"

I had hoped that they had forgotten about that. It all seemed so unimportant now. I reached for the bread basket and started buttering a slice of Mum's home-made cinnamon loaf while I worked out how I was going to get out of this interrogation.

"To The Old Town Hall in Chertsey. He thought he was doing me a favour taking me somewhere cool, and he was a bit surprised when the staff recognised me."

"Ah, he didn't appreciate that, then?"

"No, it sort of set the tone for the evening, I'm afraid." I sighed and went for the direct approach. "Do you mind if we don't talk about it?"

"Of course not, but..." started Mum. There was a muffled thump as Dad kicked her under the table. "No. Absolutely right. None of our business." She was suddenly very interested in her breakfast. Dad gave me a quick wink and I smiled in relief.

"I'm going to walk into Walton this morning," I said, putting my plate in the dishwasher. I realised too late that it wasn't a smart move.

"Oh, great," said Mum, "I need a few things, so we can drive in if you'd like. You can practise parking in the multi-storey."

"Um, actually, I wasn't planning on shopping. I could just do with a bit of time on my own." I cringed inwardly as I saw them exchange looks. "There's nothing wrong, I just fancy a walk down by the river, that's all. Don't make a big production out of it." I shut the dishwasher hard and quickly left the kitchen before they could get all apologetic. I hurriedly stuffed a few essentials into my small rucksack and ran back downstairs, by which time Mum and Dad were out in the garden. I scribbled a quick note on the blackboard in the kitchen to say that I wouldn't be back for lunch: I wanted to make sure that I had plenty of time.

I set off down the road, reaching into my bag to get the headphones for my mobile. As I tucked the end of the lead into my jeans pocket I could hear Callum laughing.

"Good idea!"

"Well, I don't want people thinking I'm completely mad as I walk down the street talking to myself."

"Absolutely, I wouldn't want anyone carting you off."

His voice was a bit patchy, as if he were talking into a microphone but periodically turning away. I tried to make sure that I was walking at a consistent pace, but it was harder than I expected. The tingle in my arm kept coming and going too.

We walked down the main road, past the fields where they were growing coriander and then alongside the back of the swan sanctuary. The swans were acting very strangely, squawking and hissing at me – normally they took no notice at all of the people walking by.

"Exactly where are we going?" he asked after we had been walking at a good pace for about twenty minutes.

"Just round the corner and over the bridge, then there is a nice towpath down the Thames from Walton to Hampton Court. Doing the loop down there and then back on the other side should take a good few hours, especially if we stop for a while."

"I can't escape from the river, it seems," he sighed.

I stopped dead. "I'm really sorry – I completely forgot you said yesterday that you didn't like the river. We can go somewhere else."

There was a silence, then suddenly the tingle and a rather loud voice in my head: "… stop like that without warning. I was halfway down the road."

I couldn't help giggling at the thought of him striding down the road without me. "Sorry," I tried to keep a straight face, "I forgot."

I pulled the small mirror out of my pocket and considered him. His dark blond hair was being gently ruffled by the wind. He pulled me out of my reverie. "You were saying something before you inconveniently stopped?"

"Ah, yes. I forgot that the river wasn't a good place for you. If we turn around we can go across the golf course. Would that be easier?"

"No, the river is fine. It plays a big part in my story, so we may as well be close to it."

We set off again, crossed over Walton Bridge and were soon free of the roads and on the towpath. It quickly became clear that even if I couldn't see Callum, other creatures could. Every dog, duck or bird we passed seemed fascinated by him: no wonder the swans at the sanctuary had been so excited. Every so often he would have to shoo various animals away, as they took no notice of me at all.

"Why do they like you so much?" I asked after a particularly enthusiastic spaniel had been reclaimed by its owner.

"I'm not sure, but they often react like this."

"Perhaps we should get off the main path and then we won't have quite so many to contend with," I suggested. "If we go over the bridge up ahead, we can sit for a while on Sunbury Lock Island." Really, I wanted to get my mirror out again. It was fine talking to him as if he was on the headphones, but it was exponentially improved by being able to look at him as well.

Sunbury Lock Island seemed as good a place as any to be somewhere peaceful. It was a long, thin island, accessible only by one public footbridge and over the weir, which was private. We had often come here as children, running around all the boat sheds and playing hide and seek in the woods. Most of the buildings were private, but it never stopped us dodging in and out of the grounds. As it was a Sunday, all the businesses in the boat sheds were shut and with no access to the other side of the river I reckoned it should be pretty quiet.

We went over the bridge and found a quiet glade to sit in, overlooking the river. There was a lot of hustle and bustle going on around us on the water and on each bank, but on the island everything was peaceful. I rummaged in my bag for a bottle of water and when I looked up again there were about a dozen small birds sitting around us. I felt like Snow White.

"You know, in a way this is the creepiest thing so far," I said, sweeping my free arm around to indicate the wildlife.

"I know, it is a bit odd. It doesn't happen quite this much in town. Maybe all the pigeons are used to us."

A finger of ice ran down my back, but I tried to keep my tone even. "Us?" I queried. "You're not alone then?"

"No ... I spend quite a lot of time with my sister, Catherine."

Sister. Sisters were always tricky, in my experience, but at least it wasn't girlfriend. "So how come the two of you are there?"

"I will tell you, but do you mind if it's not right now? It's not a happy story and at the moment I'm sitting here on a beautiful island in the sunshine with a beautiful girl," he paused and I felt him stroke the length of my hair, "and I'd rather think about happy things."

"Well, that seems reasonable," I agreed, secretly thrilled by his description of me. "So ... what do you want to talk about?"

"I was actually thinking that talking was overrated. Why don't you lie down here and let me stroke your hair. I love being able to do that, to actually touch you."

I lay down in the soft grass, turning on to my side and propping up the mirror on a small stone. From where I lay I could watch his face as he gently moved his hand down the length of my hair. His expression was completely unguarded, and so full of tenderness it nearly took my breath away.

With the sun beating down and the touch of his hand so soft it could almost be the wind, I felt my eyes close and drifted off to sleep. It can't have been for more than a few minutes, and as soon as my eyes opened, I looked for him in the mirror, but he wasn't beside me. I picked it up and used it to scan around the glade behind me.

It was quite a small clearing, but it went down to the water's edge. The grass was fresh and vibrant, and the meadow flowers were wafting in the gentle breeze. Apart from the small gap in the trees that we had come through, it was enclosed by vegetation, making it quite a private space, and my presence was likely to put off anyone else from invading.

And then I saw him. He was standing by the water's edge, staring into the depths. He looked so vulnerable, his beautiful blue eyes downcast and his long fingers absently running through his mane of hair. I continued to watch him, luxuriating in being able to see all of him. A strange contentment settled over me, and I realised that I never wanted this to stop. I wanted – no, I *needed* – to be with him, to be able to see him and talk to him, to make him smile.

He might be a ghost from another dimension, but he was my ghost, and I never wanted to let him out of *my* sight again. I thought briefly of the girls in class and everything they'd said about their feelings for the various boys in our gang, but none of them could have felt this, such a profound belief that he was right for me, whatever the difficulties. I loved him. It was almost a relief to put a name to the strange yearning which had, in truth, been pulling at me since I saw him in St Paul's.

I almost laughed out loud at the realisation. Love was why I had been so upset when he was missing; why Rob had become so irrelevant; why my whole world had turned upside down in a few short days. I had never believed in love at first sight, but that was what it had been. I just hadn't recognised it. From the minute I had seen him in the cathedral I was his.

I let out a contented sigh. Now all I had to do was wait and see if he felt the same way. I quietly got to my feet and moved up behind him. He was still lost in contemplation of the river, and didn't notice my approach.

Carefully checking in the mirror I stepped next to the space where he was standing, lining up the amulets, and felt the now-familiar tingle course through my arm. The pensive look on his face suddenly turned to one of joy.

"Hi! You woke up; I've missed you." His smile melted my heart.

"You shouldn't have let me sleep. It must have been dull for you."

"Are you kidding? This has been the best day of my life!" He spun around as if to pick me up in a huge hug, but of course only connected with air. "Even if I can't hold you, I can't believe my luck," he said, beaming.

I smiled back, suddenly shy. Having finally put a name to my own emotions I was nervous. I couldn't even begin to consider how terrible it would be if he didn't feel the same way about me.

"It's the best day of my life too," I admitted, keeping the mirror angled so I could watch the reaction in his face. There was no hint of reserve in his response, his whole face lit up, his blue eyes flashing in the sunshine.

"Really?"

"What's not to love?" I asked lightly, risking the word. In the moment's silence before he spoke I was filled with dread: he didn't feel the same way and I had made a hideous mistake. I quickly looked down at my feet.

"Alex, please look at me?" His voice was husky, and full of emotion.

I lifted the mirror so that we were side by side in the reflection, suddenly encouraged.

"I didn't want to scare you, or say anything before, but now ... I can see that there might be some reason to hope..."

I gazed at him questioningly. "To hope that you might feel something for me too." His face was open and trusting. "I love you,

Alex." And at that moment I felt my heart fill to the brim.

"Really?" I whispered, suddenly shy.

"I love you," he smiled. "I know it's too fast and I don't want to scare you, but it's the truth – I love you."

"I love you too," I confessed. "I've been yours since we met in the cathedral. I just didn't realise it until now."

"Oh, Alex," he whispered, "you have no idea how good that sounds to me." I felt the electricity run down my back as he stroked my hair, and watched as he kissed the top of my head. How I longed to be able to touch him too. I pushed the thought aside to concentrate on what I had. His glorious face just radiated joy, and mine looked equally delighted.

"I had never dreamed that this might be possible," he continued. "I would have been happy enough knowing that I loved you, but to have you love me back, well – it's so much more than I deserve."

"How can you say that? Why shouldn't you have someone to care about you?"

He looked nervous for a moment. "It's complicated, but I'll tell you. I know I must."

"Whatever you tell me, it can't be any stranger than what I have experienced in the last few days. And nothing is going to change how I feel about you."

He relaxed a little. "I hope that's true. But some of the things I have to tell you are ... pretty difficult to comprehend."

I did my best to look confident. "I can deal with all of it. You know that now. It's the emotion that's new."

His face was solemn beside me in the mirror. "Are you sure? You really want to know it all?"

I gulped. What was he trying to protect me from? Once I

knew, there was no going back – I could never un-know it. But I loved him, and needed to know all about him. I took a deep breath.

"Absolutely positive. Tell me everything. You know all about me, so it is only fair." I tried to smile, but I could feel my lips trembling.

"Well, I'll start, but you have to stop me if, you know, things get too much for you. I will understand." His smile was equally shaky. "Where would you like to begin?"

There was a sudden burst of music as my mobile phone went off, making us both jump. The spell was broken. "Bad timing," I muttered, looking at the screen. "I won't be a second." I slid the phone open. "Hi Grace."

I tried very hard to have a quick conversation with her, but it was difficult without being rude: we usually chatted for hours on the phone. Callum started to stroke my hair again, and I found it really hard to hold on to the thread of the conversation while he continued. I finally shut off the phone having promised to tell her everything when we saw each other the next day. I could tell she was unhappy about it. I had never kept anything important from Grace before, but I couldn't see how I was ever going to explain this. It would be much easier to keep it to myself. I promised myself that I would make it up to her in the morning.

"That wasn't fair, distracting me like that. I couldn't concentrate on what I was saying." I pouted at Callum as I stashed the phone back in my bag. He laughed, and continued his gentle stroking. But this time his gentle touch had quite a different effect and within minutes I found myself breathless, the blood pounding in my cheeks. I would have given anything at that moment to be able to turn round and feel his arms around me.

I opened my eyes and saw him watching me in the mirror.

"I think maybe you had better stop that for now," I gasped. "I don't think it's doing either of us any good."

"No, maybe not. I seem to be more aware of you now, though. It's not the same as touching someone in my world, but I can sense when I have made contact with your skin." He reached out and traced a line with his finger down my arm. I was aware of the lightest possible touch.

"It's definitely stronger than yesterday." I shivered. "Why do you think that is?"

"It's curious." He frowned, and I could tell now that it meant he was deep in thought. "Maybe it's because I am more and more tuned in to you. Or maybe it's the amulet. Let's hope it continues. At this rate I might be able to kiss you by Christmas."

"I hope so too," I breathed, still not sure of myself enough to look at him. The thought that one day I might be able to feel his lips on mine left me breathless again. "But now," I said firmly, "you were about to answer some of my questions."

Dirges

"Right," he said, squaring his shoulders and taking a deep breath. "Ask me."

"Let's talk about this." I lifted up my arm a fraction and the amulet glinted in the sunshine, the azure stone flashing.

"Where to start?" His voice was so gentle it was almost a question to himself. "There's such a lot to tell you."

"Let's go back to the beginning. You said yesterday that the amulet was some sort of communication device. What was it doing in the river?"

"Now that is a mystery. I have no idea at all."

"OK, so how come I got a vision of you when I held it?"

"I think that the two amulets are linked in some way." He sighed in frustration. "How can I explain this properly?"

He straightened up, and ran his free hand through his hair.

"Perhaps I should explain what happened to me when you found it," he started. "I was minding my own business when I suddenly had a blinding pain in my head and a picture, almost like a projection, of a beautiful girl who was looking puzzled about something." He smiled as I blushed at his description.

"Then it stopped, and I wondered if I had dreamt it. But later that evening I started to get more glimpses of you inside my head. I didn't know who you were or how I was able to see you," he paused as if slightly embarrassed, "but I knew that I was going to have to find out. The more I saw you, the more I realised that I had no choice – I somehow felt that I wasn't going to be complete until I found you. I didn't realise that the visions went both ways. All I knew was that I had to track you down, but I couldn't work out how. Was I going to have to walk the streets forever searching for your face in the hope that our paths would cross?

"But then the very next day you came to St Paul's, and appeared right in front of me, as if you knew."

"Not guilty." I laughed quickly, not wanting to distract him from his story.

"I couldn't believe my luck: I wasn't going to have to spend the next however many years searching: you had come straight to me. Then you smiled at me, and I realised that you could actually see me – you, a real flesh and blood person were smiling at me! I no longer cared about anything else, I just wanted to talk to you. It's been so long." The last was just a whisper.

He paused and looked without seeing into the woods in front of us. A family of foxes was sitting in the semi-darkness, watching him.

Finally Callum took a deep breath and continued. "When I saw you had an amulet just like mine it all suddenly became clear. Wrong, but clear. Amulets shouldn't be on your side, in your world. I was overwhelmed, and didn't know what to do. Then suddenly you couldn't see me any more, but I wasn't going to let you disappear. I followed you around the cathedral, then back to your minibus, and it had the name of the school on the side."

He looked up, guiltily. "That's when I really started stalking you. I followed the bus, and…"

"Hang on there! How on earth did you follow it? And why not get straight on? No one was going to see you."

"Well, the practicalities of being able to walk through things mean that things that move can also go through me. Stairs and chairs I'm OK with, but I can't use any form of transport."

"Oh, I see. I guess that makes sense," I agreed. "So how did you get to the school? And so quickly, too."

"When you can go in straight lines it is much quicker, and I'm not a bad runner either." He raised his shoulders in an apologetic shrug.

"I can imagine," I agreed, thinking of his physique. "But did you just happen to know where this school is?"

"No, but it said Hampton on the side of the bus, and I knew where that was, so I set off and when I got a bit closer I detected the amulet. I could feel that it was near me. It sort of pulled me towards you: you are a perfect conduit for its energy. That's why you see me so clearly."

I felt strangely pleased that it seemed to have an affinity for me.

"But I can still only see you in the mirror here. At St Paul's you were right there, in front of me. How does that work?"

"I'm not sure, but it could be because that is where I sort of live, so that is where my presence in your world is strongest. And the dome ... the dome is special. Maybe it focuses that presence – and you were under the very middle, weren't you? That's only a guess though. I don't really know all the rules."

"You *live* in St Paul's Cathedral?"

He sighed. "There is so much to tell you, so much you need to hear to be able to understand. I've never had to explain it to anyone before."

I composed myself, trying not to look too frustrated. "Perhaps you had better start again, and tell me who you are – or were – and how you ended up like this."

For a moment he stared out across the river, apparently distracted by the small flotilla of little launches cruising by. But his eyes were focused elsewhere, remembering.

"I only know two things from before," he whispered. "I know my name is Callum. But I have no memory of any other name, where I come from, how old I am, all the usual stuff. I'm just Callum. And I know that I have a sister. Her name is Catherine. She isn't so ... comfortable," he grimaced at the word, "with the life we have now."

"So how do you know she's your sister when you know nothing else?" I asked, puzzled. "And where is she now?" I had a sudden panic that this strange girl had also been with us all day, listening to our declarations.

"Don't worry: she's back in London. She doesn't know I am here, which is probably just as well. I can't imagine she would approve. I just know she is my sister and I know we were together when we started in this ... life. I have no idea *how* I know it." His face was troubled; this was clearly a painful subject. His gaze returned to the river, where several rowing eights were coming to the end of a run. Within a few minutes they had turned and were soon specks in the distance. I looked back at Callum, hoping I could get him to continue.

"So do you have no memory of how you got to be what you are?" I asked eventually.

"Oh no, that is very clear to me. Are you sure you want to know?"

"I want to know everything," I said firmly. "I want to know what this can do," I raised my arm, "what you are, how you live, everything."

"You deserve to know everything." He looked sad, and I could hear the pain in his voice.

"Tell me from the beginning, everything you can remember," I encouraged. He took a deep breath.

"I have no idea who I was before. When this happens to you, everything goes from your mind – it's as if your memory is wiped." He stared into the distance again. I waited a moment and was about to prompt him when he looked up.

"I know I was with Catherine, and I know…" He paused, and closed his eyes briefly. "I know that she was killing herself. We were on Blackfriars Bridge and the first thing I remember is that I was reaching for her, trying to stop her throwing herself off. I used to puzzle over why we were there, and I've been back there to see if anything came back to me, but nothing did. The river there is pretty deep and fast, so if you jumped in at high tide you would have no chance. She was on the other side of the railing, and I could see the desperation in her face. I thought I could stop her, and pull her back … but I was too late. I remember shouting to someone to get help, so we couldn't have been alone, but I don't remember who it was. I know I jumped in after her and swam to where I thought she might be. I dived deep into the murky water and after a couple of attempts I actually found her. But she grabbed on to me and pulled me down. I tried to get us both back up to the surface but it was so hard … too hard." He closed his eyes again and shuddered at the memory. "The currents were so strong and I couldn't fight them.

"We sank deeper and deeper and the darkness of the water was overwhelming. I knew that I had to get to the surface soon. I couldn't tell which way was up. I was just aware of Catherine still holding on tight. I tried not to panic, but I could feel my lungs bursting. My time was running out – and I couldn't stop myself trying to find some air. My lungs sucked in the salty water and I could feel it scorching its way down into me." He paused for a moment.

"But throughout it all I was convinced that I could save her. She was my sister after all, and I couldn't let her die. My foot brushed against something and I grabbed it with my free arm. Catherine was still holding on tightly, making it really hard to keep my grip but I hung on, swinging her around behind me. The water suddenly seemed warmer, as if we were in a different current, and I really thought we were going to be able to make it. I suddenly realised that we had somehow been swept to the very edge of the river, and that what I was holding on to was a rusty old ladder. A ladder! That meant we were safe. I was trying to haul us both up to the next rung when the pain exploded in my chest…"

I was stunned – the whole thing was just awful. My throat clenched and I felt tears on my cheeks. He was describing to me how it felt to die.

"There was a flash of bright light at the back of my eyes and every part of me pulsed with agony. Then, when I didn't think it could get any worse there was a final searing bolt through my head and then a great grey wave of fog rolled over me.

"As the fog settled I realised that the pain was gone. I was floating in the water. It no longer felt cold, but it was really murky so I couldn't see much. I was aware of a tight grip still on my arm, but then that loosened."

He paused again and looked at me ruefully. "That was when I realised that I could breathe without any problem under the water." His face clouded with remembered pain. I reached towards him in a vain attempt to comfort him.

"You really don't have to tell me all the details," I murmured.

"No, it will help you to understand us better if I leave nothing out." I felt him gathering himself together to continue.

"I knew something was horribly wrong. We hadn't made it up the ladder, so I should be a corpse floating in the river, but I felt just ... normal. The water swirled next to me and Catherine was there, a look of panic on her face, when we were close enough to see each other in the silty water. I felt for her hand then kicked with my legs to see if we could find the surface. As our heads broke through to the air there was no relief, no feeling of release. We didn't choke up lungfuls of water, and being in the air seemed to make no difference.

"I looked around and found that we were still close to the ladder, so we swam in that direction. There were plenty of people about, and I expected someone to shout as we approached, to throw us a line or send for a boat, but no one took any notice of us at all.

"We dragged ourselves up on to the embankment but still no one reacted to us, not even the passing children. I was watching one group of people when I heard a sudden, horrified gasp. Catherine was right next to me and a small child was running away from her.

"'She ran straight though me,' she cried in terror, then looked up as another pack of children were upon us. They were playing a game of tag, and they were ducking and weaving around each other. One boy was right beside me. I could see the freckles on his nose and the slightly crooked set of his teeth as he laughed at his friends. He turned and dodged away, directly towards me. I put up my hands to stop him knocking into me.

"There was a strange tingling sensation and he was behind

me, still laughing and twisting as he ran down the path. He had gone straight through me, as if he didn't know I was there."

Callum paused, remembering. "That was when I finally realised that I was no longer ... alive." He turned his eyes towards me. "What I couldn't work out was what I had become.

"'What's happened to us?' I heard Catherine whisper. 'I wanted to be dead, and now I'm back on the bank and children can't see or feel me. What have you done?' Her voice rose to a screech. 'What have you done to me? What have you done?' I looked around, but no one was paying any attention to us at all. I felt so angry with her. It was her fault we were in this situation. I wanted to leave her to her hysterics. But we only had each other..." His voice trailed off miserably.

I reached out to comfort him, but there was nothing I could say or do. I waited helplessly. Finally he continued.

"It took a long time for her to calm down, but when she did we started to walk. No one could see us. We wandered aimlessly through the city, not knowing what to do. Neither of us could remember anything before the ... fall. Catherine knew she had wanted to die, I knew that I had tried to stop her, and I knew that she was my sister, but beyond that, we knew nothing. We had no idea of who we had been, where we lived, or what to do now."

"I could see the dome of St Paul's, and when I saw it, I felt a strange compulsion to go there. I didn't know why, I just knew that's what I had to do. I started to steer Catherine in that direction, which was easy as she had pretty much given up taking any notice of where we were.

"As we approached the cathedral we suddenly found ourselves in the middle of a crowd. The sensation was peculiar – a tingling from one side of my body to the other as a stranger walked through me. I watched them closely but they seemed to notice nothing. The odd one seemed to shiver a little, but that was all.

"By then, Catherine was barely holding herself together. Her eyes were wild and she muttered continually to herself that she should be dead. I kept tight hold of her hand, frightened that she might run off. The crowd unsettled her even more. As more and more people walked through her she got more and more agitated, and she started to scream at them. They passed on, oblivious, as she stopped to rant.

"I tried to contain her, to protect her from herself, I suppose, because there was no way we were in danger from anyone else. I guess it also gave me something tangible and finite to worry about, rather than facing the enormity of the situation. I forced her to stop and look at me, to try to get her to accept that screaming at people wasn't going to help. She finally calmed down a little and we carried on to the steps at the front of the cathedral. It was busy, but the swirling mass of people had thinned out.

"I remember looking up at the carving on the facade, wondering what it was that had drawn me here." Callum smiled to himself at the memory, shaking his head gently. When he raised his eyes to mine I could see the pain in their depths.

"That was when I first saw them, at least a hundred of them on the top step: a long line of others just like us."

I gasped. "How could you tell?"

"They were all watching the same thing: us. And no one else had so much as glanced at us since we had got out of the water. But what was more shocking was the way they were all standing still while the tourists walked through them. I squeezed Catherine's hand and gestured towards them, and she was off, racing up the steps crying and imploring to the impassive line. She ran from one to the next, pulling at their clothes and shouting, 'What have you done? What's happened to me?' over and over. They stood there patiently until she had worn herself out. I watched, and then went to join her as she sank into a heap in front of the strangers.

"They were all somehow similar. They all had the same air, and, even though they wore different clothes underneath, they all had the same hooded cloaks." He plucked at his own. "They looked determined, as if they all had a common purpose, and they were completely indifferent to Catherine's pleadings.

"When she was finally silent a stocky figure in the centre stepped forward, raising his hand as if to halt any questions.

"'I am sorry for everything you have lost, but you are welcome,' he announced. 'We have had no new faces for many years. Try to be calm. There's no point in behaving like this.'

"I approached him cautiously, trying not to show the fear I felt and I tried to keep my voice strong as I greeted him. He seemed rather more sympathetic towards me than he had been towards Catherine. I found out later that he really hates emotional outbursts, so we hadn't made a good start." He smiled at me ruefully.

I tried to smile back but couldn't quite do it. This was all too strange, too horrific, and too ... unbelievable. But he was telling me with such passion that I couldn't doubt him for a moment.

"The group took us inside and explained what had happened to us." He paused, and looked straight at me. "As far as they could work out they were all people who had drowned in the River Fleet. And so had we."

I looked at him blankly. "But ... but you were in the Thames, you said. Where on earth is the River Fleet?"

"That's the first question I asked too. It turns out that the

Fleet used to be a big river, running from Hampstead down to the Thames, but over the years it has been built over, and it's covered up with buildings and roads. Now almost none of it is visible."

I continued to look at him quizzically. "But how does…?"

"I know," he interrupted, "it's really weird. It seems that all the water that still runs down the Fleet finally reaches the Thames through a culvert directly under Blackfriars Bridge. When I grabbed the ladder and pulled us around I dragged us from the Thames into the warmer waters of the Fleet, and that was enough." He paused, and looked at me again, before dropping his eyes. "Something about the water, something *in* the water, stops you dying immediately. Instead, you get stuck in the hideous half-life I have now.

"So we were neither alive nor dead, just suspended. And what was worse, we were condemned to exist forever with the feeling of doom we all felt as we realised that we were about to drown. Something else in the water damns us to be miserable for all eternity."

I struggled with the injustice of it all. "But you were trying to save someone's life. How can that be fair?"

"Believe me, I've had plenty of time to consider that point myself. But," he chuckled unexpectedly, "the others rather wish I hadn't ended up here too. It seems that, as I was so determined that I was going to be OK at the moment I actually drowned, I'm nothing like as miserable as the rest of them. They've never had a happy Dirge before. They really don't know what to do with me."

"Dirge?"

"It's our name for what we are, trapped in our half-life, neither one thing nor another."

"So you have to spend eternity wrestling with misery? Is

there no way out?" I tried to keep the rising horror from my voice.

"Well, that's a very interesting question," he conceded. "It was one of my first questions too. The key to it all is this."

He raised his arm towards his face so I could see the amulet on his wrist. The stone shimmered and danced in the light.

I raised my eyebrows in a query. "The amulet? How?"

"When we first met the others they showed us. The whole time Catherine and I had been wandering we hadn't realised that we had got these on our arms, under our clothes." He hesitated. "They don't come off us, you know; I can't even really feel it. It's as if it is part of me."

That did make me panic. "So will mine do the same to me?" I whispered. "Should I take it off while I still can?"

"I don't know." His voice was low, concerned. "I think you'll be OK as you didn't get it in the usual way, but I've not yet dared to ask anyone."

He looked away, suddenly unable to meet my gaze.

"Oh," I said in a small voice, surprised by what he had told me as well as his reaction. It almost looked as if he was hiding something, some fact about the amulet. "So why do you have them?" I asked. "Do you use them to communicate with other Dirges?"

"Well, no, not really. I mean ... well, a bit: we can tell when another one is nearby. That was how the others knew we were coming." He risked a quick glance at me then looked down again.

"Is that all they do?" I prompted, tracing the outline of mine with my finger. It looked benign enough now, the stone quiet and peaceful.

His face was a mask of conflicting emotions. This was clearly a key question, and one he really didn't want to answer.

We sat in silence for a few moments while he struggled. He finally cleared his throat, as if he had prepared a speech. "We use our amulets…" He paused again, then seemed to come to some sort of internal decision. "We use our amulets to take thoughts from people, happy thoughts and emotions, and memories," he said in a rush. "If we don't do this regularly we…" His voice dropped to a whisper, "we sink into an unbearable misery."

He hung his head as if in shame.

I was clearly missing something – that didn't sound too awful. In fact, I nearly laughed at the absurdity of it all. One look at his bowed head stopped me though. This was obviously very serious to him.

"That doesn't sound too bad," I said lightly. "I mean, people aren't going to notice if you take a copy of what's in their heads, and if they don't know, well, it can't hurt them, can it?"

He raised his head and looked directly at me, his beautiful eyes haunted. "You don't understand. We – I – don't just take a copy. We take away the memories completely. We steal them."

I felt my mouth fall open in shock.

I tried to gather myself quickly. "So you take away their happy memories permanently to keep from getting miserable yourself?"

"Yes." It was no more than a whisper.

"Do you get to keep the memories? The thoughts? Do you see what they are?" I was suddenly conscious of the thoughts I had been having about him, and remembered him reassuring me that he couldn't read my mind. "You said that you couldn't tell what I was thinking."

He put his head in his hands, and everything went silent. I could see that he was talking, but he wasn't looking at me so he hadn't noticed that he had lost contact. I had to hear what he was saying. "Callum," I called gently, "you need to be back over here. I can't hear you."

His head shot up, and he looked at his arms as if they had minds of their own. He was quickly back into position. "I'm sorry, I just forgot that I had to stay in the same place. I've never tried talking to anyone about this, and it's a bit … difficult."

"I understand. There's no rush, just tell me as much as you want to tell me." I tried to hold myself back though I was burning with curiosity about what he could do and what he might have noticed about my thoughts.

He gave a ghost of a smile. "You're being very reasonable about all this. It's not what I expected."

"Well," I tried to laugh convincingly, "you're not about to steal all my memories, are you?"

"No, no! I'm not! I would never do that to you! I'd never take something so precious from you." His voice was suddenly vehement. "Don't even think that!" His eyes flashed, angry and hurt.

"So we are OK then. There's nothing to worry about." I smiled again, trying to reassure myself that this was really the case, and to calm him down again.

"Come and tell me about it. I'd really like to understand, but I need to be able to hear this time." I smiled encouragingly.

His smile was enough to melt my heart, if it hadn't already been taken. He looked so vulnerable yet brave. "I don't deserve to have met you," he breathed, resting his head against mine. I could feel the faintest of touches, and yet again my heart leapt. I just couldn't tell if it was in excitement or in fear for what I was about to hear.

Stealing

He sat down just behind me, making sure that I could see him in the mirror, then paused to gather his thoughts. While I waited I found myself scanning across the river to the far bank.

I could see other people walking in the little park, continuing their lives as usual. It was astonishing to me that normal life was possible for everyone else when it had all changed so profoundly for me.

I turned back towards Callum and looked at his face in the mirror. It was so frustrating to be able to see so little of him at a time. He was still looking down at the amulet, frowning slightly. "It's a strange compulsion, the need we have," he said finally. "It's a bit like sliding slowly into an abyss, and the memories and thoughts give you something to hold on to, to stop that slide. We need to take happy and joyful memories. Someone's happy thoughts are good, but a happy memory – something they've thought about over and over again – they're best. They are the strongest, most powerful, and they are the best at fighting the despair."

"And if you don't get enough?"

"If we don't do it regularly, if we don't have a store of happiness and can't find enough happiness in others, we quickly sink. It's like being buried alive with a pain that will never stop." His deep blue eyes clouded over. "I can't begin to explain the horror of it. It's as if all your worst experiences have been rolled into one terrible thought that you can't get out of your mind."

"So what do you have to do?" I guessed he was talking from his own experience. It was too raw, too gut-wrenching to be purely theoretical knowledge.

"You have to force yourself to get back out into your world, to seek out someone happy and to start ... gathering. That's what we call it. You only ever let yourself get into that state once. Afterwards, you are more careful and make sure that you don't let your store of memories get too empty. That way, the feeling is manageable." He looked directly at me.

"It sounds like a terrible way to live."

He nodded slowly. "I think perhaps that's supposed to be the point. There is something about the river which causes this continuous pain and sadness, and we have no idea why."

"But how does it work? How do you go about stealing the memories, and how do you tell who is happy or not?"

"When I see people in your world, now I've had a chance to practise, I see, well, faint lights around their heads. Different emotions produce different colours, so we can tell when that emotion is good. Happy memories and thoughts give auras that are different shades of yellow – like sunshine."

"And then what happens? When you see someone thinking a happy thought about something that's happened to them?"

"It's really very simple. Frighteningly simple, in fact. I just pass the amulet through the aura, and it takes it in. The person is left wondering what it was they were thinking about. I don't really get to see the memories themselves, I just get a sense – a flavour if you like – but not the detail. Perhaps something about a favourite place, or a holiday, or sometimes a girlfriend, but nothing specific."

"Those poor people. They just ... forget?"

"It seems so. Then, once you have been here a while, you tend to acquire a preference for a certain type of memory, and I know that some of us," he winced at the plural, "like a more mature mind."

"So your friends stalk the geriatrics?"

"Yes, some of them feel that once the brain starts to deteriorate it's a waste of good memories to let them drift away. They spend most of their time in old people's homes. We have to be careful not to take too many thoughts from someone in a single go. It's very dangerous to do that. But some of us are rather less good at that sort of control." He shook his head before continuing. "Others enjoy the minds of new mothers. They are often really happy; apparently it's a good hit."

"What about you?" I lifted my chin and looked him in the eye. I had to know. "What's your preference?"

"I find that, as I am generally not as desperate as the others I can be a bit choosy about where I go. Actually, I've taken to stalking the cinemas on comedy nights. It can ruin the film for someone but at least they'll be able to watch it again in the future."

I hadn't realised I had been holding my breath and I let it out slowly. "So you don't take away real memories?"

"I try not to. I really try. And in the cinemas I just have to hope that the people in the cinema are thinking only about the film and not about their real life."

"So can you see my emotions? Can you tell if I am happy?"

He laughed, surprising me. "I'm afraid not. There is no hint of colour around you."

"Oh. Does that mean I'm not very emotional?" I was upset at the thought.

"Not at all. I'm sure your aura would be really vibrant." He

111

smiled and ran his fingers down my hair again. "It's nothing to do with you, I think. It's to do with this." He reached for my amulet. "When you wear this, I can't see anything. No aura, nothing."

"So you can't tell if I'm happy or not – other than in the usual way?"

"No, but if you were to take off the amulet I would be able to."

"If I took off the amulet I wouldn't be able to see you, so I would be miserable. No need for an aura on that one." I tried to joke to get away from the image of him sinking into despair. He looked so relaxed in the sunshine, so young and strong. I found it hard to think of him crushed by misery.

"You said earlier that you were not really unhappy, that they didn't know what to do with a happy Dirge." I stumbled over the word. "So how come you get miserable?"

"We all do. It's a bit like getting hungry. You can't help it. The amulet will store a huge number of memories and I try to keep mine reasonably full. If I then top it up with just a few memories at a time I can get back to a bearable state of mind, because I started that way. But the others, they can only get back to the level of misery they had when they realised they were about to die. They get a lot more..." He paused. "... unhappy than I do," he finished carefully.

I considered this for a moment. "How can you bear it, living with all these desperate people all the time? How can you be so sane?"

"I have no choice," he reminded me more gently than I deserved. "This is the only way I can be."

I felt myself blush. Of course he didn't have any other option. "I'm sorry. That was a stupid thing to say. I wasn't thinking."

He smiled at me to show I was forgiven, and his strong-looking hand rested on my shoulder for a moment. I had been trying to avoid one other question, but I had to ask. "How long have you been there? When did it happen?" I wasn't sure that I wanted to know the answer though. What if it was hundreds of years? That would just be too creepy. I held my breath, waiting for his answer.

"Not as long ago as you might think from my cloak." He grinned ruefully. "I'm not exactly sure, but I don't think it's been so very long." He paused for a second, the brief smile gone. "The trouble is, when you sink you lose all sense of time. I only really sank once, but I think you can miss great chunks of time quite easily when you don't need to eat."

I watched him as we sat there, him lost in his thoughts and absently playing with my hair. His eyes had a brooding look and from time to time a small frown furrowed his smooth bronzed forehead. I would never tire of looking at that face. His smooth cheek rested for a moment against my hair and for the hundredth time I wished I could rest my palm against it and feel its firm contours.

"So what's with the cloak then? Why dress up like a Tudor peasant when you could be wearing anything?"

"Not my choice I'm afraid. It sort of comes with the job."

I looked at him quizzically.

"All the Dirges wear the cloaks. Other than our amulets, they are the only possession we really have. There is a huge chest of them in St Paul's, and we each choose one. Wearing them helps us to hide a little from each other, to get a little privacy."

"So you never need to change your clothes now?"

"I don't seem to. Anyway, I don't have any more so it's pretty irrelevant. Don't you approve of them?" he added with an impish grin.

"Love the cloak, very gothic, very vintage," I agreed, "but does it..." I tailed off, suddenly embarrassed by the direction my thoughts were going.

He looked exactly as if he could read my mind at that point. "Does it what?" he asked, the picture of innocence. He was enjoying my discomfort.

"Ah, well, um..." I couldn't bring myself to say it. What I really wanted to know was whether the cloak was welded to him as well, or if it came off at all. I had only got one glimpse of his chest, but from the look of him standing by the riverbank earlier, and from the faint feel of him right behind me when we talked, I was willing to bet that his body was magnificent. I felt myself redden, and quickly looked to the floor.

When I looked back, he was still smiling gently at me, watching me get flustered. He raised an eyebrow.

I fished around wildly for something to get me out of this. "Nothing, I was just wondering about how you wash it, that sort of thing."

He knew that I was lying, but answered me with a smile. "Luckily none of my clothes seem to be able to get dirty, so it doesn't come up." He gave me a sideways glance. My cheeks were still hot and I was trying really hard to think of anything else.

"In fact," he added, in a thoughtful tone, "perhaps it would be good to be able to feel the sun and the breeze a little better. Give me a second." There was a swift tingle, and he was gone from behind me. I scanned around quickly in the mirror and he was standing a few feet away, tugging at the thick rope which was fastened at his neck. As I watched, he got it undone, pulled the cloak to one side and it dropped to the floor. The heavy material settled in huge folds by his feet.

I stifled a gasp. He was even better than I had imagined. The tailored white shirt was slightly unbuttoned, and hung casually over a pair of well-fitting dark trousers. He was tall and lean. In the real world he could be making a fortune posing on a billboard.

As I watched he stretched down to pick up the cloak and folded it loosely, his muscles flexing visibly under the light clothes. Several of the loitering ducks took off in alarm.

He turned towards me and caught me looking at him in the mirror. With a couple of swift steps he was back by my side. My arm tingled. As I watched, he smiled broadly and dropped a kiss on the top of my head.

In the mirror I could see that he had wrapped his free arm around me, pulling me close to him. I could see the strong contours of his arm through his shirt. I longed to be the me in the mirror, on his side, able to feel his touch. For a moment I let my mind wander, and pictured the two of us, hand in hand, walking along a beach, stopping to kiss...

I sighed.

He caught my mood, and stayed quiet, stroking and smoothing my hair.

"Do you think that there will ever be a way for us to be together? Properly, I mean?" I risked after a while.

It was his turn to sigh. "I can't see how. We are in different ... dimensions, and I only know one way of getting here." His voice turned bitter and I thought about his story.

"I still don't really understand why this had to happen to you," I said sadly.

"I ask myself that every single day. I can't understand it any more than you can. All I know is that, after the others had told me why they thought we were there, I went to look at the outflow of the Fleet into the Thames, and when it has been raining you can see the water pouring out. It's very clear that there are two rivers joining at that point. I guess I just took my last breath in the wrong bit of water." His face looked as fierce as it had done when I had first seen him in the visions.

"But why does it happen? And why does everyone but you have to be so completely miserable?"

"None of us knows, and they are all too wrapped up in their daily doses of misery to think about it much."

"And there's no way of finding out?" I breathed, hurting for him. He gave a bitter laugh. "Hardly. I can't see people queuing up to experiment, can you?" As he spoke the sun suddenly disappeared behind a stray cloud, and for a moment the day seemed much darker, echoing his mood.

"If there are over a hundred of you there, the Fleet must have been a big river in its time." I shuddered, thinking of all those painful deaths.

"Yes, it seems to have caught quite a few of us."

"And are you sure you are there forever? Is there really no way out?" I asked without thinking, and cursed myself when I saw his eyes cloud over again.

He hesitated and I jumped in quickly. "Don't answer any more questions. It's not what's important today." There was a look of relief in his eyes and he stooped to kiss me again.

"Thank you," he whispered.

I smiled. "There's no need to thank me. You don't have to tell me anything that you don't want to."

The relief was visible on his face and I wondered what it

was that he wasn't ready to share with me. But I guessed that I would find out eventually, if it was important.

"I've learned so much about you today. Is there anything that you want to know about me? Or did you find out everything you wanted when you were snooping about my house this morning?" I teased, determined to change the subject to something less painful.

"I want to know everything about you!" He smiled. "Your friends, what you like to do, what your school's like, everything."

"Wow. Where shall I start?"

"Family. Tell me all about them. You obviously love them all very much."

So I told him all about us, our fights and celebrations, our holidays, the house. We talked about Josh, and how much I relied on him, even if he was horrible to me from time to time. I could see a sad look in Callum's eye, and I guessed that he wished his sister felt that way about him. He carried on asking questions, and I found myself talking all about my friends, particularly about Grace and the bond we had forged after so many years at school together.

He seemed to love hearing about school, though he thought that my plans to study to be a vet were hilarious, given that I was continually getting distracted by the wildlife that was still settling around us. I told him all about my childhood ambitions to be an actress, about the singing lessons I was still taking and how dull Grade 5 Theory was. His questions slowed as the afternoon wore on, and he spent more and more time nestled behind me, sending gentle flickers of electricity through me as he stroked my hair. I was beginning to think that it was time to return home, when his tone became more careful.

"How about boyfriends?" he asked casually. "I can't imagine

117

that someone as lovely as you doesn't have a boyfriend."

It was my turn to be careful. The memory of Rob came back to me, and I realised with shock that I had been out with him only the previous night. It felt a lifetime away.

"Well," I started, wondering exactly how much I should reveal, "there was someone I had been out with a couple of times, but it had pretty much ended before it even got going. That was why I was upset when you found me last night."

His face was suddenly full of concern. "You must have cared for him a lot to be so miserable."

"Actually it turned out he was a bit ... horrible, which was why I was so upset."

"Are you sure? I don't want you trying to save my feelings. I'll ... I'll understand if he is someone special to you." His face was controlled, but I could sense the urgency behind the words; he really didn't want Rob to be significant to me.

I gave a harsh laugh. "Special? Rob? I don't think so!"

Callum gave me a sharp look.

"No, *really*," I tried to reassure him. "He thinks he's so great, but he absolutely isn't."

"What did he do to you?" Callum asked suddenly. "Did he hurt you?" The look on his face was so old-fashioned I could almost have laughed. But this wasn't a conversation I much wanted to have.

"It was nothing. He just wasn't very ... nice." I paused for a second, but I could see he wasn't about to let it drop. "Please, I'd rather not talk about it."

He hesitated briefly, and then sighed. "Whatever you want." I could see him pondering something for a moment. "Do you want me to go and scare him a bit?"

I had to laugh. "No I don't!" I didn't want the two of them anywhere near each other. "Anyway, what would you do? Aren't I the only person who can see you?"

"Well, technically, yes," he admitted grudgingly. "But I'm sure I could manage something. And he must have some memories he wants to keep hold of. I'm sure I could erase you from his mind completely if I worked at it. He wouldn't know anything about it."

"Honestly, he's not worth the bother. Why spend time with him when you could spend it with me?"

"You do have a point," he agreed, wrapping his arm around my waist again.

"So do you often scare people?"

"Hardly ever!" he laughed, and then dropped his voice. "Actually I've never done it. But I know from the others how you might do it."

I was relieved; I didn't enjoy the thought of him being vindictive. It really didn't fit the picture I had formed of him in my head.

"Why do they do it? What good can it do to them?" I asked, curious to learn more about the people he spent his time with.

"Well, some of them are just not very nice people. They don't like the fact that they are stuck in misery and others are having a good time." His voice was disgusted. "Anyway, I don't want to waste any more of the day talking about them."

I looked up and realised that the sun was now low in the sky. We had talked nearly all day.

"Actually, I'm starving," I realised, stretching my legs. "I seem to have forgotten to have any lunch. Let's get back and you can tell me more later, otherwise my parents are going to be sending out a search party."

I got up off the grass, realising that even in the warm weather sitting for so long on the ground had made my trousers slightly damp. I brushed myself down and slipped the mirror into my pocket. Callum settled into step with me as we left the glade and started the long walk back home.

True Colours

I was back just in time: Mum and Dad were beginning to worry. They were obviously concerned that I was still upset about Rob, but they were too tactful to ask about it. I found it really hard to contain myself over dinner. I wanted to tell them all about the strange and exciting things I had learned, but I knew that it was impossible. I ended up being really jumpy and Dad kept looking at me strangely. He was always much more perceptive than anyone else about how I was feeling, and I hated keeping things from him.

When the meal was finished, he asked me to help him clear up, and I knew it was time for questions. He surprised me by saying almost nothing about it, as we washed up all the big pans from the roast beef.

"So," he asked as the last pan was dried, "would you like a lift to Grace's house? I expect you two have a lot of gossiping to do."

"Um, you know, not tonight. But thanks for the offer. I think I got a bit too much sunshine today, so I'd rather stay in."

"OK, but if you change your mind in the next half an hour or so let me know. I don't mind running you over and picking you up later." He was clearly taken aback; I don't think I could remember a time when I had refused a lift to Grace's. As I went up to my room I could hear him talking in hushed tones to Mum. That would mean that she would be up for a chat before too long. I quickly went to start running a bath.

Back in my room I put on my headset and sat in front of the mirror.

"Callum?" I called gently. "Are you there?" Within a few minutes my arm was tingling and he was back by my side. I was distracted all over again by his astounding good looks and almost forgot what I wanted to tell him.

"I have to have a bath now to avoid my mother. Will you be here later?"

"I'm going to have to go back into London. Catherine will make a fuss and I have to decide exactly how much to tell her." He looked dispirited. "And also I'm hungry, if you see what I mean." He glanced at his amulet.

I was immediately contrite. I hadn't considered the fact that he had needs of his own that I didn't really understand. I felt guilty that I had asked him to stay around until after I had eaten. "I'm so sorry. I've kept you here and risked you getting miserable."

"It's not exactly been a hardship. If I can find a cinema or theatre on the way into town I won't even get that uncomfortable. I've been so happy today I guess I just feel the downside more acutely." His glorious blue eyes melted as he gazed at me.

I felt my heart lurch. "I wouldn't have missed today for the world. You will come back tomorrow, won't you?" I couldn't help remembering that he had promised to come back before and then gone missing for days. I couldn't bear not being able to see him all day.

"You try and keep me away. I don't remember being at school, so I might come with you to a few lessons."

"Don't you dare distract me! I could do without another detention."

"You'll have to practise self-control then – I'm not sure I

will be able to resist doing this to you..." With one hand he gently smoothed my hair to one side, and in the mirror I could see him bending down to kiss the side and back of my neck. A shiver of excitement ran through me.

"That'll definitely ruin physics for me," I gasped, as he gathered all my hair together and moved to the other side of my neck. I could feel gentle tickles of electricity through my skin, and a slight pressure on my hair where he had swept it up on his side. Suddenly, there was an angry banging on my bedroom door.

"Alex Walker! Get off that phone! That bath has nearly run over!" bellowed Mum.

"Oops, I'm going to have to go right now," I whispered to him, then loudly, "Thanks, Mum. I'll be right there." I looked at him longingly. "Come back ... please?"

"Tomorrow, I promise."

I had to tell him again how I felt. "I know this is a weird situation, and that it's too sudden, but I can't help it: I love you."

I don't think I'd ever seen anyone look so happy. "I love you too," he whispered. "You ... you give meaning to my existence." He paused. "And if you don't go now, your mother will kill you."

He flashed one last smile and was gone.

The next morning I went to school full of nervous anticipation. I wasn't sure when Callum was going to turn up, and what he was going to do to me when he did. I could hardly wait.

The coach ride was difficult. Grace was offended because I had chosen not to give her all the details about Rob in our phone conversation the previous day. She was positively short with me and spent most of the trip listening to her iPod. But I was too happy to care. I spent the time imagining what Callum and I could do if we were in the same dimension.

123

The first lesson was maths, and I took my usual seat cautiously, not sure where and when Callum might appear. It was a small class now, as several girls had stopped attending after the last exams and the plan seemed to be to recap on some of the basics before setting the homework for the long summer break.

He appeared halfway through the lesson. We were doing differentiation, and I was having real trouble keeping awake. Some of the class were struggling with the concepts so Mr Pasciuta was explaining it all *again*. I was doodling on the margin of my paper and realised that I was sketching the rest of a face around a pair of dark, brooding eyes. I was scrubbing it out quickly before anyone noticed when there was a chuckle in my head. Simultaneously I felt the tingle.

"Pity. It wasn't a bad likeness."

I couldn't speak, so I just snorted gently. That would tell him what I thought of his tactics. He laughed again.

"I quite like this. I get to say whatever I want, and you just have to listen to me, no butting in and no questions." His tone was teasing, so I sighed again.

"I've been listening to this guy for a while now. It's a bit dull isn't it?"

I nodded almost imperceptibly. Mr Pasciuta was writing out a long proof on the whiteboard, and my classmates were all diligently copying it down.

"Do you understand much of what he is on about? I can't understand a word."

It was my time to smile. Luckily I wasn't sitting that close to anyone else so I pulled out a fresh sheet of paper and scrawled,

I know all this. He's repeating it for the slower ones.

"OK, OK. No need to show off. I guess I wasn't a mathematician in my former life. Maybe I was good at history. Do you do that?"

It's not much use for a vet. I'm doing maths and the sciences.

"Oh, OK. Well, I have to say that sounds dull. I can't possibly sit here and listen to all these lectures. How about you skip class?"

Not easily done, I'm afraid.

"Well, in that case, I'm just going to have to distract you." With that he started to stroke my hair, occasionally letting his fingers trace delicate paths down my bare arms. It was electrifying. I quickly reached for the paper.

Stop it! You'll get me a detention.

"But I thought you liked it." His voice was slightly muffled as he was kissing my collarbone.

I love it, but this just isn't the right place. I can't enjoy it properly. Can't you just talk to me?

He laughed. I realised that my heart was racing and I was breathing heavily. I also realised as I focused on the room around me that no one was talking and every head was turned in my direction.

"Alex, come on, you know the answer to this one." Mr Pasciuta was using his exasperated tone. Then it changed: "Are you alright? You look a little … flushed."

I could hear Callum's laughter.

"I am feeling a little dizzy, Mr Pasciuta. I think maybe I

need to go to the bathroom and get some cold water."

"Yes, yes, of course. Are you faint? Do you need someone to go with you?" A number of my friends looked up hopefully, seeing an opportunity to escape from the class.

"No, I'll be fine, thank you." I needed to talk to Callum, and an audience wouldn't be helpful.

As I got to my feet to leave, a screeching bell suddenly erupted in the corridor outside, the sound echoing around the school. Mr Pasciuta swore under his breath.

"OK, girls: fire alarm. You know the drill: straight outside to the pitches, no bags, and NO TALKING!" he bellowed, as everyone abandoned the lesson and headed out towards the sunshine.

As we waited on the netball pitches two huge fire engines came racing up, and a wave of excitement swept through the crowd. There were plenty of my classmates who would cheerfully see the school go up in plume of smoke. But it wasn't going to happen today: the alarms had been set off by the girls in the common room burning toast in the toaster, and the Chief Fire Officer was not amused. I could see him giving Miss Harvey a stern talking-to.

We all lapped it up. Miss Harvey was the headmistress, and usually dished out the punishments. But our fun was short-lived. As soon as the fire engines had gone, she called the school to order. Even outside and with no PA system her voice carried across the field.

"Luckily, today it was only toast, but never forget that at any time it could be a real fire. Your evacuation today was a shambles. It took twice as long as it should to get you all out here, and half of you clearly stopped to get your belongings." Everyone started to look a bit shifty at this point, nudging their bags behind them.

"I expect a much better response next time, girls," she continued, "and I expect you to be more careful in the common room, or I will have to consider withdrawing some of your privileges. Now please return to your lessons in an orderly manner."

Callum had kept quiet while all this had been going on. In fact, I was sure that I had lost him in the scrum to get out of the school. I guessed he was taking the opportunity to have a bit more of a look around. As we started to walk back in I felt him reach me, so I slowed slightly to let the others get ahead.

"Where have you been? Find anything exciting?" I whispered out of the side of my mouth.

"Just checking out the facilities. Not bad. I can't believe my school was as great as this. Do you get to do an art lesson today? That studio is awesome."

"'Fraid not. Later in the week though, for my project."

"Come on, Alex, what are you doing?" called Alia from up ahead.

"Coming," I called. I got out a tissue out to hide my mouth. "This is really tricky. Can you come back later? I'm not sure I can keep this up for much longer."

He sounded as if he was pouting. "We were just getting to the fun bit, too."

I felt myself blush again. "Really, it doesn't work for you to be with me in lessons. But please, come back later and we can talk tonight, OK?"

"OK," he grumbled. "I'll see you later," I could hear the smile in his voice, "when it's more ... private." With that he was gone again, leaving me with an empty feeling. I ran to catch up with the others and then we ambled back to maths.

Grace stayed unnaturally quiet all morning and avoided me

at break time, but I managed to catch up with her in the corridor on the way to physics. Her long dark hair was down so I couldn't see her face but I knew her so well that I could tell that she wasn't happy.

"Are you OK today? You've not said much to me."

"It's about time you noticed. Some best friend you are," she snapped.

"Has something happened with Jack?" I guessed. It must be something big to upset her so much. It couldn't just be the fact that I hadn't given her all the details on Rob.

"I thought *you* would know the answer to that."

"What on earth are you talking about? How could I possibly know anything?"

"That's not what Rob has been telling everyone."

I was stunned. What had he done now?

"I've not said anything to Rob, and after the way he behaved on Saturday I've no intention of speaking to him ever again. What's happened? Is there something wrong with you and Jack?"

"Jack doesn't want to go out with me after all, apparently," she sniffed miserably.

"What? But he was so keen the other night. What's changed his mind?"

She stopped just outside the door of the physics lab and turned to face me. Her lips were pressed together in a hard line. "You!" she hissed and stomped into the classroom. She picked a seat away from our usual corner and got out her bags with a thump. Miss Deeley was already there, so there was no more opportunity to find out what she meant.

I was completely stunned. How could it possibly be my fault if Jack didn't want to go out with Grace any more? I knew I had been a bit self-absorbed over the last few days, but I also knew I had done nothing wrong. Unfortunately though, Grace thought that I had. I couldn't bear it that she would think that I would do anything to hurt her. I had to concentrate on helping her sort it out, and I was rather relieved that I had asked Callum to leave for a while. This wasn't going to be a great spectator event, and, especially if it had anything to do with Rob, I would feel a lot less self-conscious knowing that he wasn't standing behind me.

The lesson dragged on and on. Unfortunately it was a theory class so we didn't even have the opportunity to talk while setting up an experiment. As we listened to Miss Deeley I racked my brains to try and work out what on earth Grace could mean. It didn't make any sense to me. When the lunch bell rang, I made sure I waited for her at the door of the classroom. She paused, but then saw that there was no way to escape me, and I walked with her as we made our way back to the common room.

Whatever her problem was, I was torn between wanting to be entirely straight with her, and my conviction that I still needed to keep the bizarre events of the last few days to myself. "Grace, I don't understand. What is going on? Talk to me."

She gave me a withering look. "Are you just rubbing it in now? Isn't what you have done bad enough?"

I felt an icy stab in the pit of my stomach. Her pace along the corridor increased – I was almost running to keep up.

"Back up a bit, please, Grace. You should know I wouldn't do anything deliberate to hurt you. If Rob's been telling you things, it'll all be lies because he can't handle rejection."

"He said you would say that."

"Look, how can I win in that case? Won't you at least tell me what the problem is? At least tell me what you think I've done."

"According to Rob," she started, "you're really fixated on Jack and that is why Rob dumped you on Saturday. Rob says you've secretly been planning to make a play for Jack for years. And when you saw him with me, you decided that it was Jack you wanted, however much it hurt me. And what's worse, Jack is really pleased about it."

"So when did Rob tell you all this," I asked, astounded.

"A group of us went out last night. I did call to see if you wanted to come, remember?" I nodded guiltily. I had got her off the phone as quickly as possible so I could continue talking to Callum.

"But have you spoken to Jack about this? Was he there last night?"

"No, he's been away all weekend with his family. Grandmother's birthday."

"So you've just heard this from Rob? You haven't spoken to Jack?" I asked.

"That's right." Grace's chin came up defiantly, but there was a small quiver in her voice.

"Look, Grace, I dumped Rob on Saturday when it became clear that he was only interested in getting me down to Cornwall. He was so angry that he abandoned me in the restaurant and I had to find my own way home. He really doesn't take rejection well, so I'm not surprised that he's invented a reason for my behaviour that makes him look better."

There was a flicker of hope in Grace's eyes. "You didn't tell him that you wanted Jack?"

"Of course not. Jack's like another brother to me. You know that. I couldn't be happier that you and he are together." I reached out and took her arm. "Honestly, Rob is lying. And I don't believe for a minute that Jack would ever say that he wanted to go out with me either. In fact, why don't you call him now?" I tried to smile encouragingly, but I was too angry about Rob.

"Well ... I suppose ... I could," she murmured. "I didn't think that I wanted to talk to him at all today." She finally slowed her breakneck pace as we got to the top of the stairs in the sixth form block.

"Has he called you?" I asked. I guessed Rob wouldn't have had the nerve to tell Jack any outright lies, not if he wanted to keep his pretty nose intact.

"Well, yes, he has left a message and a couple of texts. I just assumed he was being kind." She kept her gaze on the floor.

"You see! There's no problem with Jack at all. The only problem is Rob."

She gave a weak smile, as if she was trying very hard to believe what I was saying. "But, Alex, what I still don't understand is why you turned him down. You have been talking about him for months and months, and everyone thinks he's gorgeous. I was so pleased for you when he finally asked you out. What happened? What's changed?"

I couldn't tell her, as much as I wanted to, but she needed to believe what I told her or she would continue to be suspicious. I tried to keep it as close to the truth as possible. "There wasn't really only one thing. I just got this feeling, as soon as he made his move at the cinema, that I was just part of the Rob master plan, and what I wanted didn't matter to him at all. He was too ... smooth, too sure of himself, and he was telling me what he thought I wanted to hear. In fact, when I first told him that I didn't think Cornwall was a good idea, he even told me he loved me, just to see if that would persuade me."

"No! He can't have been that obvious."

"He was. He really thought I was just being a bit difficult and that he could flatter me into doing exactly what he wanted."

"That's awful. I'm so sorry, and I'm sorry that I fell for his lies too." She looked shamefaced.

"Hey, I've forgotten all about it already. We can't let him come between us." I held out my arms and Grace stepped towards me with a smile. She hugged me back. "Now, go and call Jack. He'll be really worried that you haven't replied to any of his messages."

"Good point," she agreed. "I'll be back in a sec."

We had reached the common room, so she went off to find a quiet corner and I went to find our friends in our usual spot. This room was just for sixth formers, and following a recent campaign it was furnished with easy chairs and beanbags as well as tables and chairs. Our corner had a selection of comfortable seats, and, most importantly, a good view across the boys' playing fields next door. There were usually a few girls idly leaning out of the window watching the boys on the football pitches. Knowing this, the sixth form boys generally had their lunchtime kick-about on this particular pitch, where they could show off to an appreciative audience.

All my friends were already lounging on the beanbags so I threw my bag down and flopped into the nearest chair. I was immediately conscious that all the chatter had abruptly stopped. I looked around and most of them were obviously avoiding my gaze. The only one sitting up straight was Ashley. She was smiling in my direction, a smile of victory.

"I do hope that you aren't going to take it too personally. I mean, we're all grown-ups here."

I didn't understand what she was getting at. "Sorry, I'm not with you."

"Oh," she tittered, "surely you must have heard already?"

She had such a smug look on her face that this could only be about Rob. I sighed and tried to keep my voice even. "No. Still not with you, I'm afraid."

"I'm going out with Rob now, and he's invited me down to his place in Cornwall in a few weeks." She was visibly preening.

I had to give him credit: he was a fast worker. Poor Ashley, she wouldn't stand a chance.

"Well, he made a speedy recovery," I couldn't resist commenting. She should have some warning about what she was getting into.

"Not much to recover from, as far as he was concerned. I do hope you are going to be OK though. I know it must be difficult for you."

"I'm sure I'll be fine." I tried to strike a tone between indifference and friendliness, to discourage any more discussion, but she was on a roll.

"I mean, getting dumped on the first date! That's got to be tough." Her fake concern was beginning to get to me. If I had actually cared, then what she was doing would have been really cruel.

"I can live with the disappointment." I was pleased to see that she was irritated that she was unable to get a reaction out of me. I took several deep breaths and continued to hold her gaze. She broke first.

"I have to say you are taking it well at the moment. I really hope it doesn't get to you later."

Honestly, I thought, the two of them deserved each other. Both were equally conniving and unpleasant. I was glad to be out of it, but getting angrier and angrier about how he had manipulated my friends. I smiled tightly at Ashley and got out my books, ending the conversation.

She continued to preen with Mia and Abbi. As I tried to shut out the details of their conversation, I wished I were somewhere quiet and private with Callum, where none of this would have any relevance. I was pretending to be deep in my book when Grace dropped down on the beanbag next to my chair, her face glowing.

"You were right!" she whispered. "He's perfectly OK, apart from being a bit worried that I wasn't responding to his texts. I told him that my phone has been playing up." She considered the mobile in her hand for a moment. "Actually, that's perfectly true. It's been switching itself off at random moments for the last few days. Must be time for an upgrade."

I didn't respond, and when she looked at me I nodded in Ashley's direction. "Heard her news?" I mouthed.

Grace tuned into the conversation at the other side of the circle, her mouth falling further and further open with everything she heard. Finally she dragged herself away and looked at me in horror. "I'm really hungry, so I'm going to head down for some lunch now. Want to join me?" she asked suddenly in a loud voice.

I smiled at her in relief and got to my feet. "Sure. I'm hungry too," I lied.

Everyone else was absorbed in sharing the gossip about how I had taken the news, so the two of us walked out alone.

"I'm so sorry," said Grace. "How can he be such a pig?"

I was so angry I couldn't speak, and my eyes welled up. I tried really hard to suppress it: I really didn't want to be seen crying in school today. Everyone would think that I was upset about Rob dumping me. "You know, I'm not sure I can actually face lunch. You go ahead and I'll just take a walk over the pitches." There was

134

no way that I could sit in the dining hall and keep up the pretence.

"Oh, OK. I'll come with you," replied Grace unenthusiastically.

I did my best to laugh. "And miss lunch? Don't be ridiculous. Can you just bring me a banana for later?" Grace had a gargantuan appetite for someone so skinny, and never went without a meal. She looked relieved.

"If you're sure. I'll come and find you in ten minutes." She gave me a quick hug and ran off.

I set off for the playing fields behind the school, and after a few minutes' walk I reached my favourite spot near one of the huge horse chestnut trees. I looked around, but no one was close by. I was finally alone. I really wanted to call Callum and see his beautiful face next to mine, but given that I had asked him to come back later, I thought it was unlikely. I couldn't resist trying, though, just to check if he was still around. I called his name softly, pulling the tiny mirror out of my school bag. Nothing happened. I peered into the depths of the stone, and as usual the beautiful flecks of red and gold glittered in the sunshine, but nothing moved. He wasn't there.

Suddenly I felt overwhelmed by the events of the last few hours, and I felt the tears welling up again. This time I couldn't avoid the sobs which escaped me, and I gave in to the frustration and anger which I had been holding in check. The tears fell in fat lines down my cheeks and on to the grass in front of me.

Almost as soon as it had started I knew I didn't want to be crying. I had to get a grip. I started to root around in my bag for a tissue. "Oh, crap," I muttered to myself as I pulled out an empty tissue packet, then dived into the corners of the bag to see if one had escaped. I was so intent on my search I didn't register the tingling in my arm.

"Hey, hey, keep still or I can't talk to you." His honeyed voice was full of warmth and humour, but changed abruptly as he saw my face. "What's the matter? Are you alright?"

"Oh, Callum, I'm so pleased you're here. I thought you had gone for the day."

"I had, but then you called, and, well, I couldn't resist coming back. But what's happened?"

I was suddenly embarrassed. "It's nothing. Nothing really, I just got angry. Someone has been telling lies about me to my friends."

He was instantly angry on my behalf. "Who? Who would do that to you?"

"It was Rob. You remember I told you about him yesterday."

He was suddenly wary. "He's the one you were out with the other night." It was a statement, not a question. "He's upset you again."

"I'm just angry, not upset." I wiped away the tears with my fingers, having given up on finding a tissue, and tried to sniff unobtrusively.

Callum was silent, and I anxiously watched his face in the tiny mirror. He seemed to be struggling to find the right thing to say.

"Do you want to tell me about it?"

"There isn't that much to tell really. I dumped him, he got upset and now he's started telling people lies about me." I really didn't want to tell Callum that he was telling everyone he dumped me and that I was lusting after someone else. It was all far too ridiculous, and so unimportant.

I watched his face as he thought about what I had told him.

I knew he could tell that I wasn't giving him all the details, but it was clear that he wasn't going to ask, and I was grateful for that. "You're sure you don't want to reconsider the idea that I might give him a little visit?"

"No!" It came out rather too sharply. I didn't want Callum having to do anything out of character just so that I could get my own back on Rob, turning Callum into the sort of person he didn't want to be. "He's not worth it, believe me. Don't go and ruin your record because of him." I tried to give him an encouraging smile.

He looked murderous. "It would be a pleasure. I don't want anyone hurting you."

"Please, it's nothing. I'm sorry; I shouldn't have called you when I was upset. I just knew that seeing you would make me feel better."

"Never worry about calling me. I will always be here for you, whatever you want me for." The passion was clear in his voice.

"I'm so pleased you came. I wasn't sure if you were still around or had gone back into London."

"I was heading back, but I got distracted by the cinema in Richmond. They are showing some terrible children's film, and I thought that not being able to remember it would be doing the audience a favour." He stole a glance at me to check that I approved. "Then I heard you call, and I came straight away."

"So how far away can you be to be able to hear me?"

"I don't think there is a limit. You were as clear in Richmond as you are right here."

"But Richmond is miles away. How did you get here so quickly? It must have been less than a couple of minutes."

"Don't forget, I don't have to go around anything. As long as you are wearing the amulet, I can fix your location and run in a straight line to you, through anything."

"I'm glad," I said. "It's really good to know you are there." I smiled as confidently as I could. I didn't want him thinking I was still upset. He returned my smile and ran a gentle hand down my back.

"Do you want me to stay now, or…?" His question was gentle.

"I'd love you to stay, but I can see Grace coming, and soon it will be time to go back to class. Shall I call you when I'm free at home?"

"OK, but I'll be here straight away if you need me. Don't forget."

"As if I could," I murmured as he kissed my head and disappeared. I tried to see him go in the mirror, but he was too fast, so I put it away and watched Grace as she approached across the fields. The lunchtime athletics practice had started, so she had to make her way around the edges of the track and keep a wary eye out for stray javelins. It made for slow progress, but that gave me plenty of time to compose myself: I didn't want Grace or anyone else believing that I cared about Rob.

Even picking her way across a field, Grace was delicate and composed, her inappropriate footwear dangling carelessly from her free hand. Despite being barefoot her walk was elegant – the result of years and years of gymnastics. She had represented the county at her junior school, but when I met her as we started seniors she made the decision to quit. Her mum had been furious, having spent every weekend for years ferrying her around to competitions, but as Grace had explained to me, it was because her mother enjoyed it, not because Grace did. So my friend was never going to make it to the Olympics, but she could still drop into the splits and turn a somersault on the spot. She also always looked graceful, whatever she was doing.

As she reached me she sank elegantly to the ground, proffering the banana I had asked for. "How's things now?" she asked gently.

"I'm fine. I'm really sorry for earlier. You know how I get when I get angry, and thinking about him makes me furious. But I'm calm now, so I'm not going to think about him any more." I hoped that this would satisfy her. I absolutely didn't want to go all over it again.

"Whatever you want," she murmured, companionably. "You missed a great fight in the dining hall," she added, with a twinkle in her eyes, knowing exactly how to distract me. She then gave me a colourful description of a slanging match between two younger girls in the queue for lunch. It hadn't quite come to blows by the time the prefects had waded in, but it sounded close. Grace had a gift for telling stories, and could imitate loads of accents, and before long I was weak with laughter. It was just what I needed, and by the time we started walking back for the afternoon lessons thoughts of Rob had been firmly shoved to the back of my mind.

Reaction

There was a full house of people at home when Josh and I got back from school, including my grandparents, which made getting away somewhere quiet to call Callum next to impossible. I helped Mum make the dinner and we all sat down together. My grandparents were very keen to hear about my driving lessons. I told them that I had been past their house with my driving instructor just a few days before, and Dad immediately decided that I could drive them home, as it would give me a bit more practice. So after dinner I squeezed them into the back of the Mini and we drove back to Kew with Dad next to me in front.

After we dropped them off Dad relaxed back in his seat. "Not bad driving, Alex. What's the news on your test then?"

"Well, actually, Miss McCabe says that I should put in for it. She thinks I'm ready."

"Yes, I'd agree," he said. "And don't wait too long either, otherwise you'll start driving like a driver, not a learner, and that's bound to make you fail!"

The journey home gave me time to think up a new plan for seeing Callum. When we got to the house I parked and called out to Dad as he got out of the car.

"I think I'll just sit here for a bit and go over the Highway Code again. I'll see you inside later."

"Really?" he asked, surprised. "I thought you would have

known all of that by now."

"Just double-checking."

"You do have some strange ideas," he laughed. "Have fun!" He shut the car door and went into the house.

I waited for a moment to make sure that no one was about, then whispered, "Callum?"

There was no waiting this time. He must have been really close by. I angled the rear-view mirror and the vanity mirror so I had two views of him. "Hello," he breathed as he nuzzled my hair. "I've missed you. Did your day improve?"

"Yes ... and I'm really sorry you had to see me like that."

"Hey, don't apologise for being upset! I never mind when you call me. In fact," he paused, looking a little embarrassed, "it felt ... good, being wanted."

"Oh, Callum, you make me feel so much better."

He snorted. "I'm stuck in a different dimension. I can't see how that can improve anything." But I could see from the shy smile and the slight flush on his cheeks that he was happy.

"So what did you do?" I ventured. "Did you stay in Richmond?"

He looked into the distance. "No, I went to St Paul's. I thought I would tell them what was going on, in case one of them had anything useful I could learn."

"Ah. How did it go?"

He continued to look pensive. "They were pretty much speechless. Even Catherine, and that doesn't happen often."

"So did any of them come up with anything useful? Any thoughts on how this can be happening?"

"No, nothing." He looked away for a moment. "It seems that amulets do turn up on your side very occasionally, and it's big news for us when one surfaces. I'd never heard of it before because this is the first one that has turned up while I've been here. Everyone was extremely curious about it ... and about you."

"How did Catherine take it?"

His face in the rear-view mirror clouded. "She ... she didn't believe me at first, but I finally convinced her by telling her a bit about you. She knows that I couldn't make all of that stuff up."

I wasn't sure that I wanted this strange woman knowing too much about me, but she was Callum's sister, and perhaps his only real companion in the strange world he inhabited so I bit my lip. "I hope you didn't have to go into too much detail?"

"Nothing that would embarrass you. Nothing about how I can do this," his long fingers traced the line of my neck, "or this," as his lips found my shoulder.

"I wish I could touch you!" I exclaimed, thumping the steering wheel in frustration. "You are driving me crazy and I just have to sit here."

He stopped instantly, his face the picture of contrition. "I'm sorry, I thought you liked it."

"I absolutely love it! I just wish I could reach you too." I gazed at him longingly. "Can you feel anything I do? You said the other day that you can feel a slight resistance when you touch me. What if I touch you?"

He straightened up beside me. "No idea. Shall we give it a go?" He smiled cheekily. "Where do you want to start?"

I was suddenly very nervous, frightened that I might not be able to feel him, and also frightened about what I would do if I *could* feel him. It was dark inside the car now, so I could only see him in the yellow glow of the street light outside the house. He sat waiting patiently.

I reached up beside me and watched as the Alex in the mirror gently touched his cheek. My fingers felt the smallest resistance, as if I was touching a soap bubble. I watched myself stroke down the length of his jaw. His chin lifted slightly and I could see that his eyes were tightly shut. I dropped my hand.

"Did you feel anything at all?" I asked, disappointed.

His eyes opened slowly, and the emotion in them was almost painful to see. "You touched me, Alex. I felt your fingers on my face." A single tear ran down his cheek, and I automatically reached up to try to smooth it away. He leaned towards my hand, obviously savouring the moment. "I never believed that this could happen," he whispered gently.

I felt awed by the power I had. I could now touch him a little, in the same way that he could touch me. We sat in silence for a moment, each lost in our thoughts. I could see his brooding eyes, the colour of the sea at midnight.

"Oh, Callum, what are we going to do?" I asked eventually. "Can we live like this?" I lifted my fingers to trace the curve of his neck.

He seemed to have trouble refocusing. "I don't know. I didn't expect this." He was silent for a moment, then began, "I think that it would be best if we..." He stopped suddenly. "We've got company. Time for me to go. I'll see you tomorrow. Don't forget to keep the amulet on." He swooped to kiss my cheek and was gone.

"Crap!" I exclaimed as Josh opened the car door.

"Nice welcome! What have you been doing out here for so long? Mum wants to know if you want a cup of coffee."

"I was after a bit of uninterrupted peace, actually."

"Well I've blown that, I'm afraid," he added, sliding back the passenger seat and folding his long legs into the car. "Can I talk to you for a moment?"

I sighed. It was obvious what this was going to be about. I felt a familiar mix of irritation, gratitude and love.

"I was just wondering what you would like me to do," he started. "That prat has been shooting his mouth off, but I didn't know what your story was. And I don't want to make things worse." He grinned at me apologetically.

"I really don't know. I've not said anything to anyone, but he is saying that he dumped me, and he is now going out with Ashley. She is extremely smug about it all."

"Well, I could threaten him a bit. You know – make things a bit uncomfortable..."

I laughed. "Thanks, Josh, I appreciate the offer, but he's still not worth the bother."

"If you're sure. I'm going to tackle him on the lies, though. He can't get away with that."

I shrugged. I really didn't care at this point. Josh looked quizzically at me.

"Are you positive that you are OK? You seem kind of ... unnaturally subdued about the whole thing. Not like you at all."

I nodded. "Really, I'm fine. I mean, I'm angry with him but otherwise it's a waste of energy."

Josh suddenly sat up straight in his chair. "There's someone else, isn't there? That's why you don't care."

"Wow, that's a bit of a leap!" I returned quickly, not wanting to let him see he was close. "Where would I meet someone else?"

"Oh, it just seemed the most likely solution." His voice was disappointed.

"No, I just realised that he didn't deserve me, that's all."

"You are right there, he doesn't." He was quiet for a moment.

"Not many people deserve anything that bad," he added with a smirk, backing away from me as far as he could in the tiny car.

I took a quick swipe at him, but as ever he was able to grab my hands before I could do any useful damage. We sat in companionable silence for a bit, watching as next door's dog suddenly raced around the side of their house, being chased by a large fox. Josh really disliked the little white terrier, as it used to terrorise him every time he went round to retrieve his lost football when he was a kid, and I could hear him grunt in satisfaction at its predicament. But we couldn't leave such an unequal fight, and without even discussing it, we both got out of the car as noisily as possible to scare the fox away. The little dog growled at us when he was safe, and I vowed to leave it to its fate the next time it needed rescuing.

I went straight to my room, but Callum wasn't there when I looked in the mirror and I went to bed feeling that some important part of me was missing.

The next day was a driving lesson day, so I didn't see Grace on the coach. Ashley continued to look unbearably smug, so I avoided her as much as possible. I didn't know when Callum might appear so I was constantly jumpy. But there was no sign of him, so when it was time for my driving lesson I slipped the amulet into my bag. I couldn't risk him turning up part-way through a driving lesson. My arm didn't feel right without the bracelet, and the disconcerting feeling of loss I had had all day felt stronger.

But I was soon absorbed in the lesson as we made a circuit of the Kingston one-way system. It took every ounce of my concentration to get round in one piece without ploughing into the pedestrians who seemed to leap out at every turn.

The trip back to school was a breeze after that, and luckily there was a good parking spot available. I heaved a great sigh of relief as I turned off the car.

"Well," said Miss McCabe, "you did very well. Have you sent off your test form yet?"

"It's in my bag waiting to go. I just wanted to check that you didn't think last time was a fluke."

"You're the last person I'd have expected to be short of confidence." She laughed. "Send it in and see what date you get, then we can see how many more lessons you need."

She headed off back to the staffroom, and I started making my way to the dining hall to grab a quick sandwich, groping in my bag for the amulet as I went. As I slipped it on to my wrist Callum was instantly there in my head, shouting loudly, his tone urgent and worried. I had to stop dead and lean against a wall to stop from falling over.

"What do you think you were doing? You must NEVER take the amulet off! Never! Do you understand me?"

I staggered backwards under the onslaught, putting my hands to my head to try and stop the noise. The ranting continued and faded as he tried to catch up with my movements.

"…So irresponsible… If you had any idea how much danger…"

"*Stop it!*" I hissed as loudly as I could without attracting too much attention. "Just wait a minute. I need to find somewhere quiet to see you." I marched around the back of the sports hall and into the changing rooms. I quickly checked the toilets and then wedged the door shut. I braced myself then looked up into the mirror. He looked weirdly out of place in the white tiled room. "Right," I started, "calm down. What's the problem?"

If he could have paced he would have done so. He looked wild and distracted, and for the first time, a bit scary. Not angry

146

as he had been when I had first seen the picture in my head, but proper, not-sure-what-to-expect scary. His voice was still harsh. "You took it off. You took off the amulet so I couldn't … I couldn't protect you."

"I had a driving lesson. It seemed sensible not to be able to be disturbed. Why all the drama? You knew I'd be back at school in a little while." I couldn't work out why he was so upset.

"I told you not to take it off. It's not safe. Not now they know." The anguish in his voice seemed genuine enough, and the pain on his face was very clear.

"What are you talking about? Who?"

"The others. The people like me. I told them about you, remember? If you are wearing the amulet they can't get to you."

"What do you mean 'get to' me? And why would they? I don't understand."

I watched him take a deep breath, and wondered what was coming. "They know about you now, and it seems that some of them might want to come looking for you." His voice was tortured.

"But what for?"

He looked exasperated. "They are curious, and want to find out more about your amulet."

"So why is that a problem? Why do I need protecting? None of you can get to my dimension."

"Don't you understand? I don't want them to be able to take away any of your – *of our* – memories."

That made sense – I wouldn't want to lose a fraction of the glorious memories I had gathered over the last week, but he was still overreacting. I tried to mollify him.

"I understand. I'd prefer to keep all that too, but it's not life and death. Just relax a bit. You frightened me."

As I watched he stepped away from me, stood up straight and took several deep breaths. His eyes were closed and I hoped he was just calming himself down. After a few moments his eyes opened slowly and the scary look had gone. I smiled at him hesitantly, and he moved swiftly back towards me, settling his arm into place.

I could feel his touch on my back. "I didn't mean to frighten you. I love you so much that I don't want to lose any little part of you Alex. I'm sorry I went a bit over the top. I just didn't expect you to do it. It worried me."

Something he had said still didn't make any sense. "I still don't understand why your friends would want to come here and take my memories."

He looked uncomfortable. "I'm sorry. I overreacted – really, there is no reason for them to want to do that. It's just that, well, your recently worn – charged, if you like – amulet has powerfully attractive properties. It seems that it will summon any Dirge in the area and it'll make your memories much more tempting. I don't think they *will* do it, but when you are not wearing the amulet they *could* do it." He carefully emphasised the difference, then looked a bit abashed. "I guess I wasn't acting very rationally. Do you forgive me?"

"Of course I forgive you. I just didn't realise what a problem it would be taking this off." I looked at the amulet. "I promise to keep it on all the time, as long as you promise never to ambush me during a driving lesson."

"It's a deal." His smile was still a little strained, but as I watched his long, strong arms enfold me in the mirror, I no longer cared.

My lessons that afternoon passed in a bit of a daze. It

seemed so out of character for Callum to be so wound up. But then, I thought, how well did I really know him? It had only been a week, I reminded myself, since I found the amulet in the sand. How strange that so much could change within a week.

The double statistics lesson went on for what seemed like hours. I kept glancing at the amulet, and I could see the shadows moving across its surface, making the flecks of gold glimmer and gleam. Was that him, I wondered, or one of his mysterious companions?

I was very careful not to mention his name out loud, even in a whisper. I needed time to think.

But the more I thought about my strange and unorthodox boyfriend, the more my head began to hurt with all the questions. I tuned back into the lesson, but they weren't doing anything particularly challenging. It wasn't going to keep me occupied.

I stared out of the window, looking at all the houses opposite the school, each one full of the love, hopes and fears of the people who lived there. Every one would be different, I realised with a sudden clarity. My love was just a bit *more* different. And for all I knew, there might be dozens of people sharing their lives with someone completely out of the ordinary.

I couldn't help smiling as I thought of him. I knew I was already in too deep. I loved him, and I wanted him to know it. I guessed he wouldn't be far away, so grabbed my notebook and found an empty page.

Callum – are you there?

He must have been hovering right behind me as both the tingle and his whisper were immediate and made my heart melt.

"I'm here." His voice was hesitant. "Are you alright? I've been watching you and you have been frowning a lot. I was worried that perhaps, well perhaps I had scared you off."

Not possible. A bit surprised, perhaps, but not going anywhere.

His sigh of relief was audible, and was so real I looked around to check that no one else could hear it. They were all deep in the Bayesian analysis theory, and taking no notice of me at all. "I'm sorry about earlier," he continued, "but I just can't bear the thought of losing you, that's all. I never believed that this was possible, finding you like this, and you've turned my existence upside down. I can't lose you now."

You are in no danger of losing me to anyone.

"I know I've been a fool," he continued, "but I just wanted to keep you away from the others." I could feel him trying to lighten the tone. "After all, if you do get to see some of my companions you might like one of them better."

I started scribbling again.

Possibly. Are they all as gorgeous as you?

He gave a short laugh. "None of them is really my type."

What is your type then?

I couldn't resist asking.

"Ah, well, that is easy. It would be slim, blonde and Alex-shaped. Not much competition really."

I nestled back into his embrace, feeling the whisper of his arms gently around me. Up at the front of the class Mrs Moss was starting to ask questions and I realised I was going to have to pay attention for a while.

I need to concentrate. Can you stay without being distracting?

"Well, I like a challenge," he chuckled, but after that he was quiet. I was just conscious of his presence by the feeling that I was leaning against something light and insubstantial, and by the occasional brush of my hair.

He stayed quiet until I got back into the car to wait for Josh.

"Well that took some control, I can tell you. Not reaching up to stroke your hair or neck, like this, or running my fingers down your arm..."

"I'm very impressed." I smiled at him in the mirror. "I wasn't sure you could behave after your performance in yesterday's lesson."

I saw Josh loping over the car park, and Callum suddenly disappeared with a promise to beat me home.

"That won't be difficult," I grumbled to myself, knowing that Josh would keep to the speed limit all the way.

Josh was in a cheery mood. He only had two more exams to sit and then his party season started in earnest. I knew that he was planning on making a move on one of the upper sixth girls from my school, but had still not decided the final strategy. I took the rare opportunity to tease him mercilessly for a while, and then started offering some practical advice. The conversation continued when we got home, and I really couldn't just let it drop – I owed him for Saturday night, after all. Mum and Dad were both out so I sat in the kitchen with him for a while as he made and demolished a huge sandwich.

When I could finally get away I collected a fat book, slipped my mirror in the front cover and headed out to the garden. I made for a quiet spot by the back fence with a swinging chair - no one would be able to hear me there. I wish I had thought of it sooner.

As I settled back in the seat Callum was already there, his voice gentle and welcoming.

"At last! You seem to have taken forever today."

"Sorry about that. Sometimes you just can't rush my brother," I apologised with a grin, pulling the mirror out of the book.

"Well, you're here now, and I have the rest of the afternoon and all evening. What would you like to do?"

"Hmm, what are our options? We can't go to the pub, I don't really fancy the cinema now, and we have tried going for a walk." I grinned at him again. "Do you have any other ideas?"

He looked longingly at me. "I have one, but that's not going to work either."

I sighed. He was right, what we really wanted, to be able to fall into each other's arms, was hardly likely to happen. I went for second best.

"I really want to know more about you, and your life. You're such a mystery." I reached up and stroked his cheek.

"Really?" He pulled a face. "You might not enjoy what you hear."

"That's not very likely. I want to know all about you because I love you." It still thrilled me to be able to say it.

"Believe me, I don't want to put you off: I love you too."

My heart leapt again to hear him repeat the words. "Don't worry. Just tell me everything."

He groaned. "OK. The truth and nothing but the truth. Where do you want me to start?"

"How about a day in the life?" He raised his eyebrow at me. "Oh. Well, a day in the existence, then – an average twenty-four hours. How do you fill it?"

I could feel him settling back, so I crossed my legs up on the chair and propped the mirror on my knee to get a good view.

I could see him staring into the distance, thinking, so I kept quiet. I knew he would start when he was ready. Eventually he began to talk.

"A day in the existence... Well, we do sleep, or some of us do, anyway, so I wake up with all the others in the Whispering Gallery in St Paul's. That's our base, where we are 'home' I suppose. We wake up miserable, which is why you haven't ever seen me really early in the morning.

"But I'm not as bad as a lot of the others. Every day we go back to our base state, the mental state we were in when we drowned in the river, plus whatever reservoir we have in our amulets, but that's still pretty miserable for most of us. So we spread out and hit the commuters, always looking for those yellow auras. For most of them it takes all day, but I'm lucky: I can usually get done quite quickly, depending on what's on at the early shows.

"Most days I get assigned to help someone. I told you the other day about sinking too low. If we see someone getting that way our leader – chief, boss, whatever you want to call him – will get someone else to help them get ... well, what they need, to encourage them out on to the street, to help them search so they can start gathering. The others don't like it when I'm assigned to them: I'm too cheerful. But if we don't help the ones who are sinking then they are a terrible influence on the group – it's as if they give off misery and the rest of us absorb it, so it's in everyone's interest to get them back up out of it.

"I tend to get asked to help a lot because I am the least miserable and have less gathering to do for myself. I generally only have to pick up a few thoughts at intervals throughout the day, but most of them are searching for hours, having to collect hundreds and hundreds of thoughts and memories."

"So who is your leader – how does that work?" It was strange to think that there was some sort of social structure in his world.

"We elect one whenever the old one doesn't want to keep going any more, and give them some power to make decisions for us. Apparently the group works better that way, and not just as a random collection of individuals."

"So how many of you are there? There must have been thousands of people who've drowned in the Fleet over the centuries."

"Right now it's about two hundred, but no one has joined for years, and we don't know why. Catherine and I are the most recent, and we were unusual. So much of the Fleet runs underground now, and maybe that's the reason. Our longest residents think they have been in St Paul's for hundreds and hundreds of years."

"But you don't know when you and Catherine joined them?"

"No, not for sure. With no features in your week it's hard to keep track. And, before you, I had no reason to."

"OK, so you stalk London for the day, vacuuming up memories. What happens next?"

"After a day out gathering we all have to reassemble in the gallery at night. I don't know what would happen if we didn't. I just get a strange compulsion to be there.

"You know," he added with a laugh, "it's us who makes the gallery whisper, not the acoustics. When we are all in the gallery and you come and sit in the seats there are so many of us that we can carry the sound around. It makes the people happy, and then someone can pounce..." He tailed off, and there was a pause.

"So do you have friends over there?" I asked casually. I couldn't believe that some girl on his side wouldn't be interested in him. He looked pensive for a moment.

"No, not really. It's hard to explain. Everyone is too tied up in their own misery to spend any energy on that. There are some people I would choose to avoid when I get to St Paul's, but that's mainly because they are just too miserable all the time."

"Do you spend time with Catherine?"

"A bit, but she can be rather depressing too. I'm generally better off on my own."

"Tell me about her. What does she look like?"

"I guess you would say she's attractive. She is medium height, with long light-brown hair, green eyes, quite curvy, I suppose. I've never really thought about it. Most of the time she is scowling so much I don't want to attract her attention. She has a bit – actually a lot – of a temper."

I wasn't sure I liked the sound of Catherine, and decided I didn't really want to hear any more about her. He hadn't mentioned any other girls so I was keen to move the conversation on before he worked out why I was asking. "Tell me about your leader," I asked. "What's his name?"

"He's called Matthew, and he was much older than most of us when he came over – maybe in his fifties, and he's been with the group for hundreds of years."

"Why did you choose him to be in charge?"

"It was nothing to do with me. He's been the leader all the time I've been over here, but I think that it's because, for a Dirge, he's actually quite balanced, not too morose all the time. In fact, after I told the group about you, I talked to him on his own. I wanted to know if he knew of any way to make this work."

"I'm guessing he didn't come up with anything?" From the look on his face it couldn't have been good news.

"No, his only solution was for you to throw yourself in the river, which is a terrible idea, and as no one has joined us for such a long time maybe there's no way to be sure about that, even. It's hard to be sure that any open part of the river is the water of the Fleet." He looked at me sternly. "Promise me you won't even think about that?"

I would have to commit suicide then, to drown in the murky Fleet, and even then perhaps only have a chance of being with him. My heart filled with dread at the thought. I knew I would never have the courage, not even if I could be sure that he would be there at the other end. I loved my life and my family too much.

He was looking at me anxiously, waiting for an answer to his question.

How do you tell someone that you won't die for them? I wondered. Dying so he could live – that was a something I could contemplate. But dying with only a chance of being dead with him? No, I couldn't do that. I tried to put a teasing note into my tone. "You are gorgeous," I admitted, "but I don't think I'll be killing myself any time soon."

"Good call," he agreed. "There are some very dodgy characters over here." He was clearly happy to let the conversation take a more jovial path.

"Tell me about some of them," I encouraged.

"Well," he started enthusiastically, "there's Arthur. He loiters in churches and takes memories of weddings. And there's Margaret. She has a particular fondness for late-night parties, and is responsible for *huge* amounts of amnesia wrongly attributed to drink. Lucas, he is the most miserable person I've ever come across,

I won't be introducing you to him. Then before I got here there was Veronica, who used to stalk the university union bars. Until she left she was the worst. Rupert's speciality is…"

"Hang on," I interrupted. "What did you just say? About Veronica? Where did she go?"

His face was a picture of horror. His mouth opened but he said nothing.

"I thought you said that you were stuck, that there was no escape. What happened to Veronica?"

Introduction

I waited for him to respond. With an effort, he seemed to pull himself together.

"She was able to travel further away," he said eventually, looking out over the garden. "Very occasionally it seems that someone is able to break free of the compulsion to return each night, and that gives them the opportunity to go wandering further afield. I guess she may come back some day."

Something didn't add up. If it was this straightforward, why was he so horrified at having to tell me? And why couldn't he look me in the eye when he was explaining it?

"Do you think you could do that, break the compulsion and stay later with me?"

When he looked back his eyes were still troubled, and it sounded as if he was choosing his words carefully. "I'm afraid not, I can't resist it. I have tried a few times, but it becomes almost physically uncomfortable. I always have to return."

He could clearly see the question in my eyes.

"It's not that I don't want to stay with you, really it isn't. I'd love to be with you, but I *have* to go back to St Paul's."

Whatever it was he wasn't telling me, I couldn't doubt that he cared about me. My heart flipped again as I watched him, and I smiled. "Well, we'll just have to make the most of the time," I teased, reaching up beside me to touch his shoulder. His fiery blue eyes relaxed, and he leaned in closer.

We spent hours out in the garden, just talking about normal things, like films and music. With a free backstage pass to every gig and premiere in London he had the most amazing gossip.

He explained how he would go to the rehearsals of his favourite bands and then enjoy the concerts from the best seats in the house, sampling a quick thought or memory every now and then. His observation skills were brilliant and he had me rocking with laughter over his impressions of some of the more overrated celebrities.

I asked him about my favourite band and was delighted to hear that he liked their music too. We had both been to their latest gig at Wembley Arena, and Callum was able to fill me in on their dressing room demands – I was never going to be able to look at the lead singer in future without smirking.

"So who is next on your concert list then?" I asked, curious to know if we had any other favourites in common.

He frowned slightly for a moment while consulting his internal diary. "I think I'm planning to go to that big charity concert at the Albert Hall next week," he finally decided, nodding to himself. "Those things are usually good."

"No way!" I exclaimed. "I have tickets for that – Grace and I are going."

"Excellent – I can come with you then. I'd enjoy sitting with someone I know in the audience for a change." He gave me one of his most devastating grins. "It can be our first date."

"It'll be slightly odd to have Grace there as well on a first date, but I see what you mean," I laughed. "You'll just have to be content with teasing me when I can't respond."

"I can deal with that. Maybe I'll finally get to hear you sing too."

"It's so unfair – you'll get to see all the celebrities backstage as well."

His smile was gone and he looked at me seriously. "Don't ever forget, Alex, I get to see all this stuff, but I never really participate. No one notices me, no one asks my opinion, no one tells me I'm off-key or tries to throw me out. I'm just a ... voyeur. I would love to just go into a coffee shop and order a cappuccino, then sit and chat with some friends."

I was instantly contrite. "I'm sorry, I didn't mean to make you feel bad – you've just been selling your lifestyle very well."

It was another wrong thing to say. He stiffened and pulled away from me. "I am *not* trying to sell you this 'lifestyle'. No one should have to suffer as we do every day. When I have fun it is a very brief interlude in an otherwise miserable existence."

This was going from bad to worse. "I don't mean that I will be signing up any time soon," I reassured him. "I just like the way you make an advantage of what you have."

He looked slightly mollified, but the space between us was tense. A look of comprehension suddenly washed over his face.

"I need to go," he announced firmly. "I'm getting miserable and that makes me want to pick a fight. I've spent too long with you without gathering some memories."

I thought back; Callum had been with me almost constantly since lunchtime and it was now early evening. I smiled, relieved that something other than me had caused the tension. "You know, there is a cinema just up the road. You could be there in a minute or two."

"Nice idea, but really I need to head back into central London. I know that Matthew is going to want to talk to me again."

I pouted. "Does that mean that you won't be able to come back later?"

"It depends on how successful my gathering is, and Matthew's too. I'll have to wait for him to come back and it sometimes takes him a while. I'll come back if I can, but it's much more likely to be tomorrow. Is that OK?"

"I'd love to see you later if you can manage it, but I do understand. I don't have a really busy day at school tomorrow so just feel free to join me at any time. You'll have to behave yourself though," I teased, "I've got a long chemistry lab to do, and that would be a difficult place to be distracted."

He laughed. "Chemistry sounds even more boring than the maths. It could be fun to sneak up on you during that." I reached up and stroked his thick mane of dark golden hair. He groaned quietly, then pulled himself away.

"I really have to go now. I love you. Keep yourself safe for me until tomorrow."

"Happy gathering. I hope the conversation with Matthew goes well. See you tomorrow." I felt the briefest of touches on my lips and he was nowhere to be seen.

It was one of the longest times we had spent together. Without him I felt suddenly incomplete. The idea of not spending my future with him was becoming as inconceivable as it was impossible. I lay back in the swinging chair and watched a robin, sitting on a branch a few feet away from me and considering me with its head cocked to one side.

"What should I do then, robin? Can I live like this? Is there any way at all that we can make this work?"

The robin chirped loudly. "It's as likely as me having a relationship with you really, isn't it?" I sighed. It regarded me with the other eye, gave another trill and was gone in a flash of red.

Sadness rolled over me like a wave. However hard I tried, I couldn't think of a way around the problem. None of it fitted any of the rules of the only world I knew and understood. But the amulet gave us a gateway, I remembered. Maybe it had other, hidden properties that we could use. I looked at it in the light from the sunset, the stone flashing as the sun probed its depths. A shadow flitted across its surface. Suddenly excited, I grabbed the mirror and looked around.

"Callum? Are you there?"

There was no response, and all I could see in the mirror was my parents' vegetable garden. I must have been mistaken. Sighing inwardly, I gathered my things together and made my way into the house.

Josh was revising for his last few exams in a couple of days, and Mum and Dad were keen to watch a documentary. I made an excuse about homework and headed up to my room.

I was frustrated all over again by my inability to look up a solution to my problem on the Internet. It made me realise how much I now relied on it for answers. Perhaps, I thought, I should go back to basics.

I opened a new document on my laptop and started writing down everything I knew about the amulet, the Dirges and Callum. I felt better as I started to get it all in some sort of order. I shuddered as I wrote down what he had told me about Catherine's suicide and his failed rescue attempt. As I wrote, a thought nudged its way to the front of my brain. Of course! There was bound to be a report of a double drowning on the Internet. I quickly saved the notes and opened Google, typing in Callum, Catherine, Blackfriars Bridge and drowning. The response was instant and disappointing. Nothing useful came up at all, but I realised that this was an interesting avenue to explore further. I looked up suicides from the bridge, and then tried double deaths in the Thames, but nothing seemed to fit.

After hours of searching I came across a Coroner's Court document listing all the drownings in London since the 1970s. It was depressing reading, but numbers of fatalities had plummeted in the last decade, mainly due to the new lifeboat station nearby which was able to get out to people almost as soon as they hit the water.

But there was no double drowning listed. Perhaps he was wrong about the details. I shook my head, sat up and stretched. I hadn't realised how stiff I had got, hunched over my computer. I could hear Mum and Dad coming up the stairs, and looked at my watch. It was getting late. I yawned, saved the websites and turned off. I could work on this tomorrow.

I dropped into bed with a sigh of relief, switched out the light and nestled down under my duvet. My mind was racing but there was a warm glow in my heart where Callum now lived, and I couldn't help smiling to myself as I thought about him. The problems we faced melted away, and I felt myself start to drift off to sleep.

I was on the very edge of consciousness when I felt a tingle in my arm, one that was familiar yet strangely different. I tried to process why that would be as I shook myself awake and reached for the mirror, mumbling a sleepy greeting. "Hi. I didn't expect you. What are you doing out so late?"

As my eyes focused in the dark I felt a sudden shiver of shock. I quickly reached for my bedside light and snapped it on. Sitting behind me in the mirror was a complete stranger.

Wide awake now, I sat bolt upright. "Who are you? And what are you doing here?" I hissed as loudly as I dared. But as I said it, I knew: her face was strangely familiar. The features were rounder, but the nose had a similar line and the long thick hair was identical in colour to Callum's. This was Catherine.

"So you're Alex." There was no greeting and no question, just a statement. Her voice was controlled, without emotion.

I sat up straight and tried not to sound defensive. "Yes. And I know who you are too." I looked her up and down, as much as I could in the tiny mirror. She was petite and, like Callum, dressed in an old-fashioned cloak. Her neck was slender and she held her head at a proud angle. The gene for good looks obviously ran deep in the family because she was stunning. Her light-brown hair tumbled over her shoulders, and her dark eyes contained the familiar flecks of gold. But her eyes were not blue, they were a vibrant green, bright in the lamplight.

Although she was exquisite there was an overwhelming feeling of sadness that seemed to seep out of her. The turn of her mouth, the way she held her shoulders, the look in her eyes all combined to form a picture of beautiful misery.

"We need to talk. I'm afraid you are getting yourself into something you don't understand." Her voice sounded strained, as if it were difficult to get the words out.

I was wary. Callum clearly wasn't fond of his sister, so I didn't want to do anything which would upset him, but I could hardly ignore her either.

I pushed the hair back out of my face and pulled my pyjamas together, trying to look as if I was in control. I smiled at her as warmly as I could manage.

"Well, it's good to meet you. Callum talks about you a lot."

"Really." Again it wasn't a question, just a flat statement. Even if Callum hadn't told me about her, I was beginning to dislike Catherine.

"Yes. He's told me a great deal about all of you and why you are ... the way you are." I managed to keep my voice steady and friendly. "Does he know you're here?"

She gave a short and sudden laugh. "Hardly. He's been extremely protective of you, not telling anyone where you are."

"So how did you find me?"

"He's not as clever as he thinks he is," she said, not quite smiling, but looking a little more animated. "He wasn't difficult to follow, and then of course, when I got close I caught the pull of the amulet and you were the only one without an aura. Quite easy to spot really."

I realised that she must have been wandering about my house with my unprotected family. I tried to keep the horror out of my voice. "I hope that you didn't need to do too much gathering around here tonight."

She snorted. "There's not much joy here, so it wouldn't have been very ... satisfying." That surprised me. I never thought of the house as unhappy. Then I remembered what everyone had been doing tonight: Josh was revising one of his least favourite subjects, and my parents' documentary was about the Second World War. I heaved an inward sigh of relief, as I really didn't want Catherine to be encouraged to spend time around my family.

"Yes, well, perhaps you won't find what you want here. You may have more luck at the pub up the road."

"It's not important tonight," she muttered, then sat silently. This conversation was clearly going to be a struggle.

"Well, Catherine, it's great to meet you at last." I smiled

warmly at her. "You said that you needed to talk to me? I'm afraid that I can only whisper or I'll end up waking up the rest of the house. Do you want to meet tomorrow so we can speak more comfortably?"

If there was a delay I might be able to call Callum and find out how on earth I was supposed to deal with her. I mentally crossed my fingers as I asked.

"That's not possible. Callum will be back and I have to speak to you when he isn't around, otherwise..." She tailed off, and stared into the distance.

"Otherwise what?" I encouraged. "Is there something wrong?"

"Wrong?" she exclaimed loudly, making me jump. "How can there possibly be something wrong when a Dirge takes up with a normal girl just stuffed full of nice fresh memories and thoughts? What could possibly be wrong about that?"

I added sarcasm and short temper to the list of Catherine's character faults.

I tried to continue with my calm, friendly exterior. "I'm sorry," I said, keeping my voice calm, "that was clearly the wrong thing to say. Why don't you tell me what is on your mind" She seemed to be in the grip of some sort of internal struggle. Finally she sighed again.

"Have you asked yourself why he is interested in you?" She looked me squarely in the eye as she put the question.

I wasn't sure what she meant, so I thought it would be best to be a bit vague. "At the beginning, curiosity, I suppose. And now, well ... why is anyone interested in anyone else?"

"You don't think it's strange then, this sudden affection he claims to feel for you?"

I wanted to tell her to mind her own business, but getting her angry really wasn't going to help, and she did seem keen to tell me something.

"I know that Callum and I haven't known each other for very long, and I know that we have become very ... close very quickly. But it's not that uncommon." I shrugged and returned her unwavering stare. "We feel very strongly about each other."

She shook her head and for the first time a small tight smile broke though. "He really has got you hooked this time, hasn't he?"

"What do you mean, 'this time'?"

"Oh come on! You look like a bright girl. Do you honestly believe that the amulet just happened to be in the river? That you just happened to be in St Paul's? That you could become the love of his life in such a short space of time? Think about it!"

A cold fist of fear wrapped itself around my heart. "What are you saying?" I whispered.

"I'm saying that you have been played by a master. You didn't really stand a chance. You're too young and inexperienced."

"I'm old enough to know what I am doing." I could feel my chin sticking out in defiance.

She gave a short and brittle laugh. "Really? Let me guess. He told you that he fell off Blackfriars Bridge trying to save me; that he only takes unimportant memories from people; that he's never felt like this about anyone before – shall I continue?"

I could see my own stricken face in the mirror as I looked at her in horror. "I don't understand."

"He does this all the time." She was talking slowly and carefully, as if to a small and stupid child. "You are not the first, and I doubt that you'll be the last. Of course, he likes the company you keep too – that's quite an attraction."

"What do you mean by that?"

"He's always preferred the memories of girls, adolescents if possible. He says they have a better 'texture' than other people's. I imagine that he couldn't believe his luck that this time the amulet was found by a schoolgirl."

"No, that can't be true! That's a horrible thought." She had to be lying about this. Callum wouldn't do that to my friends.

"Yes," she continued in the same, even tone, "it is horrible, isn't it? He was telling me that your friend with the long, dark hair produced some particularly good results, as well as being acceptable to look at while he gathered."

I was stunned into silence. I really didn't believe that he was stealing memories from Grace. She must be wrong. I finally found my voice. "No! It's not true."

"There is no point in denying it. You know I'm telling the truth." For the first time she looked concerned, not just blank or angry. "Think about it – why else would he possibly want you? You're just an average girl."

The cold hand in my chest was squeezing my heart so hard I was struggling to breathe. I tried to control myself and think rationally. It was true that he was impossibly gorgeous, but that didn't mean anything. I had always been taught to be confident. I wasn't going to be easily browbeaten into thinking that I wasn't good enough for him. I took a couple more breaths to steady myself.

"No one's 'average' to the people who love them. Callum and I are just lucky to have found each other. I know that it's a bit more difficult than I imagined, but I hope we'll be able to find a way to be together."

"But you must know that it's ridiculous to believe that. He's over here and you are over there. He knows that it will never work – he's playing with you."

"But why would he? What's he got to gain?"

"I can see he's been rather ... careful about what he's been telling you. Am I right about what I said before? About how he said he came to be here?"

I couldn't deny it. "Yes. That's what he told me."

"And you believed him?"

"Why wouldn't I?"

"And has he answered all your questions about us, or has he been, more ... selective?" She raised her eyebrow in a question, looking even more like Callum as she did so.

I couldn't deny that. I thought back to the times where he had been evasive: about the Dirge who had gone away, the powers of the amulet, and when I had taken the amulet off. I looked away, and she smiled triumphantly. "You see, he's not been straight with you. Let me fill in the gaps. Callum is really only a boy, of course, but he's been doing this for so long now that he has really got very good at it."

"Only a boy? So how old is he then?"

"None of us is exactly sure, but I believe he is – or rather was – just a young teenager. He can be terribly immature."

I bristled. "But he doesn't look anything like that young."

"Our side does strange things to us, you know. It's not just the weird cloaks and the amulets. I think it changes us in other ways too. Really, Callum is just kid."

"So have you come all the way over here to warn me that he is young? It doesn't seem worth it."

She shook her head. "Hardly. I felt it was my duty to warn you of the danger."

"What danger?"

"From Callum."

"But how can he be dangerous? He's over there and I'm here. He can't hurt anyone."

"So what did he tell you about the amulets?"

"Well, that you use them to collect and store happy memories every day. He said that they appeared on your wrists when you came out of the river, and that you can't take them off." I hesitated, then plunged on. "And mine allows me to communicate with him ... and you," I added as an afterthought.

Catherine nodded as if confirming something. "Just as I thought: he's said nothing," she murmured to herself.

"What exactly are you getting at?" My whispers were getting louder.

"When one of you – on your side – wears the amulet it gradually stores up all of your best memories. Then, when it is ready he can download it all from you in one huge hit. It means that he can then go away." Her smile was thin. "On a 'holiday' I suppose. He has so much in his amulet that he can escape from the daily grind of gathering.

"He's done this a few times now. He seems very attuned to any amulets that get found, and of course he is very good at making sure that there are plenty of high-grade memories going into the store."

She looked at my horrified face and grimaced. "I can see I'm going to have to persuade you. Let me think what he might have said. Are you the first girl he has ever loved? Do you touch his heart in a way that no one else has ever been able to do before? Have you made his existence worth having?"

The cold fear was now starting to spread. I was beginning

to find it hard to focus. She *had* to be wrong. He wasn't playing me along – I was sure. But everything she mentioned he had said to me at some point. Could that make it true? I didn't want to believe it. There had to be another explanation.

"No!" I hissed, trying to stay quiet. "I don't want to hear any more about this. Maybe you mean well, but I don't believe you."

"Just think about it. Think about what he's said. Then think about what he's not said. And then ask him about Olivia."

It couldn't get any worse.

"He's not told you about Olivia, then?" she continued, shaking her head again, then tossing her long mane of golden hair back over her shoulders.

"Who's she?" My voice was dull. I wasn't sure I really wanted to know.

"His girlfriend. They've been together for years." Catherine continued to sit there, watching me carefully as my world collapsed.

"I don't believe you."

"Just ask him. He spends *every* morning with Olivia. See what he says and then make up your mind."

"Why are you telling me all this?" I could barely get the words out.

"I'm sorry, but I've had enough of watching what he does to people. He does these terrible things, and then he disappears for months on end. It's very disruptive and it really upsets Olivia, so, as she is my friend, well ... I decided to put a stop to it."

"So ... what do you suggest that I do?"

"First, stop wearing the amulet."

"Callum told me never to take it off, that it wasn't safe."

"Well, you need to decide which of us is telling the truth. You think about it and ask him those questions, then make up your mind."

"And if I believe you?" I didn't want to think it was a possibility that she was telling the truth, but I wanted to know my options.

"When you realise I'm right, just put the amulet on and call my name, and I will be there. There is a way out of this for you, you know, and I'm happy to show you. None of this is your fault."

"OK," I whispered. I was confident that Callum wasn't the monster she was describing, that she was wrong and malicious. But she didn't look it, sitting there with a concerned look on her face. I tried to sit up a little straighter. "Well, thanks for the advice, Catherine. When I talk to Callum in the morning I'll be sure to ask him."

"I know you will, and I know you'll call me afterwards. The truth hurts, but I will be able to make it better for you, believe me."

I didn't respond, just looked her in the eyes, searching for the truth. For a moment neither of us gave way, then she gave a ghost of smile and looked down.

"I'll be talking to you soon," she said, confidently. Then she was gone.

I quickly scanned around with the mirror to make sure she had left the room. I lay back on my pillow, my thoughts racing. How could I believe anything she said? But as I lay there, my mind kept coming back to all those moments when I felt he had not been straight with me. I kept flicking back over every conversation we had had, trying to pinpoint when I'd felt uneasy because I felt he'd been evasive. There was no way around it. He had misled me – or rather allowed me to mislead myself – about all sorts of things. And he definitely hadn't mentioned Olivia. I didn't want to believe Catherine, but in my heart I knew that what she had told me contained at least a grain of truth.

The only way to be sure was to check with Callum tomorrow. I clutched the bracelet on my wrist and debated taking it off. But I couldn't bring myself to do it: it was my only link with Callum, and until I knew what was going on I wasn't going to risk losing that.

Confrontation

The alarm burst into life in the morning, pulling me abruptly out of a restless sleep. I lay there for a moment, confused. Something strange had happened but I knew I hadn't been dreaming, I just couldn't remember what it was. I turned on my side and saw the small mirror open on the bedside table. Suddenly it all flooded back.

Catherine had visited and had told me things about Callum that I didn't want to hear. I pressed my fists into my eyes but I couldn't stop the memory swirling round my brain. Last night in the comforting darkness I had been so convinced she was wrong, but now I was less sure. I peered over my knuckles and checked the mirror – he wasn't in the room. Did that mean that she was right, that he was busy with – I could barely even think the name – Olivia?

I didn't know what to do. There was no one I could talk to, no way of getting any help with the decision. I realised with a sinking feeling how far I was from being able to tell Grace. I was entirely on my own.

The weather suited my mood – a fine drizzle settled over everything, drenching me on the short walk to the coach stop. I drifted through school that morning in a daze, half of me hoping that he wouldn't appear so I didn't have to face the possibility that he'd lied to me, the other half wanting to confront him, so that I would know the truth. Grace was quick to sense my mood and left me to my thoughts.

It was late morning by the time he appeared, sneaking up silently during the chemistry laboratory session. He seemed so happy, almost bouncing in his enthusiasm for our day. It made me think of what Catherine had said about him being very young. I shook my head to clear it of the thought.

"Hello, beautiful. How are you this morning? Are you ready to liven up this dull old lesson? I can't believe you choose to learn this stuff." He hardly paused for breath before continuing. "Anyway, I've been thinking about some other bands we could go and see. I've memorised a whole list of gigs so why don't you write them down as I tell you and then we can decide."

I hated squashing his mood, but I couldn't do this in the middle of a double session on the synthesis of esters. I quickly pulled my notebook towards me.

Have a headache – can't play now. Am off this afternoon. I'll call you when I'm free.

"Oh." The disappointment was evident in the single syllable. "If you are sure that I can't help? Would a massage of the forehead make it better?"

As he spoke he started to stroke my head, but I needed some self-control.

Really, that's great, but not now. Later?

"I'll be listening for you. Be as quick as you can." He kissed my neck and was gone.

It was the first lie I'd told him and it felt terrible. Could I really believe that he had been lying to me? It all seemed so unlikely.

The rest of the lesson dragged by, and all I could do was make endless lists in my head of pros and cons for believing him. I really wanted to write them down, but as I didn't know if he was watching me I didn't dare.

I didn't stay for lunch. As I had no lessons that afternoon I was allowed to use the school facilities or go home. Usually I would go to the library or the art department to work on my project, but I wanted to be alone. I also couldn't wait – I needed to know now.

I made my way over to the music department. Down a dark corridor there was a warren of soundproofed little practice rooms. From time to time doors opened and wafts of beautiful music or screeching violins filled the corridor. I checked the booking timetable and found a room which would be empty for a while. I was in luck – it was one of the ones also used by the drama department so there was a large mirror on one wall.

I carefully locked the door behind me and drew the blind over the little viewing window. I sat down in front of the mirror and tried to compose myself, to plan what I wanted to ask, but it wasn't easy. Every time I thought about the possibility of him not denying it my eyes welled up.

Get a grip, I told myself sternly. You don't know anything is wrong yet. Find out before getting overdramatic.

I sat up straight and called his name. It was time to confront him.

I had barely got the word out of my mouth when he was there, enthusiastic as ever. He must have been following me because he already understood the set-up.

"Hey, cool room! Soundproofed and private – why didn't we think of this before?" He reached for my hair and started stroking the back of my neck. "How long do you have before you have to start behaving yourself again?" His voice was a little muffled as he had started to kiss my ear.

I was torn. Part of me wanted to surrender, to take no notice of Catherine and just enjoy the moment. It was hugely tempting. But the other part of me, the practical part, wouldn't let me off so easily. I was filled with nagging doubts and kept replaying Catherine's comments. I had to do something.

I sat up and looked at him. "Callum, please stop."

He lifted his head with a cheeky smile on his face, clearly expecting this to be part of the fun. Then he saw the look in my eyes and his face fell.

"What's wrong?" he asked, full of concern.

"I need to ask you something."

"Anything."

"And I need an honest answer."

He looked confused. "Of course."

I hesitated. Once I had said it there would be no going back. I would either ruin his trust in me or destroy my own heart, but I had to know. I had to be strong.

"Callum, who is Olivia?" His face was instantly ashen and his mouth fell open. "Please. I need to know."

He recovered his voice. "How do you know about Olivia?"

"So it's true." My voice was suddenly dull and I could feel the edges of my world start to collapse. I couldn't look at him any more.

"She's just a girl, I – I – really, I don't know what to tell you. She's a girl over here."

"There's no need to explain. I get the picture." I gathered all my courage together and lifted my head. "Goodbye, Callum. It was fun, but we both know this can't continue." My free hand moved towards the amulet.

"No!" he bellowed, following my movement. "Don't go. I understand about Rob! We can work something out."

It was my turn to look confused, and my hand paused.

"Rob? What does he have to do with this?"

"Look, I know you still want him and I understand. We can be friends."

"That's nonsense, and *friends* wasn't what I had in mind."

I was getting more agitated now, and was struggling to hold my composure. I didn't want him to see me cry: it would be better to finish this quickly. "It's too late. I know you have told me nothing about Olivia and you've lied to me about where Veronica has gone."

He had been pulling himself together but the comment about Veronica clearly floored him.

"I can explain," he said, flustered. "It's not what you think."

I stole a quick glance at him. He looked wild, desperate to keep things going, just as Catherine had predicted. His glorious blue eyes pleaded with mine and for a moment I felt myself sinking, being dragged into those depths. How bad could it be to surrender to him? I wondered. Did it really matter what he would take, if I could continue to have a little bit of him?

I almost wavered, and I saw the small flicker of hope in his face as I hesitated. But that glimpse was too much for me; I didn't deserve to be treated like that. I deserved to love someone who would love me equally in return, and although my heart screamed in protest I felt a growing resolution. "I won't be lied to, Callum, by you, or anyone else."

His face fell again. "Please don't go, Alex! I can explain everything. Just give me a chance."

"It's too late." My tone was harsh, as I struggled to hide my misery. "You had plenty of chances." I kept my chin up, willing myself not to cry. "Please just leave me and my friends alone now. We don't want you gathering from us, and there won't be much joy around here anyway. I'll throw the amulet back into the river for your next victim."

"No! Don't go! I'll tell you everything!" He sounded truly desperate.

"It's too late," I repeated softly, forcing myself to look away from the face I loved, the face I was never going to see again. "Please, Callum, it's for the best. Please don't try and contact me again."

I looked up through eyes which were brimming over. His head was bowed, and I thought I saw the glistening of a tear on his face. He was shaking his head and whispering under his breath.

"No! This can't be happening. I don't believe it. It can't be happening."

He ran his hand through hair, hair that I would never learn how to touch. When he raised his head his misery was obvious; the pain on his face, the defeated droop of his shoulders, the emptiness of his eyes. The beautiful fire was gone. They looked leaden, lifeless.

I swallowed hard. Whatever he had been going to do to me and my memories was clearly extreme. He was devastated that I had found him out. I had to be strong now and finish things.

"Callum, please don't do this to people. Don't risk putting anyone else through what I am going through. Just leave us all alone. You have to go. You have to go *now*." I looked into his eyes as I ripped the amulet from my wrist and dropped it on the floor. My last glimpse of him shimmered and faded. I was alone again.

I let the tears come. They ran in streams down my face and

dripped into my lap. But I couldn't give into them completely. I might not be able to see him, but I knew he could see me and everything I was doing. I needed to get away from him. I needed to go somewhere he had never been with me. I picked up the amulet with a pencil and threw it into my rucksack. I scrabbled around in my pocket to find a tissue, mopped my eyes and blew my nose before I checked my face in the mirror, unlocked the door and made for the nearest exit. I didn't want to risk bumping into anyone. Outside, the drizzle had given way to a weak sunshine and I was surrounded by the sounds of girls enjoying themselves: the shrieks from the junior girls across the field, the cheers from the track, the gentle murmurs from the groups I passed.

I felt as if I was hardly there. It all seemed slightly muffled, slightly unreal. Inside me I could feel a writhing pain, eager to get to the surface. I forced it back down. It wasn't yet time to let it out.

My feet took me to the school gates. I scanned the bus stops, checking for people I knew, then went to stand at one where no one was waiting.

A small thought surfaced: was he still watching me? How was I ever going to know? He could be standing right beside me. Horrified at the thought, I started walking. A bus appeared going in the opposite direction and I got on automatically. I knew that I couldn't get away from Callum if he was determined to be with me, but I couldn't bear just to stand there. I needed to feel as if I was doing something. I wondered dully where the bus was heading as the driver threw it into gear and we lurched off but I didn't really care. Sitting in the corner, I forced back all conscious thoughts, and pressed my forehead into the cool glass of the window. It felt smooth and uncomplicated, so I focused on that.

The bus wound its way slowly past houses and shops where

normal people went about their business. It felt wrong that no one else could sense my misery, that life was going on regardless. After a while I realised that the houses had given way to parkland. We were heading towards Hampton Court Palace.

Hampton Court. The idea registered slowly. That would be a good place to go, I realised. I could lose myself in the maze. At this time of day and with the miserable weather earlier it was unlikely to be busy.

I made myself get up and off the bus, and walked quickly through the grounds to the maze. There were just a few tourists milling about, as I'd thought. And, as I hoped, the maze was almost deserted, and the guy at the gate looked completely uninterested as I waved my season ticket at him and pushed my way through the turnstile.

I moved between the ancient yew hedges without thinking, just putting one foot in front of another. It was quite therapeutic. All I could see was hedge, and all I could hear was the sound of my own feet crunching on the gravel. I walked without taking in anything, around corners and double-back turns, past dead-ends and open archways. All the time I willed myself to keep control of my emotions, to concentrate only on walking.

Suddenly I realised that something was different – the air seemed fresher, lighter. I blinked and looked around me; I had reached the middle. I knew this maze too well and my feet had automatically taken me straight to the centre. I couldn't even get lost properly.

I could feel my grip on my feelings starting to slip and I staggered towards the bench seat. I let my head fall on to my knees and gave in to the anguish. The waves of sadness rolled over me. I felt a huge sob forming in my chest. I gasped in enough air to feed it, and one racking sob gave way to another. I was never going to see Callum again.

I could feel the tears stream down my face, splashing on to the ground in front of me. My chest continued to heave with sobs and I struggled for breath. All I wanted was a huge hole to open up in front of me so that I could throw myself in, to be oblivious, and to feel no more pain.

As I had that thought, I realised that this was how the Dirges felt every single day. I couldn't imagine waking up to this every single morning, knowing that it was going on forever and that there was no way out. I felt a moment of pity for them. And for Callum. However hard I tried to empty my mind of thoughts of him, I couldn't escape the memory of his gentle smile, his strong shoulders, the passion in his eyes. Part of me still wanted to believe that someone who seemed so good couldn't be so heartless and cruel. But every time my mind went round in the same circle, it came back to his evasions and lies.

I had been betrayed; I felt that I could never allow myself to trust or love anyone so much again. A new haze of anger slowly started to creep over my thoughts and my tears began to dry. I would not let him ruin my life. I would find someone to love who would love me too.

But I couldn't hold on to the anger, and I couldn't hold on to my thoughts of a better future. The despair was just teasing me, just waiting to rear up and claim me again. As I thought of Callum the pain returned, causing me to gasp out loud.

"Excuse me, Miss, but I'm going to be shutting the maze soon, and..."

I opened my eyes and saw the guy from the ticket office. I could see the shock on his face as I looked at him. He took a quick step back, then steadied himself.

"I didn't want to disturb you, but a couple of people have told me that you may be stuck in here. I can show you out if you want," he continued.

"No, it's fine," I said in a voice scratchy from all the sobbing. I was glad that the tears had dried. I didn't want his pity. "I can find my way out. Thank you anyway."

I stood up and walked towards the exit. The embarrassed cough came again.

"I can let you through the quick exit if you'd prefer."

It was easier to give in and within a minute I was back outside the maze. I could hear the sigh of relief from the ticket collector as he scurried back to his hut, locking the gate as he went.

I looked around me. The gardens near me were deserted, but I could hear people further off. I realised that the sun was low in the sky and glanced at my watch. It was getting late.

I fished my mobile out of my bag. It had been on silent during lessons earlier and I hadn't switched it back on. There were nine missed calls from Grace, Josh and my mum. There was never going to be one from Callum, though, I realised bleakly. *Be strong,* I told myself sternly. *Don't think about it.* I made myself walk as I retrieved the messages. Grace's messages started off normally then got progressively more worried. Josh had left one when I didn't get on the coach and Mum had got in on the act when he arrived home without me.

I couldn't face talking so I sent them each a text saying I would be home within an hour. I just needed a little more time.

I slowly made my way through the park towards the palace. As it was late all the doors were getting closed up, but I could walk through the courtyards. The old buildings loomed above me, steeped in history and memories. Once more, my mind raced towards the Dirges. Had they been here, I wondered, taking the memories of royalty in the past? I had always loved the palace, it was so full of secrets and possibilities, but today it just seemed sad.

I walked out of the front entrance to the palace buildings and down to the Thames. This stretch wasn't tidal like the Twickenham section, but it was still really wide with vicious-looking currents. I stared into its depths and wished that I had never seen the amulet in there. I could now quite understand why someone would tie it to a rock and throw it in. I felt like doing the same, or perhaps smashing it with the rock instead.

I glanced around hopefully, but this towpath was far too manicured to have the sort of rock I was hoping for. Instead I turned my attention to my bag; the amulet was lying there looking beautiful and innocent. There was no trace of movement in the stone now. It was as if the fire had gone out in the stone at the same time as the fire had gone out of Callum's eyes.

If I just grasped it, I could have him back. I could make the fire dance again. The thought was there before my conscious, sensible side could squash it. I felt the tears well up again. I knew that the right thing to do was to throw the amulet into the river immediately. But what if I was wrong? What if there had been a hideous mistake? I couldn't bear to throw away my only link to him. I stood on the bank as a war raged inside me.

Finally, I made my decision: the amulet *had* to go. I reached into my bag and found a pencil, then scooped it up. It had to go. It was heavy enough to sink well even without the rock. I just needed to fling it as far as I could into the middle.

As I stretched back my arm to throw, the amulet slid down the pencil and over the tip of my thumb.

The voice in my head was sudden and loud, and without thinking I clapped my hands to my ears, clutching the cold metal tightly.

I could hear his beautiful voice, now ragged with grief, pleading relentlessly, "No! Don't! Please! Don't go! Don't..." The memory of his beautiful face, his gentle mouth, and his electrifying touch, the knowledge that he was near, all conspired to break my resolve. I knew I couldn't throw it into the river.

But neither could I listen. I dropped the amulet back into my bag and my head was suddenly silent. The anguish in his voice had been unbearable. I could almost believe that he did mean it, that he did love me, but the piercing memory of his look of panic and evasion when I had caught him out told me that he was a liar and I needed to break away.

I stepped back from the edge of the river, trying to stay calm. People were walking past with their dogs, oblivious to my turmoil. I needed to walk, I decided, so I turned and started marching back to the gate. It was a couple of miles home from here, but if I could keep up a good pace I would get back before they started to worry again.

I rummaged around in my bag for my iPod, being very careful not to touch the amulet. I let loud music flood my head and I refused to let myself think as I set off down the road.

By the time I got home I was exhausted. I didn't want to face endless questions, so I knew I had to tell them something that would keep them quiet.

"Where have you been, sweetheart?" asked my mum. "We were starting to get worried."

"I'm fine," I lied, as smoothly as possible. "I just had a bit of a row with one of the girls at school, and I needed a bit of space so I went to Hampton Court for a walk." I felt better telling her something which was as near to the truth as possible.

She looked at me shrewdly. "Do you want to talk about it at all, or would you rather not?"

"Really rather not." I tried to smile and nearly made it. "What's for dinner?" I attempted to sound interested, though I knew I couldn't eat.

"I was going to make a curry," she started, "but if you would prefer to have something simpler..."

I shot her a grateful look. "I think that would be best. Perhaps I'll just make myself a sandwich and have a bath."

"Whatever you want, darling." She smiled gently as she reached over to give me a kiss.

I kept myself busy for a couple of hours, but as bedtime approached I started to get nervous. I could feel the misery just waiting for me, ready to engulf me again. I needed something where I could lose myself, that wouldn't remind me of him at all. My eye fell on my bookshelf, and I scanned along the length of it, mentally discarding titles as I went. Too much romance. None of them would do.

Outside my bedroom the big family bookcase was groaning with paperbacks. Mum refused to throw books away as a matter of principle, so there was years of reading material available. But I couldn't risk something I didn't know, and I really didn't want the violence in all the cop and war stories. Finally I spotted something perfect: the Harry Potter books. In the early volumes there was no hint of romance, and the stories were compelling enough to keep me going even after reading them a dozen times before.

I grabbed a book and settled down in my bed. I hoped that I was tired enough to drop off while reading, although it was barely dark outside.

The plan worked for a while, but in the end my mind began to wander away from the plot. I remembered Callum's face, and his last, desperate words. The misery, spotting its chance, leapt up to bite me.

My heart felt as if was quite broken, as if no part of it would ever really function again. The pain was almost physical in its intensity, and I curled up in a ball to try and protect myself from it, but it was no good. The tears forced their way out again, running in streams across my face and soaking my pillow. Every time I shut my eyes I could see his face, that dazzling smile and those beautiful eyes. I could see them twinkle as he laughed, his head thrown back, his strong arms around me. And I could feel his touch, as gentle as a feather as he traced a line down my arm or brushed my neck with his lips.

And all of it was a lie, I reminded myself harshly, as a sob rose in my throat. I pressed my face into the pillow so the noise wouldn't carry.

As the night wore on I found myself going over each and every conversation we had ever had, looking for clues. Every time I remembered one of his evasive comments the knife in my heart twisted again. He had taken me in so completely. The more I thought about it, the more sure I was that Catherine was right.

Something else was niggling in the back of my mind, something she had said, but my exhausted brain couldn't bring it back.

It wasn't until dawn broke and the light started to filter through my curtains that I finally fell asleep.

Decision

I didn't sleep long, and when I woke up, my blanket of misery was wrapped tightly around me. My heart was utterly empty.

I got through the school morning as if I was surrounded by a thick fog, struggling to answer any questions sensibly. Grace was obviously worried about me, but there was nothing I could tell her, and in the end she gave up questioning me. I went for a long walk at lunchtime, and made it as far as the park. The stream that went through it was a popular nesting place for ducks, and I had come here often as a kid at this time of year to see the ducklings following their parents in straggly lines through the reeds.

Today a pair of swans had taken up residence and they were protecting their brood. There were six beautiful little cygnets – fluffy grey balls – and as they saw me watching them they all scrambled up on to their mother's back inside the protection of her powerful wings. The heads were bobbing up and down so quickly I could hardly count them and they looked so comical that for a moment I felt myself smile a little.

Then the misery-blanket reclaimed me, and the tiny bit of joy was squeezed from my heart.

Was this the swan I rescued? I wondered. Was it responsible for how I felt now? I knew it was ridiculous to blame a harmless bird for my own actions and decisions, but I couldn't look at it any more. I turned away and retraced my steps back to school, forcing myself to walk as quickly as possible. The afternoon was no better. It was impossible to concentrate and Mr Pasciuta was clearly getting frustrated by my reluctance to participate in the class.

"Are you unwell again, Alex?" he demanded, handing me the option to get out of the class. Although I didn't really want to be alone, the idea of struggling through more of the maths class with all its fresh and painful memories from a few days ago appealed even less.

"I think I have a migraine coming, sir. Do you mind if I go to the common room?" Even to me my voice sounded dull and disengaged.

"No, that's fine. It's probably best for you to stay there until it's time for the coaches," he agreed. "Get the homework from someone else tomorrow."

In the common room I threw myself down on a beanbag and stared at the ceiling.

Something kept slipping from my grasp. I still felt that Catherine had said something important, something that might help, but I couldn't remember what it was. I hated the thought of replaying my conversation with her in my head, but I had to know. I tried not to dwell on the details of his betrayal as I went through it all. What was it? She had been quite happy to bring my world crashing down, and then she had said she could help.

I sat up suddenly: that was it! Catherine had told me that there was a way out, that she could help me. I couldn't imagine what it was, how she was going to be able to do that, but if there was some way of stopping the pain I had to find out what it was. For the first time in over twenty-four hours I felt a tiny sense of purpose.

I had to talk to Catherine, but not summon Callum. She

had said that if I called her name she would come, but if I touched the amulet he might appear. I wondered if he was still listening to me, or if he had gone back to Olivia. I guessed there was no reason for him to be worrying about me any more, now he realised that I knew what he was planning, so it would be safe to call. The misery tightened its grip as I thought about Olivia and I realised that I *had* to try to call Catherine.

I looked around the common room – it was almost entirely empty. I decided that I could risk a conversation in here as long as I had my phone earpiece in place. I set it up and opened the pocket in my bag where I had hidden the amulet. I curled one finger around the band and called out.

"Catherine, it's Alex. We need to talk."

I took my finger away and waited for a few minutes, trying not to breathe too fast, and trying not to think about the possibility of summoning Callum instead of his sister. After I had counted slowly to a hundred I nervously slipped the amulet on to my wrist and called again.

"Catherine, are you there?"

There was a familiar tingle and I winced as I waited to see which voice would speak.

"I knew you would call." Her voice was matter of fact, and I was pleased that I wasn't looking in a mirror. I didn't want to see her face: it would only remind me of Callum's.

"I did what you said," I admitted. "And I asked him my questions. He didn't deny anything, so I have told him that I never want to see him again." Just telling her the story so briefly was unbearably painful.

"I'm sorry for you. I really am. He is a very good liar. It's not your fault that you believed all his stories."

I didn't want her sympathy, and I wanted to rip the amulet off again as soon as I could, so I pressed on. "You said that after I had spoken to him, you would be able to help me. What did you mean by that?"

"I can help you, Alex. I can make it seem as if all this never happened."

"How do you mean?"

"Think about it. What is it that we do?"

"I'm not sure what you mean." I tried not to snap at her in my haste to get through this conversation. I had no idea if Callum could hear us, or was nearby, and I couldn't bear to think about it.

"Every day, I go out and I take memories from people," she explained. "Whatever they are thinking at the time, I come along and – bouf – it's gone." She paused for a moment. "I can take away every memory of Callum from you. It will be as if he never existed."

I felt a cold chill in my heart. Would that be better? To forget everything about him? To go back to being the girl I was on the riverbank in Twickenham before I found the amulet? I had wanted that yesterday, but I hadn't thought that it was possible. Now it was being offered to me, did I really want it? I would have no memory of him at all, no picture of his face, no recollection of his touch, his laugh, his smile. I didn't know if I could bear the loss of forgetting ... but it was so hard to bear the pain of remembering. I couldn't decide, not so quickly. "I need some time," I told Catherine. "Can I call you again later when I've made up my mind?"

"I don't know why it's so tough. All your misery would be gone in an instant. Isn't that what you want?"

"I'm not going to make a decision right now. I have to think, and you'll need to tell me how it would work. I need to *prepare*."

"Fine. Call me later, but don't forget, the longer you leave your decision, the more memory I'm going to have to take, so you really need to decide quickly. I'll talk to you soon."

She was gone. I took the earpiece out and sank back in the beanbag. Around me the few girls in the common room continued reading, working and talking. I could be just like one of them again if I accepted Catherine's offer. It was so tempting. But to forget everything completely – to forget what it felt like to realise that I loved him, to not know the joy when I realised he loved me too – could I bring myself to lose all that?

But then, none of it was real. Everything he had said to me, every time he'd said he loved me, it was all lies. And what was the point in remembering lies?

I sat there for an hour, struggling with my decision. Girls came and went as the bell rang for next lesson, but no one disturbed me. Every time I thought I had my answer, I wavered. Eventually I curled up into a small ball with my arms around my head. My exhausted brain couldn't cope with all of this. It was all too difficult and I wished it would all just go away.

My eyes snapped open. I realised that my answer was held in my wish: I wanted it to go away, and I could make it go away. I would call Catherine later and work out the details. I felt a strange peace settle over me as I closed my eyes again and tried to doze.

My friends found me when it was time to go home but I continued my charade of having a migraine. It felt wrong deceiving Grace, though. She was really kind, offering me painkillers and herbal tea, but I gently refused everything. Never mind, I thought, tomorrow everything will be back to normal. Suddenly, I was very pleased I hadn't told anyone about Callum, especially Grace, as that would have made Catherine's plan much more difficult. I could deal with her obliterating all my thoughts of Callum, but

I didn't want to be responsible for others losing their memories.

The house was deserted when I got home, so I went up to my room to strike the deal with Catherine. Somewhere in my mind I was still worried. I wasn't sure I understood her motives, and I wanted to look her in the eyes as she told me her plan.

I sat down at my desk reluctantly. Memories of the time I'd spent sitting there talking to Callum flickered through my mind. I felt empty and lonely at the thought of losing it all, but I knew it made sense to let it go. I just wished that there was some way not to lose every piece of memory forever. My gaze fell on the laptop in front of me on the desk, and my thoughts suddenly clicked forwards a few gears.

I could record all my memories and save them on a memory stick. If I protected it with a password and stored it somewhere safe, then if there was a time when I wanted them back I could find them. I could use the video camera on my laptop and just talk, that wouldn't take very long, and then at least something of him would remain somewhere. He wouldn't be entirely gone.

I sat back, pleased with myself. It was a good solution, I just needed a bit of time to do it. I could ask Catherine to take away the memories the next morning, then I wouldn't be losing too much more. I didn't know if she could be selective and leave behind the memories that didn't concern Callum, but I realised that I didn't care. I wanted it to be over. I hooked the amulet carefully out of the bag and put it on the desk, still worried that Callum might appear. I touched it briefly and called her, then waited. Nothing. But when I slipped it on she was behind me in an instant. She swept her long golden hair back and smiled.

"So, have you finally decided?" she asked.

"I'd like some more information first, please. How will it

work? What would I need to do? How long it will take? That sort of thing. Would that be OK?" I tried to sound positive and encouraging.

Catherine gave a little sigh and I thought I detected impatience, but then she quickly smiled again. "Of course. I'll tell you what I can. You need to have the amulet, but not be touching it. That's very important: when you are wearing it I can't help you."

"OK, I can manage that. Then what?"

"All you need to do is relax, and start thinking about Callum." I felt she said his name with distaste. "I'll start to gather your thoughts. Then as soon as you've thought them, they'll be gone."

"Is it dangerous?" I whispered.

Catherine looked at me levelly. "Of course, nothing is ever completely without risk, but I know what I'm doing, and I know you. You want this. We know..." – she paused, and continued carefully – "from experience that to try to take a lot of important memories from anyone can be..." – she paused again – "painful, and can leave them, well, less than they were before."

I had to know. "What could happen?" I asked, and I could hear my own voice trembling.

She looked beyond me as she spoke quietly. "If we are trying to take more than one memory, and if the mind we're stealing from resists us – tries to hold on to its memories, to itself – then the person can be left a shell – barely alive. A person, but empty." She saw my face and hurried on. "But I'm just going to take memories of Callum, nothing else, and you won't resist: you're giving up your memories willingly."

I struggled to stay calm. "Empty?" I asked.

Catherine shrugged. "But that's only if I take a lot of

memories ... and if you fight me. That's not going to happen, is it? You want this, don't you? You don't want to live with the knowledge of Callum's betrayal."

I felt a sharp stab in my heart, and I knew she was right. I had to trust her and to take the risk. I couldn't bear to be so unhappy. "What about the last few days, when I haven't been happy? Can you take those memories too?"

"I don't generally gather misery, but I suppose I'll have to if this is to work for you. It will make it harder, but it's the only way."

I hadn't thought about that. "I'm really grateful for what you're doing for me, Catherine, really I am." I felt guilty for doubting her before. "So, how long will it all take?"

"Oh, only a few minutes. Once you start thinking about Callum, I'll be able to help you along a little. Then all your memories of him will all be gone, and you will wonder what you are supposed to be doing, sitting here at your desk."

"No! I'm not ready now! You can't do it right away!" I almost leapt up, suddenly concerned that she might start before I had completed my plan of recording everything. For a moment, I thought she looked exasperated, but then her face settled into a look of concern.

"You can't wait forever, Alex. The sooner this is done, the easier it'll be for you." She paused for a moment. "You're not changing your mind, are you?"

"Of course not, it's just that…" Somehow I didn't want to tell her about the recording. "I need to arrange for someone to take away the amulet afterwards, otherwise I won't know what it can do and Callum will have a way to get back to me again."

She pondered this for a moment, then nodded, her curtain of smooth, thick hair swaying. "How quickly can you do that?"

"I can arrange it all tonight. Can you come to me tomorrow morning? I can be on the school field or something, out of the way."

For a moment I thought I saw a look of triumph flash across her face, but it was gone so quickly I wasn't sure I had really seen it at all. "It doesn't matter where you are, I'll be there. Make sure you have the amulet in your bag: I need it to locate you. But *don't* wear it."

I was suddenly nervous. "Does it hurt? Will I know what's going on at all?"

"No, no. All you have to do, at the agreed time, is to start thinking about what you want to forget. Whatever you think about, whatever goes through your head, I will be able to take it and you'll never be bothered by it again."

I looked at her carefully, trying to understand. I knew she was underplaying the risk. But I couldn't see how I could bear this pain. I made my decision.

"Fine. Thank you, Catherine. I'm not sure why you are doing this, but thank you."

She looked away. "I'm doing it to teach him a lesson, really. He can't go on behaving like this. And he is my little brother, so that makes him my responsibility. I'm sorry that you have got hurt so badly, but you can be sure he won't do it again." For the first time there was real passion on her face.

"So when will we do it? Can you meet me at eleven o'clock tomorrow?"

I was stunned by the smile that suddenly lit up her face. When she smiled properly she wasn't just attractive, she was beautiful. "Oh yes, I can be there at eleven. I'll see you then. Sleep well!" She disappeared immediately, leaving me slightly stunned.

I set to work. I didn't have long to record everything and

work out what I was going to do with the memory stick and the amulet. It had to be somewhere safe, where I wasn't going to see it and wonder what it was, but it also had to be somewhere accessible if I needed it in the future.

Hiding it in the house was not an option, nor was hiding it at school. I really needed someone else to take care of it who could be trusted and who wouldn't ask too many questions. There was only one person: Grace. I knew I could trust her to do as I asked. It was a perfect choice.

With that problem solved, I had to tackle the larger problem of recording everything. I looked at my watch. I still had plenty of time before everyone came home.

I didn't do much videoing from my laptop, so it took me a while to get everything organised. I had no idea how much space I had on the memory card I had found. How long could I talk for? I was going to have to do a test to check. I set the camera running and timed five minutes while I made myself a cup of coffee. Back at my desk I checked the file. It had recorded perfectly and had only taken up a fraction of the card. I deleted it and sat back. Now I had no excuse. I had to start talking, to explain what I was doing and the reasons behind it.

I hesitated again, and in my heart I knew why: I didn't want this to be the end. Despite everything that had happened, and despite the commitment I had made to Catherine, I didn't really want to do anything so final.

I forced myself to remember his betrayal to strengthen my resolve. I looked at the little camera lens, took a deep breath, and began.

I started talking about finding the amulet on the little beach in Twickenham and left nothing out. Within minutes I was struggling to speak, the tears rolling down my cheeks. The memory of his face in St Paul's, the joy he had seemed to show, my excitement at being able to speak to him were all too much. I quickly shut off the camera and went to look for a box of tissues. I washed my face to compose myself and started again.

This time I was harder on myself. Every time I felt myself welling up I dug my nails into my palm and thought about Olivia. Even though I knew nothing about her I could dislike her intensely.

I didn't have to stop again until I was describing the moment I realised that I loved him. That took a while to recover from, and I was just drying my face when I heard a car pull in at the front of the house. I glanced at my watch and realised I had run out of time for now. I was going to have to do the rest of this later.

Mum left me alone during dinner: it must have been obvious that I wasn't going to be contributing much to the conversation. I caught her exchanging glances with Dad at one point, and I was grateful that it would all be over soon, and I wouldn't have to worry them any more.

But I still had a lot to do and I really didn't want to be disturbed. I thought about taking the laptop into the car or into the garden, but neither of these options was ideal. It would be easier to twist the truth a little. "Please just ignore any noise from my room this evening," I announced to a rather surprised table, having said nothing at all through the meal.

"Of course, darling," agreed Mum, "but what are you doing?"

"It's a project about video diaries. I have to do a sort of 'talking head' piece, and it needs to be finished tonight. I probably should have started it sooner," I said, trying to sound sheepish.

My parents exchanged another glance.

"Would you like any help with it?"

"Thanks, Dad, but there really isn't anything you can do. Just ignore the noise of me talking half the night."

"Well, don't stay up too late," Mum cautioned. "You know, I really don't understand the point of some of these projects…"

I tried to smile. "Well, it's nearly done now. I'll see you all in the morning."

Back in my room I settled into my chair. I was about to check over the last few minutes of what I had already recorded, but realised that was only going to make me even more self-conscious about what I was doing.

I sat up straight and set the camera going again.

I had to take several more breaks when emotion overcame me. If I ever got to play this back, I thought, ruefully, I was going to be horrified by my appearance. Finally, at about midnight I was finished. I had covered everything: how the amulet worked; how I spoke to him; what I could feel; and how Catherine had revealed all of his lies. I sat back in the chair and felt my shoulders slump. The idea of making a record had kept me going but, now it was done, I was going to have to occupy myself some other way. There was no chance that I would be able to sleep.

I pulled the memory card out of the computer and considered it. Would I ever look at its contents? If what Catherine was proposing actually worked I would never open it again, and would never need to know the depths of despair that I was feeling at the moment.

I had put a password on the file so that Grace wouldn't be able to read it. It would all be a complete waste of effort and emotion if she told me about Callum after I had forgotten.

I started to think about what I had to do the next day. I needed to give her the card and the amulet, but not until Catherine was finished, and at that point I wouldn't know why I needed to do that. I realised that I would have to get to her beforehand and make sure she was expecting to take it from me. My head was beginning to hurt again so I pressed my fingers into the tops of my eye sockets, just under my eyebrows. *Focus!* I told myself sternly. I thought it all through again, then to make sure I had everything covered I grabbed my mobile and began to write a message.

Hi G. This is a strange request, but I hope you won't mind doing it. I'll have a package in my bag for you tomorrow. Can you please take it, put it away and keep it safe for me? Please don't open it and don't mention it to me unless I ask you about it. Weird, eh? Love A x

I hoped that it would be enough. Even though it was late I pressed the send button. Within a minute there was a responding buzz from the phone.

You really are going mad! Course I will. Hope the migraine is a bit better now. Love G

I found a little padded envelope on my desk, and stuck a big label on it. I wrote Grace's name very clearly on the front, and put the memory card and the amulet inside, then sealed it carefully. I put my name on the back, with the instruction to leave it unopened, and then I threw it into the top of my rucksack ready for tomorrow.

Everything was done. I felt a tiny surge of relief, quickly followed by a huge wave of tiredness. I crawled into bed, hoping for sleep to come quickly, but not really expecting that it would. I was quite surprised to feel my eyelids beginning to close. As I drifted off, I wondered if I should have called Catherine as soon as everything was done, but I was too tired to change my plans. I slept.

Race

I woke to a familiar sense of gloom and my mood didn't improve when I remembered what I intended to do. Part of me still wanted to hold on to every memory of Callum, but I hoped that a different, carefree Alex would come back to this room after Catherine had got to work.

Another driving lesson was an additional obstacle and distraction. Josh drove in as usual. He was pretty tense as he had one of his last two exams that day, so neither of us was keen to talk. When we got to the school, I wished him luck and we went our separate ways.

The common room was busy. All the exams in my year were finished, so everyone was back to normal timetables. It looked as if most of us couldn't wait for the summer holidays that were only a few weeks away. The girls were lounging around with no urgency or enthusiasm for work, chatting, texting or reading gossip magazines. There wasn't a textbook in sight.

I searched around for Grace as I wanted to make sure that she was clear on when to take the package, but there was no sign of her. I sent her a quick text and the answer was immediate.

Coach late. Not forgotten plan. G x

I gave a sigh of relief, and checked the package in the top of my bag. It looked innocent enough, but the sight of it made me shudder slightly. The pain was a dull ache now, but still enough to make my eyes well up whenever I focused on it. I couldn't help thinking of Callum's easy smile and the day we'd spent on the island. It had all seemed so real, so right. I wondered what he was doing. Was he thinking of me? Would he ever think of me again?

I shook myself: this wasn't going to help. Around me all my friends were gathering, making plans for the weekend and the holidays, and to keep myself together I tried to focus on some of the conversations.

"We were supposed to be going to the cinema to see that film, but he got the days wrong..."

"If she gives us any more essays this term I'll scream..."

"Freddie says he's going to come shopping with me at the weekend..."

"What do you think of that new top? Too tight for a first date?"

"I'm going to have to beg my parents for the money to go to Cornwall, which is a problem as they don't want me to go..."

This last snippet sounded interesting so I tuned in properly. Of course it was Ashley, and clearly plans for her romantic trip with Rob were not going entirely smoothly. Mia was trying to be positive.

"You won't need too much money surely? It's his house and his parents will buy all the food. All you'll need is spending money for the evening."

Ashley looked at the floor. I quickly turned away so she wouldn't see I was listening. "The thing is," she started, picking fluff off her sleeve, "his parents won't be going."

There was a brief lull in the buzz of conversation, and everyone in the group heard her. Alia gasped.

"His parents won't be there? Are you mad?"

"So? It's nothing to do with anyone else."

I found myself agreeing with her. I noticed a couple of her friends glance in my direction, obviously still concerned about my feelings, but it all seemed so unimportant to me.

Nothing could distract me properly from what was going to happen to me. I wished that I had agreed to do it a bit earlier. I just wanted the whole thing over and done with. And now I thought about it, I was much more nervous than I had expected. The idea of someone interfering with my thoughts and memories – with what made me who I was – was a scary one, and Catherine's casual mention of what might happen should it go wrong nagged at me. What would be left of me? I calmed myself by remembering her reassurances. I wanted this to happen: she'd take only the right memories, and I'd put up no resistance. As the bell went for the first lesson there was still no sign of Grace, but I wasn't too worried; the less I saw her, the less explaining I would have to do. I would have a chance to talk to her in an hour or two.

My next lesson was chemistry, and Miss Amos was covering the theory of mass spectroscopy. I had to concentrate to make any sense of it at all, which was useful: I didn't spend the entire lesson thinking about Callum and worrying about what Catherine was going to do to me.

At break time I went back to the common room. I checked my bag again; the package was still safe at the top, ready for Grace when it was all over.

Real fear started to churn in my stomach, and I wondered once again what it would be like. Could I really trust Catherine? And another anxiety started to mount too: I only had another hour or so to think about Callum, and then he would be gone from my life forever.

I suddenly felt really ill. In fact, I was pretty sure I was about to be sick. I made a quick exit to the loos, ignoring the surprised looks from all my friends.

I rested my forehead against the inside of the toilet door and counted to ten slowly. The nausea subsided a little, and after a few more minutes I felt calm enough to leave the cubicle. At the sinks, I splashed some cold water on my face.

As I reached for a paper towel a screaming wail filled the air, making me jump. The fire alarm was even more loud and shocking than normal in the confined space of the toilets.

I quickly dried my face and joined the others heading for the door. Outside in the corridor Mr Pasciuta was shouting instructions.

"This is not a drill. Leave immediately, don't stop for your belongings. Go straight to the evacuation point."

There was a surging crowd of girls heading down the stairs, and I was carried along by the flow. Not one of us believed it was an emergency: we could smell the burnt toast coming from the common room. Someone was going to be in big trouble.

Out on the playing fields we all lined up, waiting for the register to be taken. I could see no sign of Grace. I asked a few of the others but no one seemed sure where she was, and my phone, I realised, was in the side pocket of my bag, which was still in the common room.

It took forever for the fire brigade to decide that we could go back to lessons, and while we waited we were treated to another lecture.

No one seemed at all bothered about getting back inside except me. I didn't want to be parted from my bag and the package with the amulet, and being without it was making me more and more anxious. I had no idea what would happen if the time for the transfer came and I didn't have it. Would Catherine notice and wait? Would she come back and try again later? I would have felt calmer if I had completely trusted Catherine, but there was something about her that nagged at the back of my mind. I would be glad to have this over and done with.

We were all suddenly called to order by a sharp command from the headmistress. This part of the lecture was short and to the point – I had rarely seen her so angry.

"Twice within a fortnight, girls! This is truly disgraceful." She pulled herself up to her full height and started scanning the audience. We all quickly dropped our eyes.

"The Chief Fire Officer and I are extremely disappointed with your behaviour. Every toaster in the school will be removed this afternoon and every girl in the sixth form common room this morning will receive a detention. Now, back inside. We've wasted half an hour of valuable school time."

Was it half an hour already? I looked at my watch in a panic. Catherine had agreed to come at eleven and it was ten-fifteen now. I edged towards the front of the crowd as we all started to file back into the building.

I just wanted to get to my rucksack, and I started walking as fast as I could, resisting the temptation to run. I got ahead of most of my friends, and broke into a trot as I hit the stairs. The first floor corridor was still deserted, so no one saw me sprint along it.

I was the first back into the common room, and I clutched my tatty old bag to my chest with a sigh of relief. I still had more than half an hour. I began to edge my way back downstairs, suddenly aware that my heart was pounding.

As I walked, I heaved the rucksack on to my back, taking my mobile out of the side pocket to call Grace. There was one new text message. I started to read it as I made my way downstairs, then stopped dead.

I whipped the bag off my shoulder and ripped it open. There was no package. I pushed aside books and files and checked every corner but it wasn't there. Everything seemed to happen in slow motion and a cold finger of fear ran down my spine. Eloïse practically fell over me as she climbed the stairs. "What is it, Alex? You look like you've seen a ghost."

"Have – have you seen Grace today?" I asked.

She looked at me curiously. "Yes, of course. We were in geography earlier, and then she was in the common room. Now she's gone on the environmental studies field visit to Kew Gardens. They left just before the fire alarm. Have you two had a row?"

"Um, no. I just had something important to tell her."

"It'll have to wait then, they'll be hours yet. I did that trip last week: it's cool. We did the Treetop Walkway. Grace's team have gone with the group from the boys' school." She was shouting the last bit over her shoulder as the queue of impatient girls behind her pushed her up the stairs. I steadied myself against the wall.

Think! I told myself. I clenched my fists until the nails dug into my palms. I hadn't thought about what would happen if Grace got the package without me being there, without me being able to control when she took it away. I had only been separated from my rucksack for a few minutes in the toilets before the alarms went off, but it had been too long.

The text from Grace had made it all very clear:

Got package. All v. mysterious. Gone to Kew. Back later. Tell me then. Gx

207

But Catherine's instructions had been equally clear: "Make sure you have the amulet in your bag: I need it to locate you. But *don't* wear it."

Now Grace was carrying, but not touching, the amulet. Catherine would start trying to take her memories in about – I looked at my watch – thirty minutes. I remembered with hideous clarity the rest of her description: "If the mind we're stealing from resists us then the person could be left a shell – barely alive. A person, but empty."

Grace could be left with nothing – empty, ruined.

I felt a creeping horror, my hands suddenly clammy and the hairs on the back of my neck rising. I knew that whatever happened to Grace, it would be my fault. I had to warn her, and warn her quickly. My fingers were shaking as I tried to call her mobile. It rang, but after a few seconds it switched to voicemail. Grace's happy, carefree voice sang in my ear. I hadn't noticed before how long her greeting was. The seconds ticked painfully past, but finally I was able to leave a message.

"Grace, it's me. It's really, really important that you get rid of that package immediately! Drop it in the bin or something, *please*. Do it right now and call me straight back."

If her phone was still playing up, I realised, it might be hours before she got to hear what I'd said. I needed a back-up plan. I racked my brain to work out who else was doing environmental studies. It wasn't one of my subjects so I didn't know the class and I was even less likely to have their phone numbers. I thought about Eloïse – she seemed to know about it. What had she said about the group? I remembered: it was a joint trip with the boy's school, and I knew someone there who did environmental studies: Rob.

I really didn't want to call him, but I had no choice. I scrolled

208

down my list of names until I found his number, and pressed the call key. I heard it connect and start to ring, and then there was a click and a recorded voice: he had cut me off.

I couldn't believe it, so I tried again. The mechanical voice confirmed it: "This mobile may be switched off. Please try later." I looked at my watch again – I had lost another two minutes. I didn't know what Catherine would do. What if I was too late, and she started to try to take Grace's memories? If she was searching for happy memories then Grace would have plenty of those. But Grace would instinctively resist Catherine, I knew that. Would Catherine stop when that happened?

My worries about Catherine and her motives, the concerns that I'd pushed to the back of my mind in my desperation to be free of my misery, came flooding in. Suddenly, I felt horribly sure that Catherine would take the memories, whether it was Grace in front of her or me. When it was my memories, my identity that had been at risk I'd been willing to silence the voice of caution in my head, but now I felt – no, I *knew* – that Grace was in dreadful danger.

I had just two choices: either I could keep trying to get a message to her or I could go there and try to get the amulet away from her myself. I realised that the longer I spent trying to find the names and numbers of the others on the trip, the less time I'd have to get there. Scooping up my bag I sprinted down the stairs and out of the nearest door. The car park was at the side of the building and I hoped that none of the teachers would notice my sudden exit.

I fumbled for the car keys as I went, trying not to think about how many laws I was about to break. It was the only way, though: Josh was in an exam so he couldn't help, and the bus just wasn't fast enough.

I looked at my watch again as I slid into the driver's seat. Twenty minutes. Luckily the school gates were open and I was soon on the road. I had to focus on keeping my speed down, though I wanted to floor the accelerator. I made it to the big junction by the dual carriageway and sat drumming my fingers as I waited for a gap in the traffic.

"Don't stall, don't stall, don't stall," I found myself chanting as I spotted my chance between a big green lorry and a delivery van. I was in luck – the road to Kew was almost empty. I pressed the accelerator down and tried to make up some time.

As I drove I was haunted by a vision of Grace looking bewildered and lost as her memories of Jack were sucked out of her, and couldn't shake the picture that kept coming next: of her slumped and vacant, her brain scrambled beyond repair. Cold sweat on my palms made my hands slip as I turned into Kew Road with five minutes to go: five minutes to park and search over three hundred acres of garden. My heart sank. How did I ever think that this was going to be possible?

But I knew where they would be. I remembered what Eloïse had said: they were going to the Treetop Walkway in the south-eastern part of the gardens, close to where I was now. I could still make it.

I drove along the road until I saw the first visitors' gate into the gardens. I had been in this entrance a few times years ago but I wasn't sure if I would remember the way. Cars were parked all down the side of the road, interspersed with big coaches, leaving nowhere to park. I had no time to waste. I pulled up right next to the gate and abandoned the car, looking at my watch. Three minutes.

With an apologetic glance I dodged the small queue of people, vaulted over the ticket barrier and ran for it.

The women behind the ticket office leapt out of her chair and started shouting at me but she had no chance of catching up. I ran as fast as I could. The pain in my lungs was like a fire as I gasped for breath, but I didn't dare stop.

I could see the walkway ahead of me, just past the Pagoda. I glanced at my watch: it was eleven o'clock. I was too late. Somewhere, somewhere close, Catherine was beginning to suck out Grace's memories, her feelings and her thoughts, taking things from her that she could never get back. And Grace would be beginning to fight...

I was at the point of collapse when I saw them.

Clustered around the bottom of the Pagoda, the group of sixth formers from the two schools were listening to a lecture. I could see Rob, slouching against the wall and looking bored. I couldn't see Grace.

I had no breath to shout, but I found a final burst of energy. I sprinted behind the Pagoda, away from the rest of the group, where she had to be. I had no time to explain: the sooner I got to her, the less she would lose.

Finally I saw her standing in the shadow of the strange, oriental building. She was alone and had her back to the wall. For just a moment, I thought that I was in time, but then I noticed her unnatural stillness. She was standing bolt upright, hands held out a little from her sides and with her head angled up. Her eyes were glassy.

I was too late.

As I ran the last few metres I saw her body jerk as if it were being electrocuted. I slid to a halt and reached for her bag, shouting, "Catherine! Stop. You've got the wrong person!"

My voice had no effect. I fumbled at the fasteners on Grace's bag. There was the envelope. Hands shaking, I tore it open and the amulet fell into my lap. I scooped it up and thrust it on to Grace's wrist, calling again as I held it.

"Catherine, stop! It's me you want."

As I shouted, I let go of the amulet and immediately Grace collapsed on to the ground in front of me. For a moment, I felt terror: whatever had happened to Grace could now happen to me, but I had no time to think about it properly. I felt sure that Grace was safe: the amulet would protect her, but in a single frozen second, I realised that my careful plan for the safekeeping of the amulet had gone horribly wrong. Grace wouldn't know that she shouldn't wear it, or that she shouldn't give it back to me. On the grass in front of me I could see the memory card, thrown out of the envelope when I had ripped it open.

It was too late to worry about that now, I couldn't stop this happening. A spark of comfort flashed through my head: I was about to get my old life back. Thoughts of Callum tumbled through my mind, and I waited for Catherine. I thought of his touch, his smile, his embarrassment at being complimented. Like a speeded-up video, the memories whipped through my mind, dissolving before I could grasp them. I realised with a flicker of panic that somehow Catherine was there and pulling them out of my mind, unravelling the most important part of my life like a thread on a spool.

I tried not to fight, to make the process easy for her and safe for me. The memories continued scrolling past: I saw myself on the beach by the Thames, examining the dazzling blue stone in the bracelet I had found, but then I realised I was thinking about my recent exams ... my plotting with Grace to catch the interest of Rob and Jack ... Christmas ... our family holiday last year in Spain... The memories came faster and faster, and then they were gone. I was now a gawky young teenager, now a child. I saw myself in the playground of the reception class, my long blonde plait flying in my reflection in a window as I tore around with my friends; my parents, shockingly young, teaching me to swim in the pool at Josh's primary school; my favourite toy, a tattered puppy. All of them were there for an instant before they streamed away from me.

My whole life was disappearing. Everything that made me who I was was being ripped from me. I was watching a video being played along the wall of a tunnel, and I was racing towards the black hole at the end.

Too late I knew that I had been tricked. Through the confused whirl of my past, I could sense a malicious presence standing next to me laughing with delight and triumph.

The blackness advanced and all I could remember was that someone, somewhere had loved me. I clung to that as the last of my memories swirled past me, and I felt myself falling to the floor.

Hospital

I tried to struggle out of the blackness, groping my way through the strange fog in my mind. But however hard I tried, everything stayed dark. My body felt heavy, my arms lying useless by my sides. Where was I? The fog swirled and thickened and I felt my mind wander – it was much easier than trying to focus on anything. But I knew that I had been somewhere for something important. Someone was waiting for me. I wanted to go back, but I just wasn't sure how.

I tried to concentrate, but it was no good: nothing was coming to me. My mind was just ... blank. I could feel little whispers of thoughts but every time I turned to catch them they were gone like ghosts.

With no real response from my mind, I decided to see if I could get my body to work. I took a deep breath and felt for my fingers. They were there alright – I could feel something pressing down on one of them, but they wouldn't move. I tried my feet, but couldn't persuade them to move either. I certainly couldn't see, I knew that, but maybe I could hear?

Almost as soon as I had the thought I became aware of a noise in the distance – a short bleep. Then another and another. Now I was aware of it, the sound banged away like a drumbeat. As I listened it got faster, until I felt almost breathless. I tried breathing deeply again, and eventually the bleeping returned to its earlier pace. I couldn't make it stop though, however carefully I concentrated. I wished that I could go back to the silent fog – it was rather less irritating.

I slowly became aware of another beeping noise, this time slightly further away. Then a slight squeaking noise, like rubber-soled shoes on linoleum.

"Oh dear," a voice wavered, "oh dear..."

"What is it, Mrs Moyse?"

"Oh dear, oh..."

"Does it still hurt?"

"Where am I supposed to be, dear?" asked the feeble voice.

"You're in the hospital, Mrs Moyse, don't try to get up. You are in the intensive care unit. You gave us all a bit of a fright. Your family are outside if you want to see them. Shall I get them for you?"

"Oh dear, I suppose so..."

As the squeaking footsteps disappeared into the distance I became aware of another noise, an almost silent sobbing, as if someone had cried so much there was nothing left.

"Oh, Alex, come back to us," the woman whispered. "It's Mum," she said, her voice catching. "I don't know if you can hear me, but they don't know for certain that you can't, I'm going to keep talking to you until..." Her voice broke, and I felt something wet on my hand.

After a short pause and a lot of sniffing the voice continued. "I wish I knew what happened to you and Grace at the Pagoda. Grace has no memory of it at all. The ambulance men think that maybe you'd been exposed to some kind of fumes or something toxic, but all your tests are negative. I just wish I knew – maybe then we could work out how to help you."

I tried to clear my head of the creeping fog. Mum? Grace? I felt that I ought to know these people, but there was nothing in my head where the picture of their faces should be. What had I been doing in the Pagoda? What pagoda? The fog was creeping over my thoughts again but I forced myself to keep listening.

The bleeping noise was getting faster again, and something someone had said made an itch inside my head. What was it? There was some connection between the strange beeping and what I had heard.

"We have had lots more cards," the woman's voice continued gently, "and loads of flowers, but they won't let us bring them in here. There is a huge card from your class – I'll read you out all the messages later – and a very nice one from Rob." The voice became more reflective. "He was very upset about something when he spoke to me. Did you two have another fight? I thought you'd split up but he still seems very keen." The voice paused. "He seems to think that you were pretty upset, but I don't believe that you would do anything silly. Not you. You are always so full of…"

The voice suddenly dissolved as she began to sob. What was so wrong? Who was this Rob and what had happened between us? Why would it upset her so much?

Eventually her breathing became more even. I waited to see if she would continue.

"I'm sorry," she murmured, "I'm not supposed to do that. But you know me… It's just so hard. We have no idea what happened to you. If we knew that, maybe we would be able to make it right, get you better, bring you home…" The voice caught again, and I could tell she was struggling to regain control.

I could hear the bleeping again, and a couple of pieces of the jigsaw finally clicked into place in my confused and foggy brain. I was in hospital, and it didn't sound as if my prognosis was good.

But I was fine – I just needed to tell this woman that she had the wrong bed, that I just couldn't move for some reason. And as soon as I could work that out I could get on with .... what? I began to have a vague sense that something was really quite wrong.

I tried to concentrate. The woman was starting to talk again, but in a rather different tone.

"No, there is no change that I have noticed."

"It's very strange," said a new voice. "The printouts show that her heart rate went up dramatically just a few minutes ago. Are you sure there was no change in her colour, or..."

"I've been watching all the time for anything different, but she is just the same. Do you think that the heart rate is a good sign?" the first voice asked hopefully.

"Rather the opposite I'm afraid. It may be a sign that her system is stressed, and, given her condition, that's not a good development. We have talked about the possibility..."

The woman interrupted, and there was desperation in her voice. "But not so soon? I … I … thought we would have more time. Time to work out what to do."

"As we've said, it's very, very hard to predict," soothed the second voice. "With the machines these days people – like Alex – with irreversible brain stem dysfunction can be kept alive indefinitely. But you know that it's important to come to terms with the fact that, even if we work out what happened to Alex, she won't get any better." The tone changed, became softer, less professional. "I've seen the scans." A doctor, then.

They can't have been talking about me. They must have the wrong bed, I reasoned. There was nothing wrong with me. I just couldn't move and I couldn't think very clearly. Surely the scans could see that I was really alright. But what if they *were* talking about me? What would they do to me if they didn't know I could hear them? If they didn't know I could think? I tried to keep calm. The second voice was talking gently again and I had to concentrate hard to catch it all.

"Did you know that Alex joined the organ donor register when she got her provisional driving licence?" The question was hesitant.

There was silence. Then the first voice spoke again, so full of pain it was a miracle she could continue.

"We talked about it. She was so sure that she wanted to be able to do something good if..." Her voice petered out.

"I know it's very hard, but I think you should give it some thought. Whatever happened to Alex, it only affected her brain. All her organs are in perfect condition and she would be an ideal donor." The voice softened again. "There are a lot of other parents waiting for a miracle too."

There was a moment of silence, then the woman made a strange sound, of misery so deep, so absolute that I felt my heart would break for her. She couldn't speak, but I could feel her rocking against my bed. The other voice kept quiet, letting her grieve.

I really needed to concentrate now. There had been a hideous mistake and the woman who thought she was my mother was thinking about letting them take out my organs. I had to let them know that I could hear, that I *was* here.

I tried again to focus all my efforts on moving my hand. She was holding it, so all I had to do was twitch it a little. I took a deep breath and willed all my strength to my fingers. For a second I thought it might work, that I could get through to her, but there was nothing. It was as if I was trying to push water uphill: all my efforts slipped away.

"You don't have to decide now," the calm voice murmured. "There is still plenty of time. But it really doesn't do any of you any good to keep her in this state. We've done the assessments and with no prospect of recovery you have to let her go. We can either use her organs to help others, or, switch off the machines and let nature take its course. Either way you will be able to get on with the grieving process."

There was silence. Why wasn't she responding? I desperately wanted to be able to see. What if she was nodding?

"Thank you for being so honest," she choked. "Her father and I will decide what to do when he gets here later. He's been with our son today. He's taken it really badly."

A reprieve then, for a short while. "I'll be back later," said the second voice, "and the nurses will alert me immediately if there is any change."

"Thank you," breathed the woman, and I felt her squeeze my hand. Shoes squeaked across the floor again and it went quiet, except for all the bleeping noises.

I had some time to think.

So I was paralysed but conscious; someone I didn't know was making decisions about whether I lived or died; and I had no proper memories at all. Even my confused brain knew that this was very, very bad. I fought rising panic with an effort to be logical. The woman thought she was my mother. One possibility was that she was right. If I accepted that, then I had to assume that she would have my best interests at heart. She certainly sounded as if she cared. I guessed that she was unlikely to switch off the machines – switch *me* off – if there was any other option.

But the doctor had suggested that there was no other

real option. A surge of panic flooded through me. If there was no other option, I was going to die, and die soon.

I became aware of the bleeping noise again, getting faster and faster. Finally I worked out what it was: a heart monitor. I was listening to my heart's desperate, futile efforts, and I was listening to my only communication with the outside world.

As I listened to the rhythmic noise, counting down towards my death, I realised that I did have an option: maybe I could make myself understood by changing my heart rate. I tried to relax, and see if I could stop it racing.

I concentrated on slowing my breathing and started to feel calmer. In response, I could hear the monitor beginning to slow a little. I started to get excited with the thought that it might actually work, and the monitor's beeping speeded up. I had to get the woman to notice something. Perhaps if I could make myself as calm as possible, any change would be more dramatic.

I let myself drift. The fog I had been fighting earlier began to seep back around the edges of my mind. I let it unfurl and felt myself relax as its long tendrils began to wrap themselves around me. Giving into it was strangely comforting and I felt my concerns slip away. The fog soothed and stroked. There seemed to be nothing to do but give myself to the fog. Had I ever wanted anything else? Nothing else seemed to matter. There was a sudden noise which seemed to come from a thousand miles away, and for a second the fog parted. I could hear the woman's voice again, urgent now.

"Alex! Don't go! Fight it, come back to me."

I struggled to understand. Go where? What was she so upset about?

The fog swirled and writhed.

"Alex, don't give up, please. Please! Not just yet. Wait! Wait for Dad, at least!" She sounded so desperate that I began to fight. I gathered all my strength, forcing the fog back into the corners. It retreated, but I could sense it was there, waiting to come back. I realised I couldn't risk letting it in again.

I remembered my plan. Had it worked? Had it been worth inviting the fog to take me? Had the woman noticed any change? Had something I had done prompted this emotional outburst? I listened to the bleeping. It seemed so placid, giving no hint of the emotional turmoil going on inside my head.

"Alex, please," she begged, "you need to keep fighting. I can't believe that you can't hear me. You look almost as if you're sleeping." She paused. "I remember when you were little and every time I told you not to do something you'd do it. For a while I was able to get you to do all sorts of stuff by just telling you it wasn't allowed. But then you got wise to my trick. I'm not sure that you have ever really done anything that you didn't want to do since then. It makes me wonder how you have ended up in here, in this state."

She hesitated again. I waited to see if she was going to give me any more clues about that, but she was off in another direction. "You have been acting so strangely lately though. Always off on your own." She took a deep breath. "So secretive. Grace doesn't have a clue either ... unless she's somehow in on it. I can't imagine she would keep anything from us now, though." Another pause, then another deep breath.

"Grace will be coming later. I thought you would want to see her. The doctors won't usually let anyone except family in here, but I have been able to get her special permission. You two have always been so close. It will be hard on her, especially as she seems to blame herself, although I can't think why she should."

I listened intently, desperate to hear something which might jog a memory and help me to let her know that I was still in here, still fighting, still wanting … what? It was gone: the ghost of a thought slipped past me before I could catch it. What was it I was yearning for? Or who?

The woman talked on, recalling a childhood I couldn't remember, a brother who meant nothing to me, a boyfriend I didn't care about. In fact, a boyfriend I *really* didn't care about, I realised: whenever she mentioned Rob, I felt a vague stirring of anger. If it wasn't a memory, at least it was something. What had he done to me? I searched and searched for anything which would tie the feeling to the name, but yet again, nothing came to me.

Eventually I heard her sigh and get up from my bedside. I felt her hair brush my cheek as she leant in to gently kiss my forehead.

"I'll be back in a little while, sweet-pea," she murmured. "I need to go and talk to the doctors with Dad. Grace will be here in a minute." She leaned closer, putting her mouth close to my ear. "Keep fighting," she whispered, urgently. "Just find enough strength to give me a sign. I know you are still in there." She kissed me again and was gone.

Could she really tell, or was she just as desperate as I was? How was I going to communicate with her? As I worked fruitlessly through my non-existent options, I heard someone approach. The step was hesitant. "Alex?" whispered a new voice, younger than the others. "Your mum has got the doctors to give me ten minutes with you. It's not really allowed, but, well, they can't see what harm it can do."

This must be the Grace my mother had mentioned. Apparently she was my best friend. "I came to tell you that I'm really sorry." It came out in a rush, as if she had been building up to it. "I don't remember what happened, but I have a dreadful feeling that it was my fault in some way." She hurried on, as if the quicker she said it, the less terrible it would be. "I took the package, and I was in Kew Gardens with the environmental studies group. All I remember is that I was by the Pagoda one minute, and then coming round in A&E, wearing your bracelet. I know how much you love it, so how it ended up on my wrist I can't imagine..."

She finally paused for breath, and I felt her hesitate. "I – I think there is something really odd about it. It makes me feel a bit ... strange, wearing it. Like someone is watching me. But somehow I don't feel right taking it off, or at least I didn't – not until now."

She was making no sense to me at all. What package? What bracelet?

"And now the package is missing, I'm really sorry. I don't know what happened to it. When I came round it was gone from my bag. But as the bracelet was so important to you, I thought you would want it back before ... before..." Her voice faded for a few seconds. "In fact, I won't really feel right until I've got it back on your wrist. I'm not sure what the rules are about jewellery in here, but your mum can always take it off later."

This time her voice caught. There was a moment as she seemed to struggle, then a deep breath.

"My time is nearly up," she choked, "I want you to know that you were the best friend I could have had, and that I will never forget you. Please forgive me if somehow I caused all this. I will miss you horribly." She dissolved into sobs.

I felt my arm being lifted and something cool and comfortable being put around my wrist. Grace leaned over and kissed me, two hot tears dripping on my face.

There was a long pause, and her voice cracked as she tried to speak again. Eventually she pulled herself together enough to speak. "I love you, Alex. Be happy, wherever you go," she sobbed. Then she was gone, and I felt the cool breeze on my face as the tears dried.

I was as good as dead. She was saying a last goodbye. How could I let them know that I was still here? As the thought went through my mind, I was aware of something strange: I felt no panic. The bracelet on my wrist felt cool against the skin of my wrist, and somehow soothing. It felt as if a wave of calm was flowing out of it, up my arm and around my body. The wave came closer to my head. What was going on? Was this it? Was this what death felt like? I felt the wave slowly surge into the only bit of me that was still me. As it reached my mind, I had a sudden blinding vision of a face, a face I knew I loved, and wanted. I felt a searing pain, a pain so harsh I felt myself straining up to try to get away, to try and call out, to make it stop. Then everything went blank.

Memories

I slowly became aware of a lot of noise. People were talking loudly, the machines were bleeping and there seemed to be an argument going on.

"But I can assure you Alex sat up for a moment." The voice sounded really aggrieved. "Just look at the monitors. Something's happened: the printouts have gone crazy."

"Thank you, Nurse Price. I'll take over. Now don't let me keep you from your duties." There was a huffing noise and the sound of retreating footsteps.

My mother's voice cut in, breathless. "Doctor, what's happened? I heard that there was a change, that Alex moved. Is that right? What does it mean?"

The doctor sounded weary. "As I have explained before, Mrs Walker, Alex has suffered irreversible brain damage. We've given her all the relevant scans, and there is nothing to indicate any form of consciousness. If she did do anything, which I cannot believe for a moment," and here the voice became dismissive, "it can't have been voluntary."

"But she sat up! The visitors at the bed over there told me."

"I am afraid that's just not possible. They must have been mistaken."

"But surely, Dr Sinclair," said a new, deep voice, "isn't it worth checking this out? I mean, shouldn't we at least run some more tests? What have we got to lose?"

"I can assure you that more tests would only raise your hopes unnecessarily."

The argument went on and on. I wanted peace to think. Something had changed completely, in a way I couldn't quite define. If only my dad would stop shouting at the doctor.

My dad? How did I know that the voice belonged to my dad? I could picture him with his kind and mischievous eyes, which I was sure would now be narrowed in anger as he squared up to the doctor. What had happened? I really needed to think, and there was too much going on.

"Please be quiet," I tried to mutter, before realising that I had a large tube down my throat. I tried to cough it out. There was a stunned silence, and then pandemonium broke out.

"Alex, was that you?" cried my mum, grabbing my hand. "Baby, can you hear me? Say something!"

I could hear the doctor in the background. "It's not possible! Not with a scan like that. Let me check her."

I felt a hand on my face as someone opened one of my eyes and shined a bright light in it.

"Get off me!" I coughed. The light retreated and I felt hands pulling at me, checking my pulse, my reflexes, and finally taking out the tube. It was all too much. "Stop it!" I shouted with as much force as I could muster. "I need to think." The hands disappeared.

"I'll fetch the consultant," said a voice, and several pairs of feet clicked away. There was silence broken only by a quiet sobbing.

"Oh, Alex, thank you! You came back!" sobbed my mum. "Just rest now. We can talk when you are ready." I could hear some very unfamiliar snuffling noises. I opened my eyes cautiously. The light was unbearably bright, but Dad was sitting by the bed, tears streaming down his face and over a huge smile. I smiled back, then shut my eyes so that I could think. They would wait for me.

Memories were flooding back to me now: my parents, Josh, Grace, school. My head felt as if it had been shaken and all the memories were still confused, but I wasn't complaining: at least I had some now. But I sensed something was still missing.

As I had the thought, I became aware of him. I could see his beautiful face, his smile, his blue, blue eyes. I knew I loved him. Then, like a crushing weight falling on me, I remembered everything: I loved Callum, but he didn't love me. I had been trying to forget, and it had all gone horribly wrong.

Callum. My heart ached unimaginably. I was going to have to live with this pain forever. Had he already moved on to another conquest? I clenched my fist and felt a single tear leak from my eye and roll down the side of my face. Someone gently tried to wipe it away, stroking my cheek with feather-light fingers.

My eyes snapped open.

My parents were together on the other side of the bed, deep in a discussion with the doctor. I was suddenly conscious of a tingling in my arm, and I turned my head. Standing by the side of my bed was a shining sheet of metal: part of a box-shaped piece of medical equipment. I could just see part of my reflection in the chrome. Right beside me was Callum, with a look of profound relief and love on his face and I was swamped with love for him. I smiled back and I felt his gentle touch on my face before I remembered his betrayal. How could I let myself smile? I couldn't believe that I was going to put myself through all that pain again. I know that however much I wanted him, he wanted something else.

"Alex?" his voice was cautious. "I know that you can't speak to me, but I have to explain to you what happened. But I have to tell you the most important thing first: Catherine lied to you about so many things, and her biggest lie was to say that I didn't care about you."

I tensed, unable to let myself feel the hope that was already welling up inside me.

"I have only ever loved one person, and that person is you. Whatever she told you is nonsense. You are the single positive spark in my miserable, dark existence. I had no idea I could feel like this about anyone. My heart is yours and yours alone."

His eyes were burning into mine, full of passion. Could I believe it? Could I risk letting that tidal wave of hope overpower me? If it was a lie, and I fell for him again, I didn't think I could survive another betrayal. He saw me hesitate and his hopeful features crumpled into a mask of misery.

"She convinced you, didn't she? I was too late to stop her. I can't believe she was so cruel…" His voice tapered off, catching with emotion.

A posse of doctors was suddenly back at my bedside. I risked another glance at him. Whatever had happened, I couldn't dismiss him. I needed to understand the truth. "Come back. Come back soon," I quickly mouthed, and saw him nod once, briefly, his eyes still full of sadness, and then he was gone.

I took a deep breath. It was time to convince the doctors that I was OK. And it was time to give my parents a hug.

It took hours to persuade them all that I wasn't dying, and that I had no idea about how I came to be in the hospital. I hoped Callum would be able to fill in the gaps when he came back – if he came back. I tried to push that thought away. They sent me for another scan, and then puzzled over the results. I heard the consultant muttering about it being an amazing case study, and wondering if he could get the details into *The Lancet*. They peered into my eyes, tested my reflexes, and asked me endless questions. I answered them as honestly as I could. Some were easy. What month was it? Where did I go to school? What was the head teacher's name? Others were trickier. Why were you in Kew Gardens? What happened to Grace? What happened to you? I couldn't tell them the truth as I hardly knew the truth myself. Once they had decided that I was out of danger, they moved me out of the intensive care unit on to a normal ward, where I could be kept under observation for a while. The new ward had rather stricter visiting hours, and the ward sister sent my parents home in the early evening. There was a huge amount of noise and clattering as the nurses did the evening drugs round, then finally the lights were dimmed, and the snoring around me started. I really hoped Callum would turn up before I fell asleep. I moved the pillows so that I was sitting more upright, and instinctively rubbed the amulet, whispering his name.

Almost immediately I felt the familiar sensation in my arm and a light touch on my hair. Suddenly, I was afraid of what I was about to find out. Wasn't it better to think that he might really love me than have my hopes shattered again? For a second I considered ripping off the amulet and remaining ignorant of it all, but I forced the thought aside, and looked for his face in the tiny make-up mirror I had begged my mum to leave with me.

I gulped as I saw him behind my shoulder. What if he hadn't meant what he had said earlier? As I watched his familiar, haunting eyes met mine, and I felt his hand on my arm. I felt my eyes fill with tears. I knew I couldn't bear to lose him again.

"Hello," I whispered. "You found me."

"When you are wearing this," he traced the shape of the

amulet around my wrist, "I can find you anywhere. This whole ... thing started when you weren't wearing it." His head dipped over my hand and I felt the briefest flutter as his lips touched the inside of my wrist. My heart lurched.

"You can't imagine what I have been going through. Having failed to stop Catherine, I was so afraid that I might fail a second time and not get this back on you before ... well, before it was too late." He continued to stroke my wrist. He looked up at me, and I could see the tears threatening to brim over. Could he really mean it? I hardly dared to let myself hope. I needed to know more before I could risk that.

"I don't understand," I muttered, trying to keep as quiet as possible in the sleeping ward. "What happened? I remember racing to get to Grace, worried that Catherine would start to transfer memories from her, but it was my choice that she took my memories." My voice had become barely audible, and I needed to be strong. I straightened up and looked squarely at him. "My choice. I wanted to forget all about you." I raised my chin, challenging him to deny everything.

"How can I convince you that you have it all wrong?"

"Catherine could tell you. Why don't you just ask her?"

"She's gone." His voice was bitter.

"Gone?" I asked. "How can she go anywhere? I thought that was the point, that you were trapped." My voice was harsher than I intended.

"She used us both. She took what she needed to escape."

"I really don't understand."

He drew a deep breath. "When I told you about us, about the Dirges, I told you how the amulets work for us, that we use them to collect good memories – individual good memories –

from strangers. We collect the happiness of others, but we never have any of our own." He stopped, as if struggling to go on. "I never wanted you to know this; I thought it would make you afraid..."

I stared at him.

"I can see now that I should have told you the truth from the start. Then you'd never have listened to Catherine's scheme." He paused.

"Go on," I whispered.

His voice was bleak and he spoke slowly and reluctantly. "There is a way to move on for us, but it is extremely rare and difficult to achieve. We need a combination of the amulet – the amulet on your side – and a willing mind and then we can..."

"Wipe it?" I hazarded.

"Take all their memories." He paused. "Then our amulet is full, and it's as if we're whole again, I think. And when that happens we can move on. Veronica was the only Dirge I've heard of who had done it."

"What else do you need to tell me?" I asked, coldly.

"I promise – I promise you – that I've only just found some of this stuff out, but it doesn't make it any better." He shook his head miserably, and then straightened up. "It seems there is only one amulet on your side, and we never know when it is going to turn up. It always appears in the Thames, and when it does appear it means that one of us can escape. When whoever has found it touches it, the amulet creates visions in the Dirge who will have the best connection with the finder. This time it was me." He paused and I felt myself shiver, thinking of that sunny afternoon when everything changed.

"I didn't tell the others because I usually keep myself to myself, so no one told me the implications. It wasn't until I mentioned you to Matthew that I realised the danger you were in, and by then I loved you too much to let anything happen to you."

"And Veronica?" I prompted.

"That time the amulet had been discovered by a man, and she was able to persuade him to do as she asked. She had no compassion, just took what she wanted. We don't know where she went, but at least she didn't have to live as a Dirge. Matthew warned me to be very careful around you and to make sure you kept your amulet on your wrist, to stay safe. He could see that you were in no danger from me. What I didn't know was that Catherine had been listening, and she realised that if she could get you to take off the amulet so you were cut off from me, and persuade you to offer her some memories, it was her chance to go. She'd hated normal life, it seemed, and she hated life as a Dirge more. She was willing to do anything – anything – to leave." His voice was bitter.

I still didn't understand. "So how did it all happen? What does the amulet actually do to me?"

"We can feel when we're close to an amulet. It's a kind of pull, like a magnet. But while you wear it, it will protect you from us, but being close and not touching it ... well, we know where to find you, and you have no protection. That's how whole minds are stolen. It's why I never wanted you to take it off."

"So why didn't Catherine just swoop on me as soon as I *had* taken it off?"

"If the mind is willing, and memories are given freely, taking them is easier and more complete."

"What happens to the people, the victims?" I asked, horrified.

"They're left with nothing. No thoughts, no memories. Nothing that makes them *them*. The shock to the brain is terrible."

He looked straight at me. "They die, I think."

"Why didn't you tell me all this before, when you first found out about it?" I tried hard to keep the edge of anger out of my voice but wasn't entirely successful.

Callum looked down guiltily. "I was selfish. I thought you might get too frightened and decide to throw the amulet back. I knew that you were in danger just by having the amulet, but I knew that it was the only way I could be with you. I thought that I could keep you safe, keep you wearing it ... I couldn't bear to lose you." I looked at his face, which was filled with self-loathing, and couldn't stay angry with him.

"Have you no idea what happened to Veronica?"

"No one really knows," he whispered. "Maybe she died, properly this time. Perhaps that is our final escape."

"So Catherine is gone? Do you think she's ... dead?"

"Yes," he answered, looking down. "She wanted to be free, but I think that there was something else too." There was a pause, and I felt his gentle caress on my shoulder. I struggled to hold myself back, when every part of me was longing to welcome him back. He felt me stiffen, and abruptly his touch was gone.

"Catherine was a very complicated person. She was filled with envy and jealousy. I've always known that. She understood what you and I had, and she realised that she would never be as happy. She couldn't bear it." His voice was scarcely more than a whisper.

"What we *had*?" I needed to know if it was all in the past.

"She saw how much I loved you, that happiness was possible, at least for me. And she saw you, young and fresh and beautiful, undamaged, untainted by our world, free from the tedium and degradation of hunting out and stealing memories one by one."

There was a tentative stroke on my arm, and I felt the involuntary tingle of goosebumps at his touch.

"What we *had*," I repeated, "was built on lies. You didn't want me – how could you? We don't even live in the same dimension. All you wanted was my memories."

I had said it. I looked directly at Callum and his face was twisted with grief. "Who told you what I wanted?" he questioned.

"Catherine of course." He stared deep into my eyes as he waited. "She was lying to me about that as well?" I gasped. "But what about the other girls? What about Olivia?"

"Do you remember me telling you that I'm often assigned to help other Dirges start gathering in the morning?"

I nodded mutely.

"Well, I'm most often assigned to help Olivia. She is very young, and very unhappy and without help she slides into a terrible state. She relies on me to help her almost every day. I suppose I'm like a big brother to her. Anyway, most of the others, like my sister, think she's a pain and won't help."

"So why were you so horrified when I mentioned her?"

He looked embarrassed again. "Catherine. It was Catherine again. She advised me never to mention Olivia, that if you found out about her you would be really jealous and tell me to leave."

"So there really is no one? No one for you on your side?" Could I really believe him?

He sighed. "I can't really begin to tell you what it's like. Our emotions are so flat. Life just isn't like that for us. We just ... exist with each other, nothing more." He looked at me sadly. "You are the only colour in my completely grey life. Somehow, being in touch with your emotions let mine resurface. I don't know how it works, but I will be grateful to you for the rest of my existence."

I still couldn't let it go. "And the girls on my side? Other girls? What about them?"

He smiled as he answered. "I've never really looked at any of them. I just see the colour of their emotions, and take no more notice of them than that. You, on the other hand ... well, I can't take my eyes off you. And you have the most beautiful emotions I have ever seen. I love you more than life itself, Alex. No one will ever compare to you."

Then a strange look crossed his face. "Of course, I'll understand if you don't feel the same way. I know you have Rob and…"

"Rob!" I almost shouted into the silent ward. I hurriedly coughed to cover it up. "You've said that before. Why would you ever think that I cared about Rob?"

This time the realisation dawned on both of us at the same time. "Catherine," we said in unison.

"When did you first start to realise what she was doing?" I asked.

"After you told me to go and took off your amulet. You were obviously devastated, but I couldn't work out what had happened. You were in so much pain – it was awful to watch and be able to do nothing." His voice had dropped to almost a whisper. "Then I thought about what you had said, and remembered that you had mentioned Olivia. You couldn't have known about Olivia unless you had talked to someone from over here, and that's when I started to think about Catherine."

He smiled ruefully at me as I raised an eyebrow at him. "I know ... a bit slow, wasn't I?"

"Definitely," I agreed.

"I went to find her immediately," he continued, "and she told me that you had called her and asked her advice on how to break with me because you loved Rob."

"And you believed her?" I was astounded.

"It always made more sense for you to want him, not me. What can I offer you?" His eyes bored into mine. He entirely believed what he was saying.

"I don't love him! I never have. I love you!"

"Is that still true? After all this? After all the trouble and pain I've caused?"

Looking at him, I didn't even have to consider my answer. "Of course it's still true! I've never stopped loving you. I only did what I did because I couldn't bear the thought that you didn't love me." I reached up and ran my fingers gently down the line of his cheek, wishing I could feel it properly. He caught hold of my hand, and his long fingers played up and down my arm. There was one last thing I needed to understand.

"But ... but why am *I* not dead?" I asked. "She took my memories and left, so how am I here, remembering everything, talking to you?"

"It was hard." His voice was barely a whisper. "But there was a way."

"How?"

He took a deep breath. "You got to Grace just in time. Of course, Catherine had just realised that it wasn't you with the amulet, and she thought you'd tricked her. She decided she would try to take whatever she could from Grace in the hope that it would be enough, because she couldn't risk waiting. I think she was scared that you'd see through her lies, so stealing Grace's memories might have been the only chance she was going to get to escape. But of course Grace didn't want to give up her memories, so she resisted which made it much more difficult and slower for Catherine, and at the same moment you appeared and rammed the amulet on Grace's arm.

"I think she couldn't believe her luck: here you were after all, begging her to take your memories. She pounced immediately, and, of course, she took everything she could. Once you'd opened your mind to her, she was able to get at everything, and she sucked it all in." He shook his head. "I can't believe that I managed to cause you such pain, that you'd be willing to expose yourself like that." His voice wavered and his gaze dropped to the floor.

"And then?" I urged. I could feel him pull himself together.

"Catherine was able to fill up her amulet with your memories. All the happy, sad, excited, peaceful and exhilarating thoughts you have ever had." He paused, as if struggling to work out how to put it. "Everything that made you really you – it all streamed into her amulet. Finally her amulet made the most terrible, awful sound, like metal tearing, and I was blinded by a shower of sparks which seemed to start inside Catherine and then envelop her.

"Afterwards, there was nothing of her left to find except her cloak," he continued. "Catherine and her amulet were gone." Callum ran his fingers through his unruly hair. "She was my sister, so I ought to feel sad, but I can't. She's the reason I am what I am, and she caused too many people too much pain. I'm not going to miss her."

"But I still don't see..." I started. He put his finger to his lips to remind me to be quiet. The ward was now very dark.

"I was obviously worried about you because you were not wearing the amulet, and Catherine had been acting very strangely. She was almost excited, not like her at all. So I followed her. But I was too late to stop it happening: I just wasn't close enough." His eyes closed, but after a second he continued. "As soon as I realised what you were doing, giving your amulet to Grace, I tried to get in the way. I couldn't stop Catherine, but I had to try to save you." His voice was barely above a whisper.

"What did you do?" I asked with a creeping horror, not sure I really wanted to know.

"I did the only thing I could do. I took your memories at the same time that she was stealing them."

"But why? And how could you do that? Why didn't you die too?"

"I had to act quickly, so I took the only option: I emptied my amulet completely first," he admitted.

"You let them all go? All the memories? The happy thoughts? Everything that keeps you from sinking into despair every day?" I could hardly believe it. All he'd told me about the amulet, about keeping sane in his awful existence, all of it relied upon having a store of memories in his amulet. And because of me, because of what I had done, he had lost them all.

"But I thought that an empty amulet was impossible, that you would sink into unbearable despair. That's what you told me."

He looked into my eyes. "That's all true, but I had to try. It was because of me that you had put yourself in Catherine's power, so I had to try to make things right."

"So how did you do it?" I whispered.

"I wasn't sure what to do, but I knew that I had to be fast. I also couldn't risk filling it up completely as that would have taken me with Catherine, and I wasn't going to leave you." He smiled at me, almost shyly. "Releasing the existing memories turned out to be pretty straightforward," he continued. "Much easier than I expected, actually. It's through our will that the memories are stored there, and it turns out we can set them free when we want to. I don't know what happened to them. Maybe they find a home in someone's mind and I added a little bit of false happiness to their life." He smiled. "I only had a second; a fraction of a second. Once I had cleared the amulet I took a copy of every memory that Catherine was pulling out of your mind."

"Could you see it all?" I whispered, mortified.

"Well, I tried not to look at them," he said apologetically, raising his eyes to mine. I couldn't hold his gaze.

"After Catherine had disappeared," he continued, "I waited with you until the ambulance arrived. You were unconscious. Luckily Rob had seen you fall to the ground, and when he got to you, he found Grace too." He spat out Rob's name. "When he couldn't revive either of you he got help.

"They took you both to the hospital. Grace was wearing the amulet so I was able to follow easily. I could see you," he said wistfully, "but I couldn't get into your head, only hers. I sat by you for days, watching as the doctors argued over whether you had any chance of recovery. Then they started to talk about switching off your life support." His voice was tight with pain.

"I knew my only chance was to get your amulet back on your arm. I just felt that the connection that it gives us would make it easier to transfer all the memories back into you. But I was running out of time. My only choice was to find a way of persuading Grace to give it to you, but it wasn't as easy as I had hoped." He paused. "I had to get a bit creative," he smiled a little as he looked up, guiltily.

"What did you do to her?"

"Well, I didn't have the quality of the connection with her that I have with you, so it wasn't easy to manipulate her. But she was wearing the amulet a lot – she just couldn't stop thinking about you – and I kept talking to her. I couldn't risk her seeing me – I didn't want to frighten her – but I could tell I was getting through somehow. When the doctors gave in to your mum and let Grace visit, I began to feel more hopeful.

"The second she put the amulet back on your wrist I was able to start getting all of your memories back from my amulet into you, back where they belong. All of those years of gathering came in useful in the end: I thought through how to reverse the process, and I just hoped it would work." His smile was apologetic.

"So you were able to put all my memories back? That means your amulet is empty – surely that's not safe?"

He looked even more sheepish. "I'm sorry. I had to keep one, and it had to be a good one. That is enough to keep me going for now."

"Which one?" I was torn between embarrassment and curiosity.

"The moment you realised you loved me," he admitted quietly, staring deep into my eyes.

I searched back: the sensation was peculiar. I could visualise the riverbank, remember the warm sun on my skin, waking up from that few minutes' sleep, then everything went fuzzy and the perspective changed. Suddenly I was looking down at *me*, listening to *my* words, and bursting with love for *me*. "I don't understand," I admitted.

"I had to take your memory to put it in my amulet, but I couldn't leave you with no recollection of that moment: that wouldn't have been fair. So I gave you mine." He looked up at me almost shyly. "I hope that was OK."

I suddenly felt with complete certainty that everything

he told me was true. Catherine had lied. Callum loved me. As I looked into his eyes I could tell that he could see the conviction in mine. The anguish in his face faded and was replaced with joy. I had never seen anyone look so relieved and so content.

I felt his touch on my face and yearned to be able to hold him tight. "I love you, Callum," I whispered, reaching for where his ghostly face shimmered in the dim light. "I am so sorry for what I have done to you, for not trusting you."

"Don't be sorry," he soothed, "I wouldn't have believed that I could love you more than I already did, but I do." He paused as a nurse walked by to a bed at the end of the ward.

I gazed back at him, full of emotion. He loved me just as much as I loved him. It felt as if my heart would burst it was so full.

As he said the word love I became aware of the tiredness which was creeping up on me. I nodded in agreement, but had to get one last thing straight.

"You will be here, won't you?" I challenged. "Be here when I wake up? You have enough in the amulet to stay safe?"

"Don't worry about me," he laughed. "I'll be fine, and I promise that when you wake in the morning, I'll be here by your side." His tone changed, becoming much more intense. "I love you, Alex, more than you will ever know."

I saw his face come closer, and felt the briefest flutter as if his lips had touched mine. The last thing I remembered as I gave in to the sleep was the smouldering intensity in his eyes. He wasn't going to leave me now, of that I was sure, because I *did* know how much he loved me: his memory was there in my memory, and I would keep it safe forever. I smiled weakly as I drifted away.

Fireflies

The doctors kept coming to take a look at me, and I was subjected to a huge number of different scans. I could see them talking about me in hushed tones, some of them clearly wondering how on earth I had fooled them, others discussing the best way to write up my case to ensure publication.

But I didn't care. I was basking in a warm glow. Whenever he could be there, Callum was by my side. Some of the other patients probably thought I was a little strange: he could keep me amused for hours with stories of the more ridiculous things that were happening in the hospital, and his wicked sense of humour often had me laughing out loud, which was difficult to explain when I was apparently sitting alone in my hospital bed.

One morning I had to sit meekly in bed while a police officer interviewed me about the whole incident, including the fact that I had driven all the way to Kew Gardens unsupervised and with a learner's licence. The officer looked very stern as he sat there with my dad.

"Driving without a licence is a serious offence, young lady. I hope you realise that."

I nodded as humbly as I could.

"What does he mean, 'young lady'? He's only about twelve himself!" Callum was in a happy mood, and was enjoying watching me try to wriggle out of some of the problems I had caused myself.

I fell back on my – by now – standard defence mechanism. "I'm really sorry, officer. I know it was wrong so I must have had a really good reason to do it, but I really can't remember anything. It's all a complete blank." I looked up at him, a picture of contrition.

The young officer blushed. "Well, luckily you didn't hit anything. I'll have to file a report though, and you are likely to be prosecuted for at least one offence. It's not a very good start to your driving career, is it?"

"No, officer. I really am very sorry. I promise it won't happen again."

"She has always been very responsible before, officer," added Dad. "Doing something like this is completely out of character."

"You should probably go with her to the court when the case comes up," he replied, folding up his notebook. "You might get the opportunity to speak in her defence, as she is a minor."

He turned back to me. "You were very lucky not to have killed yourself or someone else," he said sternly. "We'll let you know what charges we intend to bring in due course."

"Thank you." I made myself sound as apologetic as possible.

"So is that all?" asked Dad as he walked the policeman out. I didn't catch the reply but was glad it was over for today. I was really grateful that my parents believed the amnesia story otherwise they would have been going on about this for years to come.

Finally, I was discharged. There was no good reason to keep me in, and the hospital needed the bed, so even though they couldn't work out what had happened to me, the doctors let me go. They insisted that I remain an outpatient, however, and booked me in for more complicated scans in London over the coming weeks. I didn't care – I was on my way home, where I would be able to talk to and see Callum much more easily.

My parents came to take me home, and it took a long time to move all the flowers and the cards down to the car. Mum kept finding reasons to touch me – squeeze my shoulder, or smooth my hair – as if she couldn't quite believe I was there. Dad kept catching my eye too. I was so sorry that I had given them such a fright.

Josh was waiting when we got home, a beaming smile on his face.

"So they finally threw you out, eh?" he teased, squeezing me so tightly I could hardly breathe.

"Yeah. They saw through my cunning plan to get off school until the end of term."

"It sounds like you were irritating the hell out of them too."

"Actually, they're keen to have me back. Apparently I am a particularly interesting case."

"That's a first for you, then," he said gruffly, pulling me into another hug so I couldn't see his face. "You know, I kind of missed you. It's good to have you back."

The house was full of flowers and there were hundreds of cards. Stacked neatly in a corner I saw a pile of newspapers. Dad caught my puzzled glance, and looked a bit sheepish.

"You became quite the celebrity you know – and Grace, too, of course. We kept the papers in case ... well, so that you could decide what to do with them."

"How did the papers find out about it all?"

"I really don't know. A leak at the hospital? One of the kids at school?" He hesitated. "You don't have to read them, you know. Some of the comments were a little – opinionated."

I flicked through a few and saw some of the headlines: *School Girl Suicide Pact*; *Double Dose of Kew Killer*; *Coma In The*

Pagoda. I decided I didn't need to read them right now.

I wanted to be able to talk to Callum somewhere private, and to see him more clearly.

"I really want to check my emails and call a few of my friends to tell them that I'm home. Just get back to normal, you know? Do you mind if I go upstairs for a bit?"

Mum smiled contentedly at me. "Not at all. You go ahead."

My eye was caught by a small flicker of light over her head, bright yellow and dancing around. She saw me frown.

"What's wrong, sweetheart?"

The light was gone as quickly as it had come. "I think you are attracting fireflies," I laughed. "There was one buzzing right over your head."

"As long as they don't bite, I don't care," she said, giving me another squeeze. "I'll bring you up a coffee later."

The firefly was back. It was very odd: I had never seen one indoors before, and it was daytime too. But I had other things to think about – it was time to see Callum. I made my way upstairs, carefully shut the door and put my headphones on, then set up the mirror by my desk. As I called his name I felt the familiar tingling in my arm, and there he was behind me. He looked as glorious as ever. "Welcome home, beautiful."

"It is really good to be back," I said, reaching up to touch his face. "I've missed being able to do this."

As my fingers grazed his cheek I felt the gentlest of resistance. His eyes closed and I could see him move towards my touch. I continued to stroke his face and neck, then I turned around as far as I could and kissed him gently on the lips.

His eyes flew open in surprise and he instantly responded. It was the strangest feeling, like a feather touching me.

Eventually Callum pulled away. "Do you have any idea of what you are doing to me?"

I grinned back at him. "Absolutely. And it's the very least you deserve."

I ran my hand through his hair and down his neck, and saw him lean towards the touch. I reached for his face, wanting to see his eyes. They were dark with passion.

"Oh, Alex," he whispered, "I love you so much." He pulled back a little and considered me in the mirror. "I can't believe I've actually got you back. I seem to have almost lost you so many times." His voice was heavy with emotion.

"I wish I had told you everything from the start, as soon as possible after I'd first seen Catherine. Then none of this would have happened."

"There is no point regretting it now, and no permanent harm was done." That wasn't strictly true either, but he refused to go into too much detail about the problem of his nearly empty amulet.

As far as I could tell he was dealing with it by going out early in the morning and late at night. I didn't want to ask if he was having to sacrifice his principles to keep the creeping despair away and the amulet fed.

I settled back in his arms and looked at him. I could spend hours just absorbing every feature of his face until it was as familiar as my own. I luxuriated in the view I now had: at the hospital, I'd only had the tiny make-up mirror, and it really wasn't enough to do him justice.

"Callum, how old do you think you are?" He started to shake his head. "No, hang on. I know you don't actually know, but what do you feel? What's your best guess?"

He sighed. "I wish I knew."

"It must be so frustrating, not knowing even that basic fact."

"It is. The only thing I can go on is the relative ages of the others."

I looked quizzically at him.

"The other Dirges are a very mixed bag of apparent ages. Some are young like me, others are middle aged. A couple of them are really old."

I still wasn't getting it. "How does that help?"

"I must be about as old as I look: we must keep our general appearance when we come over."

It seemed as sensible an idea as any. "So look at yourself – what do you guess?"

"Hmm, what would be a perfect age as far as you were concerned?"

I laughed. "That's cheating, you know!"

"Well, I might as well make the most of my few opportunities to have things my way." The end of his sentence was lost in a mumble as he kissed my neck.

I shook to get him to sit upright again. "Listen! I asked you a question: what do you think?"

"Honestly? I don't feel *that* young. It seems as if I was already reasonably responsible when I came over. And by comparing my face to others I see – I don't know – maybe about nineteen?" He was watching me intently to see if that was a problem. "Go on then, your turn, what do you think?"

He had managed to hit on the perfect age, exactly where I would have put him myself.

"Nineteen works for me." I smiled, looking up at him from under my lashes. "Old enough for a hint of sophistication but young enough to have fun when the situation demands it."

"But why do you want to know? What difference does it make?" he asked, puzzled.

"Oh, it was just something Catherine said – it made me wonder," I replied airily, picking up an old receipt from my desk in what I hoped was an offhand manner.

"Well, you should know by now not to take any notice of anything she said."

"I know. I'm sorry. I guess I was just curious. You know so much about me, after all."

"Do you know," he said suddenly, "I have no idea how old you are either. You've never told me."

"You've never asked," I countered. "Maybe I'm too young for you."

"I'm prepared to take that risk," he laughed. "Anyway, you'll be catching me up soon enough."

"That's true. Go on then, your turn to take a guess."

"That really isn't fair! You can't make me guess both ages."

"I'll give you a kiss if you get it right."

"Now that is a game I could get used to. OK, I'm going to go for …hmm, let's see if I can work this out. You're still at school, but nearly finished; you are learning to drive; and you think most of the boys of your age are a waste of space."

I nodded at him – he was right on all counts so far. "So?"

"So, you have to be seventeen."

"Exactly right!" I agreed. "But I bet you cheated."

"In that case I still claim my reward," he said smugly. "You didn't specify not cheating. I'm waiting for my kiss."

I turned as far as I could towards him while still looking in the mirror, and kissed where I could see that his lips were. "I can see we are going to have to practise that manoeuvre," he said. "Shall we work on it now?"

"Oh yes, I think so," I said. "We need lots of practice..."

Callum stayed with me for the rest of the afternoon, only once disappearing briefly to hit the cinemas. He had found the local multiplex and there was always a selection of feel-good or comedy films on. Gathering there seemed to take him no time at all.

When he reappeared I was sitting in the garden with Mum in the shade of the old lime tree with a cup of coffee. I felt the tingle and braced myself for fending off whatever he was about to do, but he was obviously in a mellow mood. He stroked my arm. "Do you mind me joining you when you are talking to your mother?" he asked, apologetically.

I shook my head fractionally.

"So it's OK to stay?"

I gave the briefest of nods.

"Anyway, I'm not going to misbehave that badly in front of your mother. You might introduce me one day, and I wouldn't want her to have a bad impression of me."

That floored me. I had never thought about the future like that, or about him wanting to meet the other people in my life who were important to me.

I tried to imagine a scenario where I got Dad to put on a bracelet and led him to a mirror to introduce my boyfriend. I couldn't see it going well.

I was disturbed from my thoughts by a more substantial touch on my arm.

"Alex, are you alright, darling?" Mum's voice was deliberately controlled.

"Oh, sorry, Mum. Wandered off in a bit of a daydream there for a minute. I didn't mean to scare you."

Her relief was obvious.

"When you didn't respond I was worried that I had lost you again..." She looked away, trying to hide the fear in her face.

I squeezed her hand.

"Relax. I'm sure it won't happen again." I smiled at her.

"But until we know what caused it, we can't be sure of that."

I was torn. She was going to torture herself with worry over something I knew wasn't possible any more. But if I explained why I wasn't worried, I was going to have to tell her everything, and I didn't know how to begin.

"It just feels better somehow. I'm not sure how I can convince you, but I know that it won't happen again."

She looked at me shrewdly. "What has been going on, Alex? You seemed perfectly happy up until the time you went out with Rob, and even after that you were incredibly upbeat by the next evening. But just a few days later you were behaving like a potential suicide. Your mood swings were staggering, even for a teenager. Dad and I were about to talk to you when you had your accident."

I looked at the floor, horrified that my emotions had been so transparent. "So when I heard about what had happened," she continued, "I couldn't help but wonder. You had been so down, so miserable, that I thought maybe you had had ... enough." The tears were glistening in her eyes. "But I couldn't really believe that you would ever want to take your own life. I know that you know the effect that would have on the rest of us, and that *nothing* is ever that bad."

I took her hand again and waited until she looked at me.

"Mum, I would never do that. You're right – I couldn't do it to all of you, or to my friends."

"Thank you. I thought as much, but under the circumstances it did cross my mind." She paused, then added in a different tone, "Would you tell me what it was that was making you so miserable? What exactly did Rob do?"

I still couldn't decide what to tell her. "Rob is nothing, Mum, he's really not important."

"So what was it that upset you so much?"

"I was a bit upset, I know, but that had nothing to do with my being ill. And I'm over it now anyway." I tried to sound as sincere as possible but I could tell she wasn't convinced.

"Was it a boy? A different boy?"

She clearly wasn't about to give up.

"OK, Mum, I give in. Yes it was about another boy; someone I really liked."

She started to ask another question, so I put up my hand.

"Please, Mum, leave it. I've already told you more than I wanted to. It's not a problem now." I raised my head and looked directly at her, daring her to ask more.

"Fine, fine. I didn't mean to upset you. I just wanted to be sure that you were, well, that you had resolved things."

I could feel the gentle stroking on my arm.

"I'm perfectly content, Mum, honestly. There was a misunderstanding but now that has been sorted out."

She took my hand, disturbing the rhythm of the stroking for a minute.

"So no clues for me about your mystery man?"

"No. Stop being so nosy! Anyway, it's all over now."

The stroking suddenly stopped and I could feel his lips brush my neck.

"It better not be over or I'll kiss you in front of your mother," laughed the voice in my head.

"I'm glad you got it sorted out, then, whoever it was. It's terrible seeing your child so miserable and not being able to help. It's so much more complicated these days. I always used to be able to cheer you up with a hug or a piece of chocolate."

"I'm sorry, Mum. I can't help getting older."

She squeezed my hand again. "No, *I'm* sorry: I need to learn to let go of both of you. But I'll never stop worrying though. That's just part of a mother's job description."

"I know," I laughed. "We do try not to torment you too badly."

"In that case you both fail abysmally." She smiled as she said it, but I could hear the depth of feeling behind the words.

"So what were the other guaranteed ways of cheering me up when I was little?" I asked, trying to lighten the conversation.

"Ooh, there was quite a selection, depending on your age. You were never quite as easy to pacify as Josh, but I found a number of ways. When you were very little it was..."

She started reminiscing over a brand of toys from a TV programme that had captivated me as a toddler. As I listened, I became aware of the fireflies again. There was one dancing right above Mum's head. Bright yellow, it darted about just a few inches above her hair. I couldn't see the actual insect, just the yellow light, but then we were sitting in the shade.

I reached over to brush it away, and Mum broke off from her story.

"What is it?" she asked, looking around.

It was gone.

"Just another of those strange fireflies bouncing around.

They do seem to like you at the moment."

She ran her fingers through her hair. "Maybe I should get the spray. I could do without being an insect's dinner. Be back in a sec." She wandered off into the house, where she kept a huge stash of different repellents as she hated getting bitten.

Callum was there the instant she had gone.

"See, I told you I could behave."

"I should think so, too. Do you mind that I sort of mentioned you?"

"Of course not. I just wish we didn't have to be so secretive."

"I know, but at the moment there's just no other way. And I'm sorry for saying it was all over." I was teasing him now, and he knew it.

"Hmm. I'll have to work out a way to get back at you later." His fingers danced down my spine.

"Shh." I laughed. "I can see Mum coming back out of the house.

"Yes, Ma'am, whatever you say. I might stay put though – I enjoy listening to all the ridiculous things you did as a child."

"You are so lucky that I can't throw something at you. Now be quiet!"

I started to hum to myself as Mum got in earshot, so I was covered in case she had seen me talking.

We spent a happy half-hour sitting in the garden, talking about the past and laughing about some of the mad things Josh and I had done as children. Despite the insect repellent the firefly kept returning. It was quite mesmerising, and Mum kept on breaking off from her tales to find out what I was staring at.

After a while Dad joined us, bringing some cold drinks, and we sat laughing as the shadows lengthened. As Mum and Dad went over some of the gory details of stupid things I had done, I could hear Callum laughing and commenting. It was hard to remember not to answer him out loud.

The fireflies were out in force, and Dad acquired some too, bouncing around above his head. My parents were both obviously overjoyed at having me home, and their mobiles were ringing constantly as their friends got the news that I had been discharged. It sounded as if some of them were trying to get a party together to go out for a curry, but I really didn't want to go with them. I wanted to wrap up somewhere quiet with Callum and be able to talk properly to him, not just be conscious of him at my side.

I longed to hear tales of his childhood, to know some intimate little details of his earlier life, when he was real and substantial. As I listened to my parents, it made me sad that I could never have that sort of conversation with him. It must make him sad too, I realised.

"Hey," said the voice in my head, "why the gloomy face? Is something wrong?"

I shook my head almost imperceptibly.

"It's so much harder with you, you know: I have to guess if you are happy."

I raised my eyebrows just a fraction in a question.

"Well, it's dead easy with your parents, for example, their auras are really bright right now, so I know they are delighted. You look really quite down."

As he said it, I looked up at Mum and Dad sitting together, smiling over some shared memory. The fireflies were still bouncing over their heads.

The yellow fireflies!

I could feel the piece of the jigsaw click firmly into place, and sat up with a jerk.

Mum and Dad looked over at me in the same moment, as if they had been pulled by strings. The fireflies popped out in an instant.

"I've just remembered that I haven't been able to speak to Grace yet. Is it OK if I go inside for a while and call her?" I said quickly.

They looked at each other.

"Not at all, darling," said Mum, visibly relaxing. "Take as long as you like. I'll sort out dinner later. Any special requests?"

I really didn't want to debate dinner so a quick decision was needed. I picked Mum's favourite. "Could we have a takeaway curry?"

"Of course." She nodded contentedly. "I'll order the usual."

"Great," I agreed over my shoulder as I finally got away.

I could feel Callum keeping pace with me as I strode into the house. His voice kept coming and going.

"Hey, Alex, what's all this about? Are you OK?"

"You and I need to talk. Right now!" I couldn't keep the excitement from my voice.

"OK, OK, hold on, let's get to your room."

I took the stairs at a trot and quickly set up everything I needed. The room was beginning to darken so the table light threw long shadows across us both. Callum's face appeared next to mine, a deep frown creasing his forehead.

I wasn't sure how to start, but I was pretty sure of my suspicions.

"When you see an aura," I started, ignoring his puzzled look, "what exactly do you see?"

"Well, it depends."

"On what?"

"Give me a second and I'll tell you!" His impatience was good humoured and I could tell he had no idea what I was getting at.

"It all depends on the emotion. When people are sad I see a deep purple mist around them. If they are angry it is red and more contained. Happy people have concentrated yellow specks of light. That's what makes it so easy for me to collect them. If it were a more diffuse sort of mist it would be really difficult."

I was almost bouncing with excitement.

"What is it? I don't understand." He was looking really bemused.

"I can see them! I can see Mum and Dad's auras! I've been thinking it was fireflies, but it's not, is it?"

The expression on his face changed from one of shock to one of wonder, then slowly to one of absolute horror.

Talents

"What's wrong?" I asked him, puzzled. "I thought you would be pleased. Could it be that you somehow transferred some part of you with my memories when you gave them back to me?" I could hardly contain myself with excitement, so why was he looking so aghast? I tried again.

"Callum! Do you think I could be right?"

He stayed quite silent. I felt like shaking him to get a response, but of course I couldn't do that. Instead I did the next best thing and took the amulet off for a second. His face shimmered and disappeared, then was back the instant I slid it back into place.

His eyes immediately refocused. "Don't do that," he muttered under his breath. Then he nodded slowly. "I think you *are* right. This is awful."

"But why? It sounds like fun to me." He was beginning to scare me. "Why do you think it is a problem?"

"Being like us, being the way we are ... it's not a good thing, Alex. I thought you understood that." His face was ashen. "When did this start?"

"I'm not really sure. This morning, I think, when I came home. It's been getting stronger though."

"So it wasn't immediately after you recovered then?"

"No, I don't think so." I was starting to get cross now. What was up with him? "Talk to me, Callum, explain what you are worried about."

He put his head in his free hand for a moment, then looked up at me with anguished eyes. I couldn't believe I had found something else to make our lives more difficult again. Finally he spoke.

"What if it's the amulet changing? It could be that it's starting to exert its influence over you, even though you are over there. It's over there with you after all, so why shouldn't it have its usual effect?" His voice was flat, and he looked at his own amulet in disgust.

"So explain why that is a problem."

"Do you want to be miserable, do you want to have to chase those yellow lights, steal those memories, just to keep sane?"

I didn't want to hear this. "But I don't feel depressed any more! I feel happy!"

"You don't know!" he almost shouted, making me jump. "I won't be responsible for dragging you into this."

"What do you mean?"

"You have to take the amulet off, now, and throw it far away before it does any more damage."

"What are you saying? Then I wouldn't be able to see you at all, and what's the point of that?"

"I know, but it's too dangerous: we don't know what's going to happen, how it's going to change you."

I felt a small shiver of fear run down my spine, but I wasn't going to give up. "But only a few days ago you were furious with me for taking it off in my driving lesson. We know that it is dangerous, and Catherine could only do what she did because I had it but wasn't wearing it. Now you are insisting I take it off. It doesn't make sense."

I could see him about to object again, so I stopped him. "Look, let's both calm down and try to work it out. OK?"

I watched him struggle to control himself, but he bit his tongue and waited a few moments.

"OK," he agreed, "but I just can't bear it if you get hurt again."

"I know, I know." I reached up for his face and tried to smooth away the frown which was etched into his brow. "And I can't bear it if I have to lose you again, so let's work it out ... yes?" I looked up at him, waiting for his answer.

Finally, he nodded in agreement.

I pulled a piece of paper across my cluttered desk and found a pen. The first one I picked up didn't work, so I had to scratch around for another one. It was a luminous green colour with a feather attached, left over from some long-distant party bag. But it worked, so it would have to do.

"Right." I put on my most efficient manner. "What exactly do we know? What are the facts?"

He looked as if he was humouring me but he did start. "First fact: you lost all your memories. Catherine and I both caught them. I stored them in my amulet and then transferred them back to you."

"Right, and they are all fine – a little disconnected maybe, but all there. Well, except for one notable deletion and addition." I smiled at him, but his answering smile didn't quite reach his eyes.

"Fact two: you can now see yellow lights above people's heads."

"Yes," I agreed, scribbling it down, "and it's been happening all day."

"What might have triggered it? Anything?"

"Well, coming out of hospital, I guess. I didn't see any in

there."

"Maybe it was being in your home. Perhaps that's the key."

I thought about it for a second. "I suppose it could be," I agreed doubtfully, writing it on the list.

He was on a roll. "Do you only see the lights over people you know?" he demanded.

"I've no idea. I've not really had the opportunity to test it."

"Right, let's try it out. Look out of the window."

We went to the window to see who was passing on the road outside. I peered out into the early evening, waiting.

Soon a woman walked past with a nervous-looking Irish terrier. I watched her carefully. There was nothing unusual to see, and then the dog stopped and looked up at her, licking her hand. She bent down to stroke the top of his head and a little yellow light popped into existence. I couldn't help gasping.

"What do you see?" Callum demanded.

"There was nothing at first, but then I saw a sudden yellow light above her head as she bent down. What did *you* see?"

"Pretty much the same," he admitted grudgingly, "although I got a bit of purple mist first before the dog cheered her up."

We sat and watched the road for a while, and I tried to spot those thinking of good memories. They were remarkably few and far between.

"Is this usual?" I asked after the fifth person walked by without any sign of a firefly light.

"Oh yes, in fact I'd say that round here the people are *more* cheerful than other places, especially London." He paused. "That's why it's so hard for us to track down enough happiness to keep going. It's a constant struggle to find and capture them."

I still didn't understand why he was so bothered by the

whole thing. I moved back to the table so I could see him again in the mirror.

"So why is it a problem that I can see this now? Why are you so worried?"

"I think your amulet must be changing, and I don't like that. Amulets aren't exactly ... benevolent things. I can't imagine that yours is changing in any way that's good."

"OK, so what do we do? I'm not going to take it off again when we are not sure. And I can't bear to be without you." I could feel his touch as his arms went around me and he rested his head against mine.

"I couldn't bear that either," he said softly, tightening his grip on me in the mirror.

"So what other options do we have?" I persisted.

Callum looked thoughtful for a moment. "Perhaps I could ask Matthew," he said slowly. "He may have heard of something, have some idea…"

"Excellent plan," I agreed.

I saw Callum steal a glance at my watch. "If I want to get him in a good mood I had better get going." He hesitated for a second. "I might not make it back again before my curfew. I'm sorry."

I pouted at him but then smiled. "Don't worry. This is important. You need to find out what you can. Go and find Matthew and come back to me as soon as you can in the morning. I don't believe I have any plans to be in school."

He gathered me more tightly and kissed the top of my head. "I love you. Wish me luck!" For a second one of his dazzling smiles banished the worry from his face, and then he was gone.

I remembered what I'd said to Mum and Dad, and I picked up the phone to call Grace. However glorious it was to spend time with Callum, I missed her.

Grace was at my house in minutes, obviously having had no problem persuading her dad to give her a lift. After a quick hello to my parents, we retired back up to my room. We had had a few conversations when I was in the hospital, but we'd never been alone, and I could tell she was dying to know all about the package and what I knew. I was still unsure of what I should tell her. She settled herself down on her usual spot on my futon chair, mug of coffee in her hands. "Well, what was all that about then? You must have a theory."

I hesitated for just a second. Could I tell her, or would she just think I was mad? For a second I had a picture of her knowing everything: I'd introduce her to Callum and things could almost be normal. I hated keeping things from her: she knew every single other detail of my life. And of all the people I could tell, she would be the most accepting, I was sure. But then my courage deserted me. It was all too strange, and I couldn't begin to find the right words. "You know, I was going to ask you the same thing. My memory of that morning is a bit patchy."

"It's frustrating, isn't it?" she agreed. "I have a very clear memory of being there, but then it goes a bit fuzzy and I can't sort of pull out any details."

I nodded furiously, hoping that I might get away with it.

"But the really peculiar thing," she continued, "is the bracelet. How did I end up wearing that? It's barely been off your wrist since you found it."

"I've been wondering about that too. It does seem really odd."

"And then when I put it back on your wrist, you came back from the dead!"

I was in trouble: she had made that connection. "But that's just ridiculous. Bracelets can't do that."

"No, but there is something *truly* odd about that one." Her voice was almost fearful and I saw her steal a glance at it and shudder, then look away.

"What do you mean?"

"Well – don't laugh when I tell you this – but I did wonder whether it was a bit ... possessed."

"Possessed? What, by a ghost, or something?" I tried to look as if I was finding this amusing.

"Not exactly, more of a presence. I know it's silly, but when I was wearing it I had the strangest thoughts – almost as if someone else was speaking in my head." She sighed, then muttered to herself, "I should never have started this," before taking a deep breath. "It was a man's voice," she said reluctantly.

"How exciting! It hasn't had any effect on me; I just love the look of it." I paused, but was unable to resist. "So, what did the voice say that made you want to give the bracelet back?" I asked as nonchalantly as I could manage.

"It was very odd. It just kept saying that the bracelet wasn't mine and that I had to get it back to you. It was never exactly threatening; I just knew that I had to do it."

"Well, I'm sure it had nothing to do with my recovery, but thank you for looking after it and for giving it back to me anyway."

"But why did I have it in the first place? And I have a vague memory of an envelope from you. Was it in that?"

I thought quickly – I had sent her a text about the envelope, and left a voicemail, so I couldn't deny its existence "Yes. I wanted you to look after it for a bit, but I can't remember why now."

"As long as that was all that was in there, because the

envelope's gone. There was no sign of it in my bag when I came around."

"Oh well, it doesn't really matter now." I tried to sound offhand about the whole subject while hoping that no one would ever find that memory card.

She shook her head and sighed again. "I guess not." As I looked at her a small yellow light popped on over her head. "Hey, did I tell you that Jack came to visit me in the hospital?"

"No, you didn't! Come on, tell me everything: did seeing you vulnerable and helpless propel him into super-boyfriend mode?"

She blushed scarlet, and nodded mutely, the yellow light growing stronger and stronger. "And...?" I prompted, keen to hear about her news but also keen to observe some good memories in progress.

"He told me he loved me." It came out in a slightly embarrassed squeak and she hid for a moment behind her curtain of long dark hair. I had to smile.

Grace giggled her way through the details of her conversations with Jack. I wouldn't have thought that he had that much romance in him, but from what Grace was saying he seemed completely smitten.

Throughout, the yellow light danced over her head, sometimes flicking briefly on and off as she moved on to a new story. Finally though, the yellow light snapped out. I couldn't help but look at her with a question on my face before she even had a chance to speak.

"Did I tell you I had a visit from Rob as well?" she asked.

"No, I don't think you mentioned it," I replied hesitantly. I wasn't sure I wanted to hear what he had been after.

"He said he noticed that you had tried to call him but it

looked like the phone had cut out. He said there was a desperate-sounding message from you which he picked up later."

"Huh! He cut me off! He saw who was calling and cut me off. I was furious."

"I'm afraid that's not all. He's convinced that it was some sort of suicide attempt because he finished with you. Sorry," she added meekly, looking at the rage on my face.

"The little...! I ... I ... words fail me! I wish he was here so I could smack him in the mouth."

"I think both Jack and Josh are planning to get there before you."

"No one believes him, surely?"

She looked quickly at the floor, and started picking imaginary fluff off the cover of the futon. "No one knows what to believe, Alex. You'd been acting pretty strangely, and hadn't told anyone – not even me – what was going on."

She looked directly at me. "What is it, Alex? Why all the strange messages, the peculiar mood swings, the sudden loss of interest in Rob? What's the story?"

I didn't know what to say. I hated deceiving my best friend, but how could I start to tell her the truth? I had to tell her something, though. It wasn't right to carry on deceiving her. As I searched for something – anything – to tell her which wouldn't raise more questions than it answered, I realised I could expand on what I had told Mum.

"Do you promise not to tell anyone, not even Jack, if I tell you?"

Grace looked nervous but nodded anyway. "Of course, you know I always keep your secrets."

"The thing is, it's a bit embarrassing really."

"Go on," she urged, leaning closer.

"Well, I met someone, someone special."

"Really? When?"

"About the same time that Rob asked me out. The trouble is...." I paused, trying to appear as reluctant as possible, "I met him on the Internet."

Grace's hand flew to her mouth in horror. We had all been really well drilled in the potential dangers of dating over the Web.

"I know," I filled in as she floundered, "dumb, huh?"

"Have you met him?" she managed eventually.

"Not in the flesh, but we talk all the time on the webcam." It was close enough to the truth.

"So where does he live? How did you meet? What are your plans?"

I laughed. "I can only answer one question at a time, you know."

She looked a bit sheepish. "Sorry, I'm just rather surprised."

"I know, and I'm really sorry I didn't tell you earlier, but I didn't want to have to say anything until I knew it was serious."

"So is it, then? Serious, I mean."

It was my turn to look away. "Absolutely. He's the one for me."

"Wow. I mean, WOW! How did that happen?"

"It just crept up on me really. Suddenly I realised that I didn't care about Rob because I had fallen for someone else." Even though I was talking to my best friend, I could feel myself redden. I was really glad that Callum wasn't around to eavesdrop on this conversation.

"So come on: name, details, dirt – all that sort of stuff!"

"There is no dirt. He lives abroad so there's no chance of a quick meeting. But his name is Callum and he's nineteen." It felt great to finally say his name out loud to someone. I liked the way it sounded.

"And what does he look like? Tall, dark and handsome, I hope," she teased.

"Close: tall, dark blond and exceedingly handsome."

Grace made a move towards my laptop. "Come on then, let's see the photos."

"Ah, sorry. I don't have any at the moment."

She looked at me suspiciously. "No photos?"

"Um, no. He's not keen on photos. He's very ... shy, really." That sounded lame even to me. She was never going to buy it.

"Unusual, especially when Internet dating, wouldn't you say?" Her perfect eyebrow was raised in a question.

"Well, you wanted to know. You don't have to believe me." My voice was a bit sharper than I had intended.

"OK, OK! Sorry. I'm just disappointed that I don't get to see the guy who finally stole your heart," she said soothingly. "So are you absolutely sure that this Callum is on the level, not some sort of crazy old bloke axe-murderer?"

"Look, I'm seventeen. I'm not going to fall for that kind of thing."

"So are you going to introduce us? You could get him up on the webcam and show him to me that way."

"Ah, he's ... um, he's out right now, working. He's got a meeting with his boss."

Grace sighed. "I see. Never mind. Some other time, when things are easier." She reached out and grabbed both my hands. "You'll be really careful now though, won't you? I've already said goodbye to you once in hospital and I really don't want to do it ever again."

"I promise, Grace. Really, he's not like that, it's quite safe." Well, it was now we had got rid of Catherine, so I wasn't really lying.

"I'm so glad you have found someone. I promise you I'll squeeze the details out of you sometime soon, but I'll let you off tonight: I'm in too good a mood." The light was buzzing around her head again.

"Thinking of Jack, are you?" I hazarded. She laughed.

"Of course. He is the most gorgeous guy in the school, no question. Hey," she looked around in a conspiratorial manner, but my old soft toys didn't seem to be listening. "I'm giving serious thought to breaking the pact…"

It was my turn to squeak. "Ooh! What have you got planned?"

Soon we were deep in complicated plans to launch on the unsuspecting, but probably very willing, Jack, and I managed to keep the conversation on safe topics until Grace's dad appeared to collect her.

I hadn't realised how tired I was, and I was pleased to be climbing back into my own bed where I wasn't going to be disturbed by nurses and drug rounds. For the first time in ages I was able to drop into a peaceful, dreamless sleep.

Possibilities

When I woke the next morning I stretched luxuriously, knowing I had had a very good night's sleep. The curtains fluttered at the window and through the gaps I could see the sun beating down on the trees outside. I had been woken by the smell of coffee – a large mug was resting on my desk – and by the smell of freshly baked bread that was wafting up from the kitchen.

I turned over and felt a long stroke down my arm.

"Good morning, gorgeous, are you awake now?"

"Callum! How long have you been here?" I rummaged quickly for the mirror I kept stashed nearby at all times now, trying not to notice how awful I looked when still half asleep.

"Oh, hours," he answered mischievously.

He looked surprisingly at home on my tatty old duvet. I finally managed to drag my imagination away from the thought of him actually being in – or at least on – my bed, and remembered to speak. "Well, while you are here you might as well tell me about last night. How did it go?"

I felt him settle down on the bed behind me, and I could watch his face as he stroked down my arm to my hip. He had a look of slightly bemused wonder which pretty much matched my own expression. I pulled his mind back to the important question.

"Come on now, concentrate! How was it? What did Matthew say?"

"Now that conversation was interesting," he mused as he continued the exploration of my back. It was becoming increasingly difficult to concentrate.

"What? Come on!"

He stopped stroking and looked me in the eyes, and I could see the excitement on his face.

"Matthew thought it was very curious. We spent quite a long time discussing the implications. His view," he paused as he made another sweeping movement down my side, "was that you are probably not in any danger. He can't see how the amulet could compel you when you have the ability to take it off at any time."

"Well, that's a relief. Of course, you're a pretty good incentive to keep it on..."

"Then I guess it depends on whether you think I'm dangerous." He gave a mock snarl and pretended to gnaw at my neck. Nice as it was I had to stop him: we had things to discuss. "Oh, I must tell you! I mentioned you to Grace last night."

He was instantly wary. "Really? How did that go then? Are we expecting the men in the white coats to come any minute?"

"I didn't tell her the truth! I told her I had met someone fabulous called Callum who I loved."

He beamed at me. "I like the sound of that. But didn't it raise other questions?"

"No, I told her that I met you on the Internet."

"Hmm, you'll have to explain that to me. I've heard about the Internet at the cinema but I've never seen it."

"What! You've never seen the Web?" I couldn't believe it.

"How would I have?" he countered defensively. "I know the general concept from what I hear, but I don't know if I ever used it before I came here. It's a place where you can ask questions, right?"

I was stunned. How could I possibly start explaining the Web?

"Where do I start? You really don't want a lecture on it now, do you? Don't we have more interesting things to discuss?"

"I suppose. I'd just quite like to ask it some questions." He sounded disappointed.

"I've already asked it about you."

"Excellent!" This clearly pleased him. "Did you find anything interesting?"

"Well, no. I looked up drownings and Blackfriars Bridge to see if I could get a clue to your identity. I thought that as there were two of you involved it might have made the papers."

"Oh. Was there nothing there?"

"Lots about drownings in the Thames, but nothing that seemed to relate to you. I was thinking about it later, when I was in hospital, and I wondered if maybe they didn't find your bodies. What if they can't find your bodies because you take them with you?"

"I suppose it's possible," he agreed dubiously. "Shame though, I thought I might be able to find out something."

"We could try a search of missing people, there must be sites for that. If they didn't find the bodies you ought to be listed as missing."

"Interesting thought. We should try that later. Right now though I need to tell you the rest of Matthew's theory."

I was suddenly nervous: what if Matthew thought all this was a bad idea? I wasn't sure if Callum would be able to disobey him and his rules.

"OK. What's the deal?"

"He thinks you should come to St Paul's. If the amulet is

making you more like us, then the effects ought to be stronger there. He thinks that there's a chance we might be able to communicate more easily inside the cathedral walls."

Meeting Matthew. The whole idea made me really twitchy. It was a bit like having to meet the parents. I swallowed hard and smiled. "That would be great. When could we do it?"

He seemed tremendously excited – almost bouncing in his enthusiasm. "I think we should see him straight away. What do you have planned today?"

"Callum, be sensible! I was only discharged from hospital yesterday – without a diagnosis as far as my parents are concerned. They won't let me go into London unsupervised for weeks."

He looked crestfallen. "Oh, I see. Is there any way round that?"

"I guess I could sneak out, but it depends on what my parents are doing. If one or other of them is working at home I've got no chance, but if they have meetings I could maybe get away for a while."

"Do you have any idea of their plans for today?"

"I haven't got a clue. I'll have to go downstairs and find out. Do we have to go today? It's already halfway through the morning."

Some of the excitement faded from his eyes. "I'm sure it will wait. I'm just curious about what you might be able to do."

"What are you expecting?"

He gave me one of his most devastating smiles. "Who knows? I'm just really interested in finding out."

I had to confess the concept was intriguing. There was obviously something he thought I might be able to do which he wasn't telling me about. The only way to know would be to go.

I told him to go and gather for a bit while I checked out the family's plans. Mum was working in the office downstairs and Josh, having finished all his exams, was lying in the sunshine, listening to his iPod. Dad's car was gone.

Mum seemed delighted I was awake, and got me some breakfast. She hovered around while I ate, obviously still overwhelmed by the fact that she had got me back from the dead. This wasn't going to be easy.

"So what are the plans for today then?" I finally had to ask when the subtle approach failed.

"You just get to relax, sweet-pea. The doctors have signed you off for another week, so there is no need to do anything." I winced a bit at the old endearment and wondered if Callum was listening.

"Are you home all day too? I expect you have loads of work to do after a week camping at the hospital."

"I'm pretty busy, but I can manage from home. I don't want to leave you, not so soon."

"Honestly, Mum, there's no need for that. I'm not going to keel over if you go into the office."

I could see the indecision in her eyes, so I nudged her in the right direction. "And Josh is here, so I wouldn't even be on my own."

With perfect timing her BlackBerry buzzed, announcing another email. She quickly scrolled down through the list and sighed. "Well, if you're absolutely sure... I really could do with going in for a few hours to sort some of this stuff out."

"I'll be fine, Mum. What could go wrong?" I crossed my fingers as I said it: I had no idea what weird things Matthew had in mind.

"OK... As long as you are sure." I could tell she was beginning to feel guilty now, and would beat herself up about it until she got into the office. Then she would get completely absorbed in what she was doing and be gone for hours.

"I'm positive," I soothed her. "I really don't need to be babysat: I'm OK."

"Fine. I'll get going then. The sooner I go, the sooner I'll get back." I knew this was nonsense, but she seemed to have deluded herself into thinking it was true so I nodded in agreement.

"I'll see you later, Mum. I'll call you if I feel odd or need anything, I promise."

"Alright, darling. Thank you. I'll see you later. Tell Josh, will you?"

"Of course I will. Have fun at the office!" With a flurry of papers and charger cables she was through the door and off. Sometimes there were real advantages to having a mother with a career.

With Mum out of the way, I only had to deal with Josh. I ambled casually out into the garden, where he was still lying with his headphones on. There was no sign of consciousness at all.

I quickly ran back into the house and got ready to go out, and he was still sleeping when I approached him twenty minutes later.

I shook him gently to wake him up, hoping that this wasn't going to annoy him too much. He peered at me from under his shades. "Uh, you up now then, are you?" he grunted.

"Sorry to wake you, but I just wanted to let you know I'm popping out for a bit. Oh, and Mum's gone to the office so you are on your own. Got your mobile on you?" I said the last bit over my shoulder as I started back to the house, hoping it would discourage a conversation. He patted his pocket and gave me a thumbs-up as he sank back.

I knew it was going to take me a while to get to London, so I called Callum to tell him I was on my way and to meet me at Waterloo Station. The timetables were with me: a bus arrived just as I was walking past the bus stop, and as I arrived at the local station I had just enough time to get a ticket and jump on the next train. As I sat on the train I considered all the possibilities ahead of me, but I couldn't think what would get Callum so excited. Then I realised what he'd been thinking about: our first meeting! Directly under the middle of the dome in St Paul's I had been able to see him without a mirror.

The journey dragged on, stopping at every tiny station on the line, and I counted them off until we got to Waterloo. The station was huge, with a vast glass roof where I could see some pigeons making themselves at home. I searched around for somewhere to buy some water and ended up paying a fortune for a tiny bottle from a coffee stall. It was deliciously cold though. I looked around the concourse to find somewhere unobtrusive to call Callum. Even at this time of day there were hundreds of people milling about, some obviously commuters off to meetings, some harassed parents with fractious children, and several elegant ladies who were clearly going to be lunching. Watching the crowd was mesmerising. I could see yellow flashes around the heads of several people, particularly above people who were arriving, and I guessed it wouldn't be like that in the rush hour, though: these people clearly had exciting places to go. I smiled to myself: I realised that no one was watching me, so there was no need to find a quiet corner. I put on my earpiece and called his name.

There was a moment's hesitation when I thought I was going to have to call again, but then he was there. I realised as I felt the welcoming sensation in my arm that now it felt odd when he wasn't there: the tingle was now what I expected to feel.

"Hello. I made it. What's the plan?"

"I'm so glad you're here. But there is no plan. We go up the front steps of the cathedral like everyone else. I just don't have to pay like you do – I hope you brought some cash!" His fingers tickled my back and I resisted the compulsion to wriggle – that would have looked a little odd.

"We only need to get you there," he added. "How long before you are missed at home?"

I looked at my watch and did a quick calculation. "I've only got a couple of hours before I need to start heading back. I'd like to avoid Mum finding out that I've sneaked off."

"OK, then, we need the most direct route, not the scenic, tourist approach. Waterloo and City line to Bank, then a very brisk five minute walk round the side of the cathedral. I'll catch up with you outside the tube station." The excitement in his voice was infectious.

"Oh, please tell me why you're so excited! What should I expect?"

"Let's find out when we get there. You need to get down to the underground." If he could have pulled me along, he would have.

"OK, OK! I'm coming. See you in ten minutes."

I quickly ran down to the tube and found that the Waterloo and City line went from a different part of the tube station. Muttering crossly to myself, I finally found the right place and jumped on the first train. It was a weird little tube line with only two stops, and I noticed that in the tube there were far fewer yellow lights: most people were dressed in formal suits and looked as if they were on their way to meetings. The little train shuttled along to Bank very quickly, though, and I was soon running up the escalators into the sunshine.

Callum was with me almost as I got to the street. He must have been watching out for me. He directed me down the road, giving me details of some of the sights we were passing. It was like having a personal tour guide in my head, except that he also kept up a running commentary on the auras of the people we passed.

He was right that the majority of people were gloomy, and I didn't get that much chance to practise my new skill. I thought as we rushed along that if I looked really hard, I could perhaps detect a hint of red in the air around some people.

Callum got more and more twitchy the closer we got to the cathedral. I tried to think of things I could say to calm him down, but given how nervous I was feeling I wasn't able to do much good. Finally, we made it to the front steps. The imposing portico loomed up above us and I suddenly felt very scared.

"Callum, can the other Dirges see me? Are they expecting me?"

"Relax," he whispered. "Most of them are out gathering."

I really didn't believe him. If this was an unusual event in an otherwise completely unchanging daily grind, I was willing to bet that most of them would be watching.

"You are such a liar! Come on, how many are looking?"

He gave a nervous laugh. "OK. I was just trying to make you feel more relaxed. I think they're pretty much all here."

"Oh! I wish I hadn't asked. Is Matthew there too?"

"Yep. He's there waiting."

"For you, I hope."

"No! For you, of course. He sees me every day." He was trying to sound casual but was failing miserably.

I took a deep breath. "What do I have to do?"

"Once we get to the top I'll get out of the way and Matthew will join you." It sounded as if he was as nervous as I was.

My heart pounded. "Have you any last minute advice, or anything?" I asked as we started climbing up the steps.

"Just be you. It'll be fine." He kissed me quickly and then whispered, "Stop behind the pillars by the main doors. I promise I'll be right by your side."

The steps were dotted with tourists, some standing looking down Ludgate Hill or poring over maps, some sitting eating ice creams or sandwiches, and still others just enjoying the sunshine. I worked my way around them all to the top, and then went past the immense pillars. It was relatively quiet as the tourist entrances were to either side. The big doors here obviously only opened on special occasions. I stopped where there was a reasonable amount of space around me: I didn't want too much of an audience for what I was about to do.

My mouth was dry with nerves. I got out my water and had a quick swig before I pulled out the little mirror. My earpiece was already in place. I swiftly scanned around me and almost dropped the mirror as I suddenly realised that I was in the middle of a huge crowd of dark-cloaked figures. For a split second I was frozen with fear and an urge to run almost overcame me, but then I caught sight of Callum watching me anxiously and tried to calm down: I was doing this for him, I remembered. I adjusted my earpiece and spoke clearly. "Hello, Matthew, Callum tells me you would like to meet me."

There was the tingle in my wrist, subtly different from the one I was used to, and I glanced in the mirror. Matthew was standing in front of me with his hand extended towards mine, our amulets occupying the same space. He was shorter and stockier than I expected, with close-cropped grey hair and fierce, deeply-set eyes. I almost stepped back and broke the connection, but I recovered myself in time. I smiled at him. "I'm Alex. Callum has told me a lot about you."

I couldn't really follow his expression in the mirror without it appearing odd to ordinary onlookers so it was hard to see his reaction. The voice that suddenly boomed in my head was brash and tough, but not unfriendly. "Welcome, Alex. We're all very happy to meet you."

The volume nearly made me stagger back, and I was too surprised to properly notice the warmth of his voice. "Oh ... me too. But, please: – I can hear you very well if you talk quietly," I tried to say at a normal volume.

"Ah, right, sorry." The deafening voice reduced in volume to an almost bearable level. "I've not spoken to anyone real this way before – not really sure of how it all works." I could hear the East End accent in his voice and wondered how long he had been a Dirge.

I smiled weakly. "Of course. I understand." It felt a little lame, but what could I add? Where could I possibly start?

"Now, I've got plenty of questions for you, but I know that it's not me you want to talk to. I'll let you and Callum work out what new talents you've got, and we can talk later." The tough voice was almost chuckling so I had to sneak a quick peep at him. He looked as if he had surprised himself by laughing. It was clearly not something he did every day.

"Thank you, Matthew," I whispered. "I'll call you."

I saw him give a brief nod, then the tingle stopped and I was alone.

St Paul's

Callum was back with me in an instant, and I gave a quiet sigh of relief. "Can they still hear what we are saying?" I whispered.

"Uh-huh," he mumbled. "Let's go inside quickly, and then we can relax."

I walked along the front of the cathedral away from the huge ornamental doors to the tourist entrance on the left. The place was full of people milling about, speaking a multitude of different languages, and staring up in awe at the inside of the building. Almost all had a bright yellow light flickering above their heads and the effect was mesmerising. I shuffled along in the ticket queue totally absorbed in watching their visible thoughts. There was no doubt that whatever talent I had was stronger here: I could see differences in the intensity of the yellow lights, and the hints of red that I'd seen on the street, and which here were mostly over the people in the queue, were much clearer. I also got my first glimpse of a purple mist that surrounded an elderly lady who was leaving.

I was starting to get pretty excited. When I finally made it to the ticket desk, the man looked up from under his red cloud.

"Yes?" he asked in a bored tone. I had no idea where in the cathedral Callum wanted me to go, but he was still with me so I would have to ask.

"Oh, now, where do I want to go? What are the options?" I smiled sweetly at the man hoping Callum would take the hint.

He looked at me as if I was mad, the red cloud intensifying in colour. "Options? What do you mean? You want an adult ticket, right?" The line behind me started to fidget, but finally Callum got it.

"Sorry! I forgot. You want to go up to the very top of the dome."

"A student ticket including the top of the dome, please." I smiled again and flashed my student ID card as he scowled at me.

"Whispering Gallery's open, Stone Gallery's open, Golden Gallery at the top's shut for maintenance," he announced in a bored tone as he took my money. "All one ticket price anyway. 'Options'..." He tutted to himself as I moved aside for the next customer.

Finally I was in the vast emptiness of the belly of the church. The concentration of visitors at the entrance suddenly gave way to the stillness of the enormous space. I walked up the nave towards the dome and almost jumped when I heard Callum's voice in my head.

"You need to go to the stairs."

"Can't we go under the centre of the dome first? It would be great to be able to see you in front of me again."

"Later. We can't do that right now, anyway: there is a service in progress."

I looked up the nave and saw that he was right. There were a number of people sitting in the chairs surrounding the central star, and the minister was up by the altar.

"OK. Let's go up the stairs, then. But I can't get to the top: the man said it was shut."

"I don't think we need to worry about that. I can sneak you through. Head over towards that woman in the red."

As I located the woman, I was conscious of other movement,

of insubstantial cloaked figures just disappearing out of sight. I turned to look at Callum and there was a hint of him in the air, like a reflection in a pane of glass, a ghostly, half-transparent shape with the face I loved.

"I can see you!" I exclaimed, far too loudly. "Did you know?" I added in a whisper as a passing tourist gave me a disapproving stare.

"I hoped it might make a difference. The effect should be greatest at the top." He was trying to sound cool and calm but I could feel the edge of excitement in his voice too.

We had walked to the entrance to the stairs, so I showed my ticket and walked in. There was a notice warning that it was five hundred and twenty eight steps to the top. "Couldn't you have arranged something a bit lower?" I joked.

"Well, I guess if I'm not worth a bit of effort..."

"I'm going, I'm going." I laughed as I set off.

"I'm going to go ahead. Carry on up, and just ignore any barriers. I'll see you at the top."

The stairs up to the Whispering Gallery were in a wide spiral and very shallow. In my impatience I took them two at time, passing struggling tourists easily. It seemed as if the staircase would never end, but finally I was working my way through the narrow corridors to the gallery itself. I paused for a moment and looked down at the view to the beautiful floor below. The pattern was spectacular from here, and lit with long beams of sunlight dancing in from the windows.

As I looked up from the view below me, I gasped. Sitting around the gallery on the thin stone bench running round its edge were dozens of shadowy, cloaked figures. Most had their hoods up, concealing their faces. It was as if they were superimposed on another scene, as the more solid tourists played with the acoustics around them.

For a moment I experienced another wave of fear, the sense that I should have nothing to do with this strange, ethereal group. But then I glanced behind me, and caught a glimpse of a few of the faces hiding in the nearest hoods. They were just ordinary faces wearing looks of wonder and puzzlement as they looked at me. I smiled at a brown-haired girl who looked younger than me, and she immediately blushed and looked down, but I did see a brief twitch of her lips before she hid her face.

The tourists could see nothing. As they sat on the stone bench, the Dirges seemed to glide out of their way. I had to walk past them to get to the entrance to the next stairway, which was right on the other side of the gallery. Most of them shrank back towards the wall as I passed, but some acknowledged me with a nod.

Through the next door, the stairs carried on relentlessly upwards. At the Stone Gallery, which circled the base of the dome on the outside, I stepped out into the welcome breeze, and I quickly looked around me for cloaked figures, but there were none. I only stayed long enough to let the pain in my calves settle, and then I headed on to the entrance to the stairs for the Golden Gallery. As the grumpy ticket man had predicted, there was a barrier by the entrance with a sign saying that the gallery was shut. I glanced around me. All the tourists were concentrating on the view, so I quickly jumped over the barrier and into the cool gloom beyond.

I remembered from my previous visits that this was the strangest and scariest part of the climb to the top – the open-tread iron stairs winding up between the inner and the outer domes, intertwined with the huge cage of massive timber beams that held the whole thing up. The drop below was dizzying, and I kept my eyes firmly fixed on the steps ahead of me.

The muscles in my legs screamed in protest as I finally approached the top, and I stopped at a small room with the peephole through which you could see all the way down to the star on the cathedral floor directly below – the point where I'd stood when I saw Callum. I waited for a moment to catch my breath, but I could feel my heart pounding in my chest and the butterflies in my stomach. I tried to persuade myself that I might not be able to see Callum properly, and told myself that I shouldn't be too disappointed if what he seemed to be expecting, whatever that was, didn't work. I took another swig of water, ran my fingers through my hair and squared my shoulders. I walked up the last dozen or so steps and pushed open the door into the bright sunshine.

As my eyes adjusted I could see the panorama of London laid out before me, the glass buildings glistening in the light and the river meandering past the London Eye. In front of me there was only the gold-coloured iron railing. I looked around – the Golden Gallery was tiny, a miniature balcony set on top of the dome and around the base of the tower holding the huge ball and cross. There was very little space between the stone structure and the circular railings and I could see immediately that Callum wasn't by the entrance, but my disappointment quickly gave way to hope that he might be round the other side, overlooking the eastern part of the city.

I called out tentatively. "Callum? Are you up here?"

"Over here!" My heart leapt, and I just had time to register that there was something different about the familiar voice that answered that I couldn't define before I squeezed my way round to the far side of the gallery.

Callum was standing by the battered old railing, waiting for me. I could see him perfectly. His cloak was on the ground and the sunshine caught the fire in his eyes. I could see every fold in his shirt, every hair on his head, every detail of the long, strong arms that were held out to me in welcome.

His beauty and his presence stunned me, and for a strange moment I was overcome by shyness. And part of me wanted to stay where I was – just far enough away to believe that he was real – to avoid the disappointment of finding that I couldn't touch him however well I could see him. But then I looked into his eyes and was overwhelmed with the love I could see there. I couldn't resist: I stepped towards him and reached up to stroke his face.

It felt as if a bolt of electricity went through me as I touched – *actually touched* – the firm skin of his cheek. I felt its warmth and contours and the bones below, and then I felt it move underneath my fingers as he smiled and pulled my hand down to his mouth and kissed my palm.

I was speechless. I put out my other hand and touched his chest, and I could feel his heart beating as fast as mine. He looked down into my eyes and suddenly pulled me to him, wrapping his arms around me. I felt faint with the pleasure of it. It was so much better, so much *more*, even than I had imagined. His strong arms held me tight and for a second he lifted me off the ground.

"Oh, Alex, I can hardly believe it! We've done it!" he breathed, his lips brushing my forehead.

I pulled back in astonishment. "I can hear you, too! Properly, not just in my head."

He smiled at me indulgently. "I'm all yours now. We can talk all you like."

"Actually, talking is not at the top of my list. This – *this* – is what I've been wanting to do since I first saw you," I said, and I put my hands behind his head and pulled his mouth down towards me. His lips finally found mine: I never wanted the kiss to stop.

"That was worth waiting for," I murmured as our lips finally parted, and I rested my cheek against his shirt.

"Really?" he asked. "You know, I've no idea how much experience of all this I have. I don't want to let you down."

I stole a quick glance at him. He was looking down at me with such openness and honesty that I thought my heart would burst with love. His deep blue eyes burned with passion. "I didn't think it was possible to love you any more than I already did, but to have you here, to hold you in my arms, to kiss your lips ... I can't believe my luck." He pulled me even closer to him and I could feel the muscles of his chest beneath his shirt.

"I can't believe that we came so close to losing each other, but it was worth it to find that we can actually do this." I ran my hand lightly over his bicep, then under his elbow and round to the back of his waist. Every part of him was perfect. Callum kissed the top of my head and reflectively stroked the full length of my hair to the base of my spine. I shivered with pleasure.

"Just think," I murmured. "Perhaps Catherine did us a favour. We might never have got to this without her interference. We could have spent the rest of our lives just looking at each other in a mirror." I leaned back to look at his face. "This way I get to know rather more of you." My hand pressed into the small of his back as I pulled him towards me again.

"So how can this all work?" I asked as I sat on his lap, resting my head against his shoulder. I couldn't stop touching him, feeling the sinews and the muscles in his arms, running my fingers through his hair at last.

He was just as compelled to touch me, and couldn't stop leaning in to kiss me again every few minutes. "I really don't know, but when I told Matthew yesterday that you could see the auras, he seemed to think that this might be a possibility. That first time you saw me – when I was directly under here – you didn't need a mirror then. We think that there is something about the dome which concentrates the energy – the essence – of us, and at the very top it's at its strongest. And when you combine that with the effects of the amulet on you – and, of course, the strongest possible connection," he kissed me again, "well, this is the result." He smiled briefly. "At least, that was Matthew's theory, but I really didn't know whether to believe it, and I didn't want you to be disappointed if it wasn't the case, so I'm sorry that I didn't warn you."

I traced my finger down his jawline, admiring the contours. "I forgive you. It was the best surprise I could ever have been given." I luxuriated in the feel of him. He was sitting cross-legged on the floor of the balcony with me nestled into his lap and I was conscious of being warmed by him as well as by the sun. I felt like purring like a cat, I was so content.

"Do you know I was up here the very first time I saw your face," he said reflectively, twirling a lock of my hair around his finger as he spoke. "I come up here a lot – it's one of my favourite places. I love to stand here and watch the light change over the city. Really early morning is the best time." I stole a quick glance at his face – his eyes were focused in the distance, remembering.

"It was mid-afternoon and I had had a good day of gathering. I was up here alone with none of the others around, and I was leaning on the railing looking at the river when your face suddenly jumped into my head."

"I had no idea how I'd find you, or even whether you were

in your world or mine. You were so beautiful, I think I started to fall in love with you then," he admitted. I turned to look at him and caught his look of happiness. I would never tire of that face, especially now I could reach up and kiss the hollow of his jaw. He was so real, so gorgeous, and he loved me. I wanted to stay with him forever, but I knew that wasn't possible. I glanced at my watch and groaned as I realised that I was going to have to start making my way back home. I looked back at him and could see the love and longing I felt mirrored there.

"Come on," I said gently, as I hauled myself upright, "I'm going to have to go soon, and we need a plan."

We stood locked together watching the sunlight play over London, seeing the windows sparkle and the soft light glitter on the river snaking away into the distance. All around, the city was thrumming with energy and noise and business, completely oblivious to us above it. On a nearby rooftop I could see a lone figure with a large sketch pad. From the direction he was facing it looked as if he was probably drawing the cathedral. Would we both be in it, I wondered, or would he see a lone figure on this balcony?

As we watched the city I felt his gentle lips kiss the top of my head again and I leaned back against him contentedly. Here he was, someone I could see and touch and smell and hear. I examined his hand which was so tightly held in mine, the long fingers and the smooth palm, and raised it to my lips. I kissed it gently. "What do we do now?" I whispered. "How can we make this work?"

"I have no idea," he murmured in my ear, "but I think we can have some fun trying."

I looked down again and saw his wrist next to mine, with the matching amulets side by side now, two identical blue stones glinting in the sunshine. The fire in them seemed intensified somehow, as if the two together had a greater power than they had individually. I knew I would never take mine off again, and smiled to myself at the thought. I turned around in Callum's embrace and lifted my face to kiss him again.

Epilogue
Guy's Hospital

It was quiet in the ward. The nurses had finished preparing all the patients in good time for the impending ward round. There was a new consultant, and he was known to be a stickler for details, so all the staff, from the registrar down, were keen to impress him with their knowledge of the patients.

It was a general medical ward, dealing with a variety of patients and conditions. At any one time you could hear conversations in at least ten different languages between the patients and their visitors, who came in to leave a card, a bunch of flowers or food in fancy bags or plastic containers. Only one bed was different. The patient in bed twelve had had no visitors and had been given no gifts. She lay silently, staring at the ceiling while the buzz of the ward went on around her. Her eyes were empty.

Earlier the social worker had tried to get her to speak, but had got absolutely no response. After a while he had sighed, scribbled something on the chart at the end of the bed and returned to the nurse's station.

"I can't get a thing out of her. I've no idea who to inform. She doesn't match any of the missing person descriptions either. And that injury! Who did that to her? No one would do that to themselves."

"Well at least the silence is better than the noise," replied the young nurse. "I could do without that on the ward round."

She was interrupted by the social worker's bleeper. He read the message quickly and pulled a face.

"Let me know if anything changes, will you, Penny? I have to get over to A&E now."

"Sure, I'll take her over a cup of tea later, and maybe some magazines. Perhaps she likes to read."

The sheer curtains in the staffroom fluttered as the summer breeze stirred the hot air. Penny was sitting at the corner desk and looked up expectantly as the door opened. A harassed-looking young doctor rushed in, then looked at his watch and swore under his breath.

"Have you lost something, Dr Luck? Can I help at all?" She rose from her chair, keen to take this opportunity to do a favour.

"Thanks, Penny. I've just lost my notebook and the ward round starts in a few minutes. I have to mug up on the amnesia patient in bed twelve. Do you have any notes at all? I wasn't on yesterday's round and don't want to be seen getting the update from the desk this close to the event." The young medic ran his hands through his hair distractedly.

Penny smiled. "Of course, Dr Luck. Would you like a full history?" She tried to sound as efficient as possible. Dr Luck nodded, his pen poised.

She consulted her notes. "Found in the Thames near Blackfriars Bridge three days ago, unconscious. Only visible injury's a burn around her wrist. Vitals are all good. Given she was found in the river there was surprisingly little water in her lungs. I mean, physically, she's fine.

"She's had a full tox screen but it came back completely clean. She's got no identifying marks apart from her injury and she carried nothing.

"Yesterday she regained consciousness, and for a while we thought we would have to ship her off to the psych ward. She wouldn't stop screaming and ranting until we got ready to sedate her earlier today. Then she suddenly quietened down, but when we tried to talk to her we got nowhere. Her memory seems pretty patchy. She spent all of yesterday shouting that she should be dead, and ranting about someone called Callum, and the fact that he was responsible for everything, but then she couldn't – or wouldn't – give us any idea who he is. She's just been staring into space since mid-afternoon."

Dr Luck looked up from his scribbled notes. "Psych consult?"

"We've requested one, but they've not been over yet."

"Great. Just what I need: a suicidal amnesiac." He sat back in his chair, his long legs stretching out towards her.

"There was some improvement later this afternoon though," Penny added, pleased to be able to give the doctor some new information. "I think maybe something is coming back to her. I opened the windows near her bed to get some fresh air in, and you could hear the bells ringing the hour. She suddenly sat up and asked me, quite rationally, what church it was. 'St Paul's Cathedral,' I said. 'Have you ever been there?'

"There was a moment of silence and then she said, 'Catherine. I am Catherine.'"

The story continues in

Perfectly Reflected

publishing June 2011

Turn the page to find out what happens next …

Caution

Breaking glass exploded into my bedroom. The cold, early morning air rushed in as I leapt up and pushed my feet into my flip-flops, not sure for a moment if I had been dreaming. The crunch of glass under my soles proved I was awake. Switching on the light, I quickly scanned the room, but it didn't look as if anything had been thrown in. I raced over to the window. The drawn curtains had held back a large part of the debris, but piles of lethal-looking shards of glass on the floor by the window meant that I didn't want to get much closer without proper shoes on. Leaning over, I pulled back the curtain. The early dawn light showed that the road was completely empty.

At that moment my dad burst through the door, closely followed by Mum. "Alex! What on earth was that? Are you OK?" He surveyed the damage as he spoke, and then carefully picked his way over to join me by the window. "Did you see anyone?" he asked, peering out in both directions.

I realised that my heart was racing and had to take a deep breath before I could answer. "No. By the time I got there, whoever did it had gone."

"Don't get all over-dramatic," interrupted Mum, obviously trying to keep everything calm. "It could have been a bird flying into the window. Don't assume that someone was responsible."

Dad and I exchanged a quick glance of perfect understanding.

We both knew that what she had said was nonsense. Still shaking slightly, I looked through the window down to the ground below. "I can't see a dead bird from here. Maybe you should go and look. If there is one, it might need putting out of its misery."

"OK," Mum nodded and backed out of the room.

"Is there anything in here?" asked Dad as soon as she was out of earshot. "I mean, what was it? A brick?"

"I can't see anything," I said. "But there has to be something somewhere. Whatever it was that hit it was either very big or very fast: the window's completely disintegrated."

He grunted in agreement, taking another look down the road. "We need to get this cleared up", he said, giving me a quick hug. "I'll go and get my trainers on and I suggest you do the same. I'll be back in a second with the dustpan and a sack." His voice changed as he went through the door. "Oh, hello. I didn't think you were actually alive at this time of day."

My brother tried to give him a withering look but at five in the morning he was too sleepy. "Thought maybe we were under attack. Coming to see if you needed help," he mumbled in my general direction as Dad disappeared.

"You play too many computer games. What were you planning to do – throw your game controller at them?"

"Ha ha. Very funny. What's happened then?"

"We don't know yet. My window's been broken, Mum thinks it was a bird strike, and Dad and I think someone threw something, but I can't see a stone." I tried hard to keep my voice light, to not show him how shaken I was.

"If you don't need me and my superior fighting skills, I'll just be resting then," he mumbled as he turned around and headed back towards his room.

I picked my way over to my desk and sat down to change my shoes. Despite the flipflops, my right foot was already studded with tiny shards, one of which had drawn blood. I pulled a tissue from my box and wiped it clean. The wound was hardly more than a scratch, not worth getting a plaster for. I pressed the tissue against it until it stopped bleeding, and then fished around under the desk for my Converse. I was about to put them on when I realised that there was something in one of them, so I turned it upside-down. A small, heavy, white ball dropped on to the carpet.

I looked at it for a second, then hesitantly reached down for it. The ball was covered in paper which was secured by sticky tape. I carefully peeled back the corner of the tape and the paper unravelled. The golf ball inside dropped on to my desk while I turned over the crumpled sheet, holding my breath. I didn't recognise the handwriting on the sheet, but my blood ran cold as I read the words:

I know your secret, Alex.

My heart pounding, I shoved the piece of paper under my maths textbook as I heard Dad come back up the stairs. I had no idea what it was about, but I was pretty sure I didn't want to involve my parents.

My day didn't improve much. The clearing up and waiting for the guy to come and board up the window meant that I was late for the school coach, but then that was late too, so I spent half an hour standing at the bus stop listening to the inane chatter of the junior kids. I longed to be able to drive myself in to school, but that was a pretty distant dream: I was due to visit the police station that afternoon to answer to various driving offences, and fully expected to lose my provisional licence.

None of my friends was on the coach either, not even my best friend Grace, so when I finally got to school I walked over to the sixth form block on my own. As I rounded the corner my way was blocked by a familiar figure. I began to smile but her face was stony. Without warning, she suddenly slapped me across the cheek. My head flew back with the force of it and the stinging feeling crept outwards from my cheekbone towards my ear.

I tried not to stagger backwards as I turned back to face her again, tears pricking at my eyes. The thin veneer of friendship between us had gone; she looked ready to kill me. She was standing facing me, balanced on the balls of her feet, preparing to swing again. As the ringing in my ears subsided, I became conscious of the absence of other noises around us. In this corner of the school there was little activity; everyone else was already inside the building, and it wasn't yet time for the younger girls to be out on the pitches. No-one was around to step in.

I could feel my cheek starting to redden. The stinging was slowly being replaced by a hot burning, and I could feel the welts rising where her long fingernails had scratched my skin. I knew that I couldn't reach for it, to press it as I desperately wanted to. I stood up straight and lifted my chin.

"I have no idea why you think I deserve that," I said as evenly as I could manage, though I could hear my voice trembling.

"Don't play any more of your stupid games with me!" she hissed. "I thought we were supposed to be friends."

"Well we *are*... friends." It wasn't exactly the way I would have described our relationship, but I didn't dare disagree with her. I stood up even straighter. "And I've done nothing wrong."

"Ha! Then what are you doing with my boyfriend? Why is he so interested in you? You're nothing special."

I closed my eyes briefly. "Honestly, I'm not after him, and I really can't imagine that he is after me."

"You're bound to say that, aren't you?" she spat with real venom in her voice.

"What do you mean?"

"You two have got some secret little pact going on. I know it."

"That's such rubbish. Why would you think that?"

"Why else would he have a whole bunch of secret stuff on his computer about you?" Her voice was sneering now.

"About me? What sort of stuff?"

"I don't know. Lots of files."

"Why would he want files about me? What's in them?"

"I don't know yet, but I will, just as soon as I break the passwords. In the meantime you keep well away from him, do you understand me? Rob's mine!"

"Ashley, I know he is! And after all, it's you who's going to Cornwall with him, isn't it?" I gazed at her steadily.

"How do you know about Cornwall?" Her voice had turned low and ominous. That had touched a nerve. I cursed myself silently and tried to think of a suitable response.

"Oh, you know: gossip in the common room. Some of the others were quite keen to share the news with me."

The thought that some of our friends saw her holiday with Rob as evidence that she'd beaten me in some competition between us obviously pleased her, and the look in her eyes reminded me of a look I had seen before, in a face that, thankfully, I would never see again: Ashley wore the same look of triumph that Catherine had worn weeks ago when she had me completely in her power in Kew Gardens. The memory chilled me so much that I took a step backwards and looked away. Ashley knew she had won.

She turned and started to walk away, but before she had gone more than a few paces she wheeled around and shouted: "You keep away from him, you hear me. You go *anywhere* near him and there's going to be trouble!"

Curious eyes from some passing kids swivelled in my direction, but I kept mine firmly on Ashley as she walked away, still battling with my tears and a growing sense of injustice. I wondered briefly if she could have thrown that ball, but why would she then slap me? Two enemies before nine o'clock. Fear clutched at my stomach, and for a moment, I seriously considered going home to hide in bed. The sharp pain in my cheek was turning to a dull ache, and I knew I should get something cold on it. With a groan I realised that I really had to sort it out quickly: my appointment with the police was only in a few hours, and I didn't want to look like I had been in a fight. Cursing Ashley under my breath I made for the nearest toilet block.

The police officer looked over the top of her glasses at me, shook her head a little and returned to considering the papers in her hand.

"Well Alexandra? What do you have to say for yourself?" she asked eventually.

I swallowed hard, wishing that there was a tumbler of water on my side of the desk. "I'm truly sorry for everything. I just can't remember any more. All I know is that it was vital to get to my friend Grace quickly. The rest is blank."

My eyes dipped to my lap, and I fiddled with the bracelet on my wrist. I couldn't hold her gaze any more, not when I was lying so comprehensively. "The doctor's report – does that help?" I added lamely.

Luckily my dad jumped in at that point. "We have provided all the relevant medical reports, officer. You should have them there."

The police officer started turning over the sheets of paper in her file, pursing her thin lips as she started to read. It was getting uncomfortably warm in the featureless room in Twickenham Police Station that doubled as the Restorative Justice Centre. The open windows did little to help move around the stale air as the protective mesh stopped them opening more than a chink. I tried very hard not to fidget as she turned the last page, and kept my eyes down.

"Well, it's certainly very curious," she said, tapping the file with one long skinny finger, then picking up the medical report again.

"We have submitted a reference from Alex's headmistress," Dad added, pointing at a letter which could just be seen sticking out of the back of the file. "As you can see from that, Miss Harvey felt that the most appropriate response to the incident was to strip Alex of her prefect's privileges."

I think I had been a prefect for the shortest time in the history of the school. They had added my name to the list for next year when I was dying in hospital in a coma following the incident in Kew Gardens, then promptly stripped me of it when I regained consciousness and got hauled up for driving on my own with a provisional driving licence. I never even got to see a badge.

The policewoman, who had been looking as if she was going to tell Dad off for talking out of turn, fished the letter from the back of the file and scanned it.

"Keep calm; you're doing really well," said the soothing voice in my head. "Don't overdo the grovelling though."

I sighed in relief: Callum was back. It had been a long and stressful morning and I hadn't had a minute to call him to me, but he was finally here, making my wrist tingle as usual, as he moved his arm so that the identical bracelets we wore overlapped, his in his world, and mine in my own. I glanced up briefly at my reflection in the reinforced glass door and caught a glimpse of Callum's blindingly handsome face behind my shoulder. All my worries faded away as my love for him swamped every other emotion. He saw me looking and winked, then looked stern.

It had been a fortnight since I got out of hospital, and his voice in my head was a source of love and comfort, commentating on my world.

"Concentrate! Don't mess it up now!" He was right. The end was in sight. I looked briefly at the policewoman but made sure that my face didn't reflect my sudden contentment.

There was a knock and a young PC appeared nervously at the door. "I'm sorry to disturb you, Inspector Kellie, but you wanted to know when that forensic report was in."

I looked quickly back at the policewoman and her absolutely stony exterior was now belied by the yellow light which was suddenly bouncing around above her head. I knew what it meant: she was either very happy about getting the report, or was very happy about seeing the fit-looking policeman. I hoped for her sake it was the policeman.

I was still astounded by the difference it made to me, to be able to tell when people were thinking happy or miserable thoughts. It seemed to be an unexpected side effect of the miraculous recovery I had made from my vegetative coma. Only two of us knew what had really happened to me: me and Callum, whose mysterious reflection only I could see.

Callum was waiting patiently, as he always did. I tried hard to not look at him in the shiny surface of the glass, and instead to concentrate on the police officer as he advised. But it was so hard to ignore him. My love for him felt so profound, and I knew, given what he'd risked for me, that he loved me too. The fact that we were separated by – I swallowed and forced myself to remember – the fact that he had drowned, made no difference to the intensity of my feeling for him. Ever since we'd seen one another under the dome of St Paul's Cathedral, I had loved him completely. I shook myself mentally, then re-focussed on Inspector Kellie; as I watched closely I could see a slight softening of her gaze as she looked at the young policeman. "Thank you, constable," she said formally. "I'll be with you shortly and you can take me through the main points."

I looked swiftly at the PC; he too had a bouncing yellow flicker just above his head. I wondered if the two of them would ever admit anything to the other. Whatever happened next though, it was enough for me that the inspector was in a good mood: maybe I was going to get away with it.

She looked back at me, and pushed the file away.

"Well, Alexandra, I see that you have clearly already been punished by your school. And I think that, under the circumstances," and she waved her hand at the medical report, "There is little to be gained by prosecuting you for these offences."

I felt my heart lift at her words but tried to continue to look contrite.

"However," she continued, and my heart sank again, "I shall have to issue you with a formal reprimand. You have expressed regret, and as your driving didn't cause any accidents we won't take it any further. We will keep the reprimand on file, though, and if there is *any* repeat offence, there will be no leniency shown."

Dad wasn't quite so happy when we finally got outside. "I have no idea what a reprimand will do to the insurance policy," he grumbled. "It may be best for you to give up driving for a while until the dust settles."

"I'm sure I'll manage, Dad." I grinned at him briefly, unable to contain my joy. "I'll enjoy having you both ferry me around, even more so once Josh is off in the autumn."

He groaned again as he realised I was right. If he didn't insure me to finish my driving lessons he was definitely going to get stuck with a lot more driving as soon as my brother Josh went off to university. He was in a no-win situation and he knew it, so I was surprised when he suddenly smiled back.

"I'll talk to the insurers today," he said, "and get an update on the increase. Then you can give me a cheque for the difference."

I had no quick answer to that. He had won after all. He knew that I had quite a lot of money saved up to buy my own car when the time came, as I had been putting away all the babysitting money I made. I felt my arm tingle and could hear Callum chuckle as he caught up with the last part of the conversation.

"He's right you know. It's your own fault you are in all this trouble. If you hadn't believed Catherine's lies about me in the first place none of this would have happened."

I made a non-committal noise which would convey my feelings to Callum without alarming Dad. As we got into the car I considered the changes in my life. Less than a month ago I had been a perfectly happy, normal teenager, out celebrating the end of my exams. Now I was lying to the police and finding every opportunity I could to be alone with a strange and gorgeous apparition who was summoned by the bracelet I'd found in the

Thames. I glanced down at the amulet on my wrist, its fiery stone glinting in the light, and felt overwhelmingly grateful to have found it and discovered its extraordinary power.

I settled back into the passenger seat and couldn't help smiling as I thought of him. He was tall, dark blond and extremely athletic. I could see him beside me in the mirror or in other reflective surfaces, and hear him when the amulets on our wrists were in the same space, but most of the time I could only feel the faintest of touches as he sat behind my shoulder when we talked. He was a Dirge, a soul caught in a terrible half-life of misery after falling into the River Fleet and drowning. These days the Fleet was mostly covered over, and very few Londoners even realised it was there, but centuries before it had been a busy river running from Hampstead in North London, and something about its water, still flowing into the Thames, had a mysterious power to transform those who drowned in it, though none of the Dirges understood what it was. All they knew was that day after day they were compelled to feed on the happy thoughts and memories that they stole from unsuspecting people, and stored in the amulets they all wore. And every night, another fierce compulsion drove them back to St Paul's Cathedral, the place they now called home.

They knew of only one way out of their misery, but it carried a huge price for the living human who trusted them. Callum's sister Catherine had made me believe that he didn't really love me. In my despair, she had very nearly succeeded in tricking me into sacrificing myself. She had sucked away every memory I had ever had and left me for dead. I was only alive because Callum had been prepared to risk himself to save me, emptying his own amulet of stolen happiness so he could capture a copy of all my memories as Catherine spooled them out of me. And after she disappeared, he gave them back to me, leaving himself with nothing. Every time I thought about it, I felt breathless with love and gratitude. Most of the time, at least around me, he seemed to be able to tolerate the desperate wretchedness that he must be feeling without a good store of the thing that was so essential to him. And he wouldn't tell me what he was having to resort to in order to re-fill his amulet. I didn't want to ask. Whatever he was doing, though, he was as loving towards me as he had been when we had first met.

There was no one else in when we got back to the house, so I didn't have to spend hours telling Mum all about the police caution. As soon as I could, I ran up to my bedroom to see if he was already there. The bedroom was gloomy from the boarded window pane, but as I slipped on to the chair by my desk, the tingle was back in my arm and a sense of peaceful contentment washed through me. His face behind my shoulder was perfectly clear in the mirror, his blue eyes sparkling with amusement.

"I like what you're doing with the place," he said, surveying the carnage of my bedroom.

"Well, you know, I heard that transparent windows are *so* last year." I couldn't bring myself to burden him by recounting my horrible morning. I hated to do anything that might add to the weight of his misery: it would wait until we had more time.

"I can't believe you sat there and lied so believably to that poor policewoman. You obviously have a hidden talent."

I tried to look ashamed, but failed miserably. I was too happy to see him again. "It was all perfectly true," I objected. "I did have to get there to save Grace, and I really didn't know why because I didn't have any clear idea about what Catherine was going to do. I mean, I guess I could have gone into a little more detail, but she would never have believed it anyway."

306

Callum sighed. "I still can't help wishing that I had told you everything from the beginning..."

"I know, I know. Then none of this would ever have happened. I believe you might have mentioned that before," I teased him. "But at least now we have our regular trips to St Paul's, and that wouldn't have happened without Catherine."

When Callum had saved my life, he had unexpectedly given me the ability to see him – and touch him – as a proper flesh-and-blood human at the very top of the dome of St Paul's Cathedral. It was a fabulous side effect: to be able to caress his face, hold his hand, kiss those firm lips... My thoughts wandered off into dangerous territory.

"That is very true," he agreed, his lips brushing the back of my neck in the reflection. "Although this is great for me, it's so much better to be able to hold you properly. When can you next make it into town?"

"I'm not sure. Maybe at the weekend. Term will be finishing next week too, so after that it should be easier. I still don't think Mum and Dad will be keen though. They've been so worried about me since I've come out of hospital. I'm going to have to come up with some sort of excuse."

"Hmm. Can you get Grace to help?"

"I wish I could, but I don't think it's a good idea to tell her, do you?"

"I suppose not. I wish you didn't have to keep things secret from your best friend, though."

"It's not so bad now. Now she just thinks you are some sort of cyber-boyfriend."

I hated keeping quiet about Callum to Grace. She and I had shared so much over the years that it was almost impossible to deal with the practicalities of life with Callum without talking to her about it. I had got around the problem by telling her I had met someone I really loved over the Internet, and for now she was happy with that. At last I was able to indulge in a bit of mutual boyfriend-comparing with her. She was getting increasingly impatient to see a photo, though, and I knew that there was no way I could conjure that up. And I couldn't involve her in my trips up to London to meet with Callum in person at the top of the dome.

"I'd like to meet Grace sometime," Callum said reflectively. "She seems so happy and lively."

"Steady!" I laughed. "Don't you go giving me ideas that you prefer Grace. It could just as easily have been her who found the amulet."

"Well, I suppose that's true... She didn't, though, did she? You were the only one prepared to go digging for it." He fell silent for a moment. "I still can't believe that you did find it ... and that it found me," he murmured eventually. "What are the chances of that happening? It could all have been so different."

I looked into his eyes which were soft with emotion, and tried not to think of the scenario where I had not pulled the wire out of the Thames mud to find the amulet tied to the end of it. My life would be calm, uncomplicated and, well, *dull* really, when I started to think about it. My mouth started to twitch into a smile.

"You could have got some really miserable beachcomber bloke with a metal detector instead of me, so think yourself lucky. Besides, there aren't many people who wouldn't have run screaming into the sunset once you started talking to them." I thought back to those uncertain days not so many weeks ago when I really thought that I was going mad. We gazed at each other contentedly for a while before he announced that it was time for him to go and start his usual evening task at the local multiplex. His preference for the happy thoughts generated by people watching comedies meant that he could do quite a bit of gathering pretty quickly in a full cinema. He said that the other Dirges all thought he was crazy. They said that the quality of this superficial happiness wasn't as good as real happy memories, but it made Callum feel better about what he was doing. And right now he had a lot of gathering to do. He was still trying to get back to a reasonable state of equilibrium by refilling his amulet, but it was obviously difficult: although he tried to hide it from me, there were times when I caught a look of melancholy creeping over his features.

I knew he needed to go so I smiled broadly at him. There was no point in making him feel any worse than he already did. With a promise to return as soon as possible the next morning, he was gone and my evening stretched ahead of me.

There were only a few days of term left now, and the teachers had mostly given up on setting us homework. They wanted to mark it about as much as we wanted to do it. I had some catching up to do though, as I had spent a lot of time in hospital, so my time was not yet my own.

I stretched and reached for my schoolbag to see if I could remember what I was supposed to be doing. I had been given the afternoon off to go to the police station earlier, but the long list of work I was supposed to cover was waiting for me.

I was just opening up my laptop when my mobile phone rang. I smiled as I shut the lid of the laptop back down again and pressed the answer button on the phone: it was Abbi, so we were bound to chat for ages.

"Hi, Abbi," I said. "Hey, guess what? The police didn't

prosecute me!"

There was a strange, slightly muffled silence on the other end of the phone.

"Abbi? Are you there?"

"I don't know how you can talk to me like this," bit the voice at the other end of the line, "after what you have done!"

"I'm sorry ... Abbi? Is that you?" The voice was familiar but almost unrecognisable.

"I just wanted to tell you that I never want to speak to you again, and once I've told the others, don't expect many of them to talk to you either. What made you so cruel? I thought we were supposed to be friends." Her voice cracked with emotion.

I could hardly believe that this was happening again, and this time with someone I cared about so much more than Ashley.

"Abbi, I have no idea what you are talking about! What's the matter? What's wrong?"

There was a strangled-sounding sob. "How could you do it? How *could* you?"

"Abbi," I said gently, "please, I have absolutely no idea what you are talking about. Take a deep breath and tell me what I'm supposed to have done."

There was a short grunt on the other end of the line. "Huh. As if. Check your email and see if you've had a reply from Miss Harvey yet."

From the headmistress? This was getting more and more bizarre.

"Why would I email Miss Harvey? What on earth would she want to talk to me for?"

"Go on, then. Check it. I can't wait to hear what she has to say."

"OK, OK. Give me a minute. I'm not logged on at the moment." I wedged the mobile to my ear with my shoulder and opened up the laptop again. I quickly switched it on and opened my email account. It was terribly slow as usual, and I could hear Abbi sniffing in the background. "Right, I'm in. What exactly am I looking for?" I was trying to read through the junk as I spoke, wondering what on earth she was talking about. Then I saw it, part-way down the list, a message with the subject line *Abbi Hancock*. I quickly opened it and scanned the contents, feeling more and more horrified as I went down the page.

"What on earth...? Abbi, what's all this about? How did this happen?"

"I should have known you'd try to wriggle out of it," she said tersely. "But you can't. Why would you do this to me? You'll get me expelled!"

"I ... I haven't done anything, Abbi. I promise!" I needed some time to work this out. "Look, give me a minute will you? Let me read it properly at least."

The email was long. It was addressed to Miss Harvey, and went into an extremely comprehensive list of all Abbi's school misdemeanours over the years, none of which she had been punished for as she was brilliant at appearing innocent. They ranged from breaking windows, putting green food dye in the swimming pool on St Patrick's Day, skipping school and, most recently, burning the toast in the common room which had brought the fire brigade out again. Sending an email like that was the kind of thing no friend would do, and I could feel a creeping horror as I realised why she was so upset. It had come from my email account, addressed to Miss Harvey, and copying in Abbi for good measure. It was vicious. "Abbi, what can I say? It really wasn't me. You must know I'd never do anything like this. Someone must have broken into my account."

"Really?" she sneered. "So explain why the bit about the swimming pool is in there? I only ever told you about that – no-one else *at all*. Explain that! And don't think you can talk me round. Miss Harvey is going to annihilate me tomorrow. She's been waiting to pounce on a victim for weeks about the toast and you've just handed me to her. But before she gets to me I'm going to let absolutely everyone know just what sort of a friend you really are!"

My mind raced as she spoke, and suddenly I realised something: the email was in my inbox, not Miss Harvey's. It had been returned undelivered. I checked the email addresses at the top, and then looked again a bit more closely. The address was wrong, with an 'n' instead of an 'm' in the middle of it. Abbi obviously hadn't spotted it.

"Abbi!" I shouted over her. "The email didn't get to Miss Harvey – that's why I can read it in my inbox. It bounced back. She won't know anything about it."

I could hear the tapping as she scanned through her inbox, and an audible sigh of relief followed by a prolonged silence.

"Abbi, are you still there?"

Nothing.

"Abbi, speak to me."

"If this has been some sort of joke," her usually sunny voiced hissed, "it's been in really, really bad taste. Don't speak to me tomorrow, or ever again for that matter." The phone went dead.

I sat back, appalled, staring at the handset. Fear clutched at my stomach again. What was going on?

About S. C. Ransom

Sue Ransom, the author of *Small Blue Thing* is a senior head-hunter, but on the way to work and in the evenings she's a writer: she wrote *Small Blue Thing*, her debut novel, as a birthday present for her daughter, and she composed it mostly on her BlackBerry. Serendipity led her to Nosy Crow, and she's now busy writing her second book and planning the third in what will be a trilogy. She lives with her husband and two teenage children in Surrey.

Acknowledgements

None if this would have been possible without the inspiration of my children, Jake and Ellie. I must also thank my friend and colleague Clive Sugars, who made the vital introduction, Hina, Jude and Ruth for their support and encouragement, and Meg for always being my Grace. Kate and everyone at Nosy Crow have been instructional, inspirational and an all-round delight as I have travelled on this unexpected journey, and I have loved being part of their new venture. My Mum has shown unfailing support, and gave me the drawing by Dad of St Paul's, my most treasured possession. Thanks Mum.

But most of all I have to thank my husband Pete, for being there, for giving me time, and – hardest of all – for being honest in his feedback. The story wouldn't have been the same without him.